ROMAN WILL *Fall*

New York Times & *USA Today* Bestselling Author

CYNTHIA EDEN

This book is a work of fiction. Any similarities to real people, places, or events are not intentional and are purely the result of coincidence. The characters, places, and events in this story are fictional.

Published by Hocus Pocus Publishing, Inc.

Copyright ©2021 by Cindy Roussos

All rights reserved. This publication may not be reproduced, distributed, or transmitted in any form without the express written consent of the author except for the use of small quotes or excerpts used in book reviews.

Copy-editing by: J. R. T. Editing

CHAPTER ONE

"I can't work with him." Harper Crane crossed her arms over her chest. "He's an arrogant, controlling asshole who can't follow even the simplest of directions and—"

"And I'm standing right here," Roman Smith cut into her words.

"I am completely aware of that fact." Harper huffed out a hard breath as she kept her eyes focused on her boss, Eric Wilde. "Assign him to someone else." Yes, she was nearly pleading. "Anyone else." Like, there was a whole building full of other agents. One of those unfortunate souls could be assigned as Roman's training partner. It didn't have to be her.

Unless, of course, deep down...her boss hated her. And because of that secret hate, Eric was trying to punish her by pairing her up with the way too intense Roman.

"So many other options," she muttered.

Did Eric's lips twitch? Harper could have sworn that they did before he carefully stated, "It's only been one week."

The longest week of her life. Didn't he get that? Sometimes, people just did not mesh well. She and Roman were *not* meshing. At all.

"It takes a while for partnerships to hit their stride," Eric continued. Was he trying to be encouraging? She was not in the mood for encouragement. "It's standard for a partnership's probationary period to last at least six weeks here at Wilde. You know that."

Yes, she knew it. But she'd truly hoped Eric would bend the rules this one time. It wasn't as if she'd ever asked the man for a favor before.

"Is this because of the chocolate?" Roman's low voice rumbled.

Goose bumps rose on her arms. Why did the goose bumps appear so often when he was near? She had no clue. Okay, fine, maybe she had a teeny, tiny clue. Harper whirled away from Eric's desk and let her glare land on Roman Smith.

Smith. She snorted. As if she bought that was his real last name. The man seemed to wear secrets like some kind of shroud. He never shared any information about himself, and, usually, he replied to all of her questions with one-word answers.

She liked to talk.

He didn't.

She loved to laugh.

Despite her best efforts, the man had not cracked a single smile in the week that they'd been together.

And on the job, *she* was the senior agent.

But *he* was the one being bossy as hell. That crap had to stop.

This afternoon, he'd crossed the final line. Gone just too far. Harper had to unclench her teeth as she snapped, "Those chocolates were mine."

"I can buy you more." He shrugged.

Wow. For a moment, she was impressed that he'd actually replied with five whole words. Then those words sank in. "They were a *gift* from a date."

His dark eyes narrowed. Dark, deep eyes. Ridiculously long lashes. Ridiculously handsome man.

No. Stop. Do not go there. Do not dare.

"You didn't enjoy the date." His words were clipped.

Again, five words. A miracle!

But... "How do you know that?" She crossed her arms over her chest. He was right. The blind date from hell had been a disaster. Sean had been handsy and boring, but when the chocolates had arrived, she'd been more than ready to pounce on those babies. She'd earned those delectable goodies by giving up two hours of her life that she would not be getting back. The box had been full of milk chocolate treats. Her absolute favorite. "How do you know I didn't enjoy the date with Sean? I could've had the best time of my life."

Roman's head moved in a negative shake. "Heard you talking to your blond friend."

Her eyes narrowed. "Eavesdropping isn't polite."

"No."

Wonderful. He was back to one-word replies. "For clarification, just because I didn't like Sean, it didn't mean I wasn't going to love my chocolates. You can't take stuff from a person's desk without asking. Partners don't do that. They don't eat an entire box of chocolates and then just leave the *empty* box there like some kind of tease. That's not cool. Not at all."

While she'd been talking, Roman had been standing near the closed office door. Lounging with his wide shoulders propped back against the wall. Looking as if he didn't have a care in the world. But he straightened slowly to his full, rather impressive height. He easily cleared six feet by several inches, and his broad shoulders and chest more than filled out the tight t-shirt that he wore.

A t-shirt and jeans. At the office. And it was a high-end office. Their clients included celebrities, royalty, billionaires. But he wore old, faded jeans.

He looked extremely good in those jeans but...

Roman stalked toward her. Her shoulders stiffened. Then her chin angled up. He was taller than her—way taller. Bigger. But she'd never been one to be intimidated by a person's size. She could take down men bigger than Roman. *Had* taken them down before and would again.

Behind her, she heard Eric clear his throat.

Whoops. She'd almost forgotten that her boss had an up-close and personal view of this show as—

Roman stopped right in front of her. "Let me get this straight. You don't want me to be your partner because you think I ate all of your chocolates."

"No. I don't want you to be my partner because you don't follow directions. I *told* you to stay behind me when we were rushing into the club. Instead, you grabbed *me* and pushed me back—"

"I was protecting you."

Harper snorted. "Yeah, that shit has got to stop."

He blinked.

"I can protect myself. Senior agent here." She touched her chest. Then her hand turned and pressed to his chest. His very firm and warm chest. "Junior agent."

His nostrils flared, then he looked down at her hand.

She probably shouldn't be touching his chest. Harper could see where that had been a poor life choice. Were her fingers stroking him just a wee bit? Bad fingers. Naughty fingers. She snatched them back.

Eric coughed. Loudly.

Harper glanced over her shoulder at him. "Are you coming down with something?"

He was on his feet. "I think I gave you the wrong impression of Roman."

"Uh, no, you didn't. You clearly told me that he was some distant relative that you had to hire—"

Eric winced.

"And that I should be extra careful with his training. You said this situation was all new to him and that I should treat him with kid gloves." Like that didn't scream *green agent* in her mind. "Just so you know, those gloves are not working. If he isn't going to listen to me, if he isn't going to follow orders, then he's too dangerous to have in the field." The real truth. This wasn't about chocolate or his one-word answers to most of her conversational offerings. It was about safety.

And the fact that...

She knew when she was being lied to.

Harper edged away from Roman and angled her body so that she could see both him and Eric. Oh, yes, she knew when she was being played. She liked her boss. Most days, she admired the hell out of Eric. But he was lying to her. Or, if not flat out lying, then definitely hiding some facts.

Roman was no green agent. She'd watched him. Seen the way he could move silently into a fight. Seen the coldness of his eyes when he attacked prey. Seen the *way* he attacked.

Kid gloves, my ass.

She also didn't buy that whole long-lost relative spiel. No, something else was at play. Something that made her uncomfortable.

She'd caught the way Eric sometimes eyed Roman. As if...as if he didn't quite trust the other man. *Is that why I'm really his partner? Am I supposed to be keeping an eye on Roman?*

If so, then she needed to know that info. She couldn't be walking around blindly.

"I'm not inept," Roman growled.

She rolled one shoulder.

"I can handle myself in any situation."

"That remains to be seen," she replied.

Eric's gaze darted between her and Roman. He slowly exhaled. "I need to speak with Roman alone."

"What?" Harper demanded. He was supposed to want to talk to *her* alone. He was supposed to give her the inside scoop and stop leaving her in the dark. She gaped at her boss.

He had the grace to at least look mildly uncomfortable as he reaffirmed, "I need to talk to Roman alone."

Well, hell.

"To go over some rules." A firm nod from Eric. "It will only take a few moments. Do you mind stepping outside for a bit, Harper?"

"Yes, yes, I mind. I mind a whole super lot." Her hands flew to her hips. "This is one of the problems with the partnership. Secretiveness. If things are being kept from me, how am I supposed to trust my partner? The person who is supposed to have my back? The man who is supposed to be there to help me in case of an—"

"I'd kill anyone who came for you," Roman told her. Again, using that dark, deep voice of his.

She believed him. Her gaze flickered toward him. "I don't need you to kill anyone. I need you to follow orders."

Roman's lips—oddly sensual—parted and—

"He will," Eric assured her. "He absolutely will."

Roman's expression said he would not. He absolutely would not.

A knock tapped on the door. A moment later, Eric's assistant poked his head inside. "The museum manager is here. Tomas wants to go over last-minute details for the gala, and ah..." His gaze darted to Harper. "He's looking for you."

Because the gala was her gig. Hers and her new partner's. Typical security. She could do it in her sleep. But the manager was a worrier, and she kept having to go over details with him. Again and again. Sighing, she said, "Fine. Send Tomas to my office. I'll be right there."

He ducked out.

She swept her attention back to Eric. "Get Roman on task."

Eric's brows rose.

My bad. She could see where her words had sounded a wee bit too demanding. Or, a lot too demanding. *That's what happens when you don't get enough chocolate.* She tucked a lock of hair behind her ear and offered Eric a bright smile. "What I meant to say was...I'm sure you will get him on task."

Eric nodded.

Right. Okay. She'd pushed plenty for one day. Time to get to work. Even though she would have loved to stay there and hear exactly what Eric had to say to the mysterious Roman, Harper turned and headed out. Duty called.

But with every step she took, Harper could have sworn that she felt Roman's stare on her. It was weird the way she could always tell when he watched her.

And he watches me a lot.

Almost as much as she watched him.

At the door, Harper paused and peered over her shoulder. She caught Roman staring at her, and for just a moment, as she looked into his eyes, she swore she saw—

Lust.

All of the moisture dried from her mouth. He stared at her like he wanted to—

He blinked, and the lust was gone. His controlled mask was back in place. No expression at all showed on his face or in his eyes. The change was so complete that Harper wondered if she'd imagined the lust. Because he certainly wasn't looking at her as if he were desperate to have her any longer.

Yes, she must have imagined that expression. That hunger.

Or maybe you're projecting. Dammit. So perhaps she *did* find him sexy. In that tall, gorgeous, and dangerous way of—nope. Harper cut off the thought. *Not* sexy. Frustrating. Annoying. Not hot.

She yanked open the door. Marched out. She had a job to do.

***

"So...that went well."

Roman stiffened at Eric's mocking words. "No."

"No? You don't think that your new partner coming in here and demanding that you be assigned to someone else, you don't think that's good?"

"No."

Eric sidled around the desk. "I think this is one of the issues."

Roman lifted his brows.

"You may have noticed...Harper likes to talk."

Oh, he'd noticed. She liked to talk. Laugh. Smile.

Only she doesn't smile and laugh with me. She does that crap with everyone else. It was like she sensed who he truly was. When she looked at him, there was caution in her beautiful, green eyes. The faintest trace of...fear.

She knows what I am. He swallowed. "Maybe you should assign me to someone else."

"No, Harper is great. She's exactly what you need."

He would not think about how he could *need* her in—

"But you have got to follow her rules."

"There were bullets flying," Roman gritted out. "I didn't want her shot so I stepped in front of her." He'd thought that was a good thing.

"She doesn't know your background."

No one knew his full background. Not even Eric. Eric knew bits and pieces, and that was all. Well, maybe not all. Roman tilted his head to the right as he studied Eric. *Distant relative.* That was what Harper had called him, but she was wrong. They really weren't that distant at all.

But Roman hadn't known about Eric's connection to him, not until recently. When Eric had discovered the truth, he'd offered Roman a job at Wilde. The security and protection firm had a great reputation. Eric had assured Roman that his skills could be put to use at the firm.

Just how much digging has Eric done on my past? It wasn't wise to dig up certain graves.

"Since she doesn't know about your...particular skill set," Eric noted tactfully, "it stands to reason that Harper wants you to be extra careful on cases. She needs to get to know you. Understand your capabilities."

Roman exhaled on a slow breath. "I'm pretty sure she can't stand me."

"Yes, well..."

"You told me—when you offered me this job—you swore that I would love my new partner."

"Ahem. Most people do love Harper. They find her to be very friendly. Outgoing. Warm. Charming, even." Eric's stare swept over Roman. "You're just not most people."

No, he wasn't. Because most people hadn't been raised by a sadistic psychopath who'd taught them not to trust others and to be as ruthless and dangerous as possible. Harper was like a bright light, flitting around from person to person in the company while he was...

Yeah, not. "What are *her* qualifications?"

"Harper has..." Eric winced. "A very unique background."

Roman waited.

Eric didn't offer more.

"That's not helpful," Roman told him.

"If I can't tell her about *your* past, then how is it fair for me to tell you about hers?"

Okay, shit, that actually made sense.

Eric tapped his fingers on the edge of the desk. "When the two of you build trust, when your partnership clicks, you'll tell each other all of the important stuff."

Highly doubtful. At this point, Roman didn't anticipate anything clicking. "Does her background have anything to do with the fact that she seems to always run the cases that involve jewelry, art, and high-priced items that thieves might be interested in swiping?" He'd done a little digging—pulling up her old case files to get a sense of how she worked.

Eric stopped tapping. "That's her area of specialty. Some agents here prefer to work at protecting people. Harper prefers to protect things."

Uh, huh. "So she was an art thief." That could make sense. She'd turned her stealing talents into something all new—

"What?" A bark of laughter. "Absolutely not. And stop pushing. I'm not going to tell you about her past. She's qualified. She's smart. She's a great agent. *That's* all you need to know." He pointed one finger at Roman. "Oh, yes, and stop screwing things up. Harper is the most easy-going agent here. If you can't work with her..."

He let the sentence trail off, but Roman got the picture.

If you can't work with her, you can't work with anyone.

"I get that you're not used to working with others," Eric allowed.

Understatement. Roman was just used to others trying to screw him over. How many times had he been betrayed by people close to him? Hell, he had lost count. So excuse the hell out of him if he didn't jump at the chance to tell Harper all of his deepest, darkest secrets. And they were plenty dark. Dark enough to send the gorgeous Harper running.

She *was* gorgeous. Harper had the most brilliant green eyes that he'd ever seen. And dimples. Freaking dimples that flashed when she smiled. Her hair was thick and dark, her body delicate but curved in all of the right places, and she always smelled just like sweet cream—

"Are you even listening to me?" Eric wanted to know.

Oh, shit. No, he hadn't been. He'd been thinking about Harper.

"It's a six-week probationary period, just like I said before," Eric continued grimly. "Try and make it work, will you? Try to play nicely with her."

"I have been nice." Mostly.

"This is a chance at a new life, Roman. I know you want that life. You don't have to be like him."

Roman stiffened. *Him*. His father. The sick, twisted bastard. "Yeah, I think this little meeting is over." No accent marked his words. He'd learned—long ago—to ditch the accent. Just as he'd learned to alter his appearance. His hair was blond now, a very dark blond. He kept a loose stubble on his jaw, and he'd let his eyes go back to being dark. When others had seen him in the past, well, his eye shade had varied. As had his hair color and beard. Small changes could turn a man into someone completely new.

"*Try*, Roman. I want you to be a part of Wilde." A pause from Eric. "I want you to be a part of my family."

Because they were connected by blood. By secrets.

Roman nodded. He was trying, but no one seemed to understand that. No one got how hard it was for him to trade his bloody past for...this. He was used to looking for trouble—death—in every direction. Yet now he was supposed to become a good little agent and toe the line in the blink of an eye?

Not happening.

He left Eric and went in search of Harper. As he walked through the building, everyone there seemed to steer clear of him. People suddenly remembered paperwork as they turned away abruptly. One guy even spilled his coffee as he staggered back.

What the hell? Had he really been *that* difficult to get along with at Wilde? Not like he was the big, bad, friggin' wolf.

All right. Maybe I am. But these people didn't know that.

He rounded the corner that would take him to the office he shared with Harper and—

She was hugging some jerk who wore an ugly blue suit.

"I knew I could count on you," the jerk praised as his arms lingered around her. "You never let me down, Harper."

Roman raised a brow and studied them. The man's hands were far too close to her hips. Roman debated the best way to interrupt. He could clear his throat to get their attention—that was the technique Eric had been using back in his office. Or Roman could just grab the guy and toss him across the room.

Option two. That one seemed like a winner.

He took a fast step forward—

Harper pulled away from the fellow in the blue suit. Her gaze darted to Roman. Widened.

He could almost hear Eric's words in his head. *Try to play nicely with her.*

"Roman!" Alarm had her voice rising. Maybe she'd read his intent. Harper seemed to recover quickly as she waved a hand toward him. "Roman, ah, have you met the museum manager, Tomas Archwright?"

No, he hadn't met the guy.

Tomas turned toward him and smiled.

Roman didn't smile back. He wasn't the fake smile type. He did assess the man. From the top of his head to the hands that had been holding Harper to—

"Roman is my partner, and he'll be supervising security tonight at the museum with me. Don't worry, Tomas. You have absolutely nothing to be concerned about. We will make sure that the gala is a complete success. No one will touch your jewels."

"Absolutely." Roman agreed, deadpan. "No one touches your jewels. Sure as shit not Harper. That is not on the agenda."

Harper frowned at him.

Tomas's eyelids flickered. "Do you—"

"Well, we have work to do." Harper curled her hand around Tomas's shoulder. "So glad that you dropped by, and I will see you tonight." She was determinedly guiding their client toward the door.

He was dragging his feet and eyeing her with way too much interest. "I, um, was wondering…once the event is over, if you might be open to possibly having dinner with me—"

"She's not," Roman supplied flatly. "We have a policy against dating clients here at Wilde."

Her brow furrowed.

"Oh, but I won't be a client when the event is concluded," Tomas announced happily. "So that won't be a problem—"

You're being a problem, Tomas. Roman stared at the other man. Just stared.

Tomas gulped. "I need to get back to the museum. It was, um, interesting to meet you, Roman." He finally stopped dragging his feet and nearly ran from the office.

Harper expelled a relieved breath.

"That's three," Roman noted as he shut the door.

She rolled her neck, as if her muscles ached. "Three what?"

"Three different men who have asked you out..." *Right in front of me.* "Since we started working together."

"Yes." She turned away from him. Strode back toward her desk. There were two desks in the office. Hers and his. They faced each other.

The better to distract him as he studied her far too much instead of getting shit done.

"I get asked out fairly frequently." She sat down. Crossed her legs. Sniffed. "This will come as a major surprise to you, but most people actually like me."

It wasn't a surprise. He marched forward and threw himself into the chair opposite her.

She lifted a brow. "Did you have a nice chat with Eric?"

"No."

"Did he go over the rules again with you?" Harper asked. Her voice was all hopeful. Cute.

He hated to burst her bubble. Actually, he didn't hate it. He found it a little fun. "No."

Her lips thinned. No flashing dimples for him. What a pity. She'd been smiling plenty for Tomas.

Her fingers curled around a pen, and she began to lightly shake it back and forth. "Are we back to one-word replies?"

"No—" Roman caught himself. Normally, he *did* talk more. But he'd been trying to be extra careful at Wilde, and while he learned the lay of the land, so to speak, he'd been in observation mode.

A few things he'd learned from observation mode?

Men had a tendency to fall at Harper's high-heeled feet.

They tripped over themselves for her. Maybe it was because she had a killer body. Or the most striking eyes on the planet. Or the dimples. Dammit. He was starting to think those dimples of hers were some kind of secret weapon that she wielded whenever she wanted to get something.

Except, she didn't use that secret weapon on him.

Why the hell not? Would it kill her to smile at him?

She blinked at him. Put down the pen.

Roman sucked in a deep breath. "We aren't back to one-word replies," he rumbled.

Her eyes widened. "And you're going to start following orders?"

"I'm not as green as you seem to think."

She laughed. God, of course, the sound of her laughter would be musical. "I never thought you were green." She propped up her chin on one hand as she studied him. "You have this whole extremely intense, I-get-shit-done vibe that rolls off you. I'm guessing former military or maybe you were involved in some off-the-books, covert work."

He didn't respond.

"I didn't even get a one-word response to that." She licked her lower lip.

His body tensed.

"Does that mean I'm right or wrong?" Harper wanted to know.

"Definitely not former military."

"So...covert. That makes sense. You remind me of another agent—more of a freelance guy, really—who flits in and out of Wilde." Her expression showed mock surprise. "You know what...come to think of it...I believe *his* last name is Smith, too. What a coincidence."

"The world is full of those."

"Coincidences?"

"Smiths."

Her lips trembled. He thought she *almost* smiled.

"I would like to start over," Roman told her, voice serious. "I will try not to be as major of an asshole."

"Is that a real promise? Like, one that you honestly intend to keep?"

He wouldn't go that far. "Sometimes, being an asshole comes naturally to me."

"I have noticed that." Her smile finally flashed fully. It lit her eyes. Made her dimples wink.

Fuck me. I am in some serious trouble.

She offered her hand to him. "I'm all for starting over."

He glanced at her hand. She was willing to give him a second chance so easily? Eric had been right. Harper *was* kind—the nicest agent there.

His fingers closed around hers. He felt the hot surge of attraction pulse through his entire body.

She was kind. Nice. *Good.*

He tightened his hold on her hand.

Too bad he wasn't any of those things.

CHAPTER TWO

"It's cursed, you know," Charity Hall, Tomas's assistant at the museum, told Harper as she grabbed a flute of champagne. "Anyone who wears the ruby necklace is doomed to danger. Well, doomed to face danger and desire." She wiggled her eyebrows.

Harper's fingers tightened around the champagne flute she held. Unlike Charity, she wasn't actually drinking. But if you wanted to blend in with a crowd, props were always helpful. "Facing desire doesn't sound so bad to me."

Charity laughed. "It's the danger part that gets you." Her blue gaze wandered back to the ruby necklace that was on display in the middle of the massive room. A guard stood at attention beside the priceless piece. "It's as big as a human heart."

The ruby's size would explain where the jewel had gotten its name. *Lover's Heart.* But the whole spiel about the wearer being doomed to face danger and desire? Harper figured that was simply clever marketing that someone had created over the years. All good pieces needed a curse attached to them. Curses attracted crowds.

There was certainly a massive crowd at the museum that night.

The *Lover's Heart* wasn't the only piece on display. There were plenty of other gorgeous jewels in the room. Diamonds. Emeralds. Yet nothing touched the giant heart in beauty. The collection had been donated to the museum by a big celebrity, but, originally, all of the jewels had been owned by a certain king's infamous mistress and—

"Who is that?" Charity asked. She waved her hand in front of her face. "Oh, I don't know him. But I'd like to. I'd really, really like to know him. All of him."

The sinking feeling in Harper's stomach told her that she already knew the identity of the mystery man. And, sure enough, when she followed Charity's gaze…

Hello, Roman.

He was cutting a swath through the crowd. Not wearing his worn jeans and slightly dirty t-shirt any longer. No, now he was dressed in a black suit that fit him like a glove. It hugged his broad shoulders, accentuated his golden tan, and, uh, yes, the man could certainly clean up well.

He looked up and his stare locked right on her.

"OhmyGod," Charity whispered. "Do you see that? It looks like he wants to eat you alive. That is so hot."

It wasn't hot. It was an act. Charity hadn't met Roman before. Mostly because he was a new member of the team and because he was supposed to be keeping a low profile that night. There were several "low profile" Wilde operatives in the museum. Dressed like other gala attendees, their job was to keep an eye on the jewels. They were supposed to blend. When you blended, you could see things so much better.

Except, Roman wasn't blending. He was standing out. Catching the eye of every woman in the room.

And I'm still staring at him, too.

She yanked her gaze away and returned it to Charity. "That's Roman," Harper said, aware that her voice had gone husky for some unknown reason. "He's my—"

"Date," Roman supplied as he stepped to Harper's side. "I'm her date for tonight, and if you don't mind, I would love to steal her away for a few minutes."

Charity's eyes had gone very, very wide. "Sure but, um..." She nibbled on her lower lip. "Don't forget, Tomas has plans for you soon. Stay close, okay, Harper?"

Harper inclined her head. She was well aware of Tomas's plans, and they didn't exactly thrill her. But he was the client so she'd play along.

Roman didn't speak again until Charity had disappeared into the crowd. He didn't speak, but his gaze was sweeping all over Harper's body. She could feel it.

Automatically, Harper glanced down. He was in black, while she was wearing white. The softest, silkiest dress she owned. It dipped off one shoulder, and the fabric clung lightly to her curves. She'd had to slip on extra high heels because the dress was a little long, but it flared nicely around her feet. She hadn't worn any jewelry with the dress. Mostly because...

She knew Tomas's plans. He'd sprung them on her when he'd been in her office.

"You look beautiful."

Harper shook her head. She must have misheard.

"No, you do. Though I'm sure you realize it." Roman waved one hand vaguely toward the crowd. "I'm also sure plenty of these guys have probably come up to you and told you how great you look."

Do not shatter the champagne flute. Ease your killer grip, woman. "I think you gave me a compliment, but then it got weird."

His lips tilted. Almost a smile. But not quite.

"You look very handsome." She raised her brows. "Did you see what I did there? I gave you a compliment, but I didn't tack on anything rude like… 'And I'm sure you know it because all the women here are tripping over themselves to get your attention.'"

His dark gaze drifted down to her feet. "You're not tripping."

"I'm not trying to get your attention." Why was her heart pounding so fast? *Because it's almost showtime. Because you're having an adrenaline rush. This has nothing to do with Roman. Nothing at all.*

"You don't need to try." Now that hot stare of his rose again. Held hers. "You have it."

A surprised laugh escaped her. Only the laugh came out sounding a bit too much like a gasp. "You are a very good actor."

A furrow appeared between his brows.

"I have to commend you. You're playing the role of my date admirably well tonight. You truly seem interested in me." She inched closer to him and lowered her voice even more to say, "Once I'm wearing the necklace, don't forget that we have to go into the ballroom and take one dance together. Keep up the act for that part, and then, once the necklace is returned, you can go back to mingling with the crowd and looking for anyone suspicious."

A muscle flexed along his jaw. "You don't seem overly interested in me."

Was he criticizing her acting skills? She plopped her champagne flute down on the nearest waiter's tray and curled both of her hands around those super broad shoulders of Roman's. Then she let loose her winning smile. "Darling!" Harper chimed loudly. "I can't wait to dance with you." She pressed higher in her heels and let her lips skim his jaw.

He stiffened. She felt the sudden tension in his whole body. His hands flew up and clamped around her hips, and he held her in a tight, fierce grip.

Her mouth was lingering against his jaw. She'd just been playing around. But now...now her lips feathered against his skin once more.

Alarms blared in her head. *Stop this. Do not do this. Not with him.*

She pulled back. Stared into his eyes. Harper found that she couldn't say a word.

You don't trust him! Another alarm blaring in her head. And it was true. She didn't trust him.

She'd agreed to the idea of starting over, but that didn't mean she'd stopped being suspicious.

She needed to get a grip. They were both just playing a role. That was all. Pretending to be involved. Okay, fine, maybe there was a real attraction between them. An attraction she'd noticed on day one. But she was going to ignore it. She could ignore it. She could—

"Tomas is coming up behind you," Roman murmured. "Guess it's showtime."

Showtime. Yes. Right. That was the time.

Roman's fingers slowly slid away from her.

She didn't move back. "It's time for me to get cursed."

He frowned.

"Don't worry. I can handle some danger and desire." She tried to sound flippant, but Harper was pretty sure she failed. She turned away from him.

"That's good to know," Roman assured her quietly. "I'll remember that."

She was certain that he would.

***

Tomas's fingers trailed over Harper's shoulders after he secured the *Lover's Heart* around her neck. The guy's touch was lingering a little too long, and Roman found himself glaring.

It's a role. An act. I'm supposed to be her date. A date would get jealous when some other dumbass got all touchy with his lady, wouldn't he?

Except it didn't exactly feel like he was pretending. It felt all too real to Roman.

"We have one brave woman who isn't afraid of danger!" Tomas's voice boomed out. "Or desire."

Roman nearly snorted. *Laying it on thick, aren't you?*

"She's accepted the curse."

Laughter followed Tomas's dramatic announcement.

"She was also the lucky winner of our random drawing, so the lovely Harper will be allowed one dance while wearing the *Lover's Heart*."

Such bullshit. Harper hadn't won anything. Tomas had thought it would be a great idea for the people at the gala to actually see someone wearing the ruby. According to Harper, Tomas had rambled on about how precious things shouldn't just be admired. They should be savored. Whatever. Sounded like PR bullshit to Roman, but it wasn't his call.

There was a round of applause as Harper stepped forward. The dance floor was in the adjacent room, and Roman took her hand as he escorted her through the crowd. He wasn't her only escort. A security guard and an undercover Wilde agent trailed along with them.

Roman and Harper took up a position in the middle of the dance floor. They were the only ones allowed this dance—the better from a security perspective. He pulled her into his arms. Held her easily as the band began to play. Their bodies moved slowly, in perfect time. As if they'd danced together dozens of times in the past.

Why does she feel so right in my arms?

"You aren't smiling," Harper whispered. "You aren't even looking at me."

No, he wasn't. His gaze was on the crush of people watching them. He forced a smile as he told her, "I'm searching for threats."

"You didn't want me wearing the necklace."

No, he hadn't. He'd argued against it when he heard the idea. "It seemed like an unnecessary way of putting a target on you."

"But I have you to keep me safe."

His gaze cut to her, for just a moment. Then back to the onlookers. "Damn straight you do."

She laughed. Was it for show? So that the people watching would think they were a couple and she was having the time of her life? Probably.

But what would it be like if Harper was really happy to be dancing with him?

Doesn't matter. Won't ever matter. He forced his jaw to unclench. "We've got several people who seem far too interested in you. They're staring."

"I'm sure the rest of the team is watching them."

They were.

"If I were going to steal the ruby..." she mused, her voice low as she leaned in even closer to him. "This would not be the time I chose. I mean, everyone is watching now. All the attention is focused on me. For a theft, you don't want attention. You want..." Her head turned. She stared across the room.

"You want...what?" Roman prompted.

She was still looking across the room. "Trust me."

"Ah...excuse me?"

"We're partners. If our relationship is going to work, you have to trust me. So...*trust me.*" She stopped dancing. Her hand dipped down. Her fingers stroked over the ruby. She lifted it up. "It should be heavier."

"It's a giant ruby. I'm sure it is plenty heavy and—"

"Not heavy enough." She yanked at the ruby—and the elaborate chain that circled her neck.

The chain snapped.

There were gasps from the crowd.

The band stopped playing.

Roman wondered what in the hell was happening.

"Harper?" Tomas's shocked voice. He rushed onto the dance floor. "What are you doing?" His eyes were wide. Utterly horrified.

Harper simply smiled her charming, dimpled smile. She lifted the ruby up even higher—the priceless, big as a fist ruby—and then she threw it onto the dance floor.

It shattered into a hundred pieces.

Holy shit.

There were screams. One lady in a blue, strapless gown even slid to the floor in a dead faint.

"Do you know what you've done?" Roman asked. His voice was mild. Curious.

The security guard was running straight for Harper.

"Yes." She nodded. "I saved the day."

Perhaps her definition of saving the day was way different from his?

The museum's security guard made a grab for Harper. "Hell, no," Roman snapped. He caught the man's outstretched arm and sent him hurtling to the side.

Then he realized...

Harper was running. She'd hitched up her dress and was racing straight toward Tomas. Except Tomas—he was running even faster. *Away from her.* He'd whirled around and was rushing through the crowd.

"Stop him!" Harper yelled. "He's got the real ruby!"

The real—

I'll be damned.

But most of the guests ignored her. They were too busy diving for the floor and trying to scoop up what they thought were pieces of the shattered ruby. Harper leapt over several men and one woman, and she kicked her high heels off as she gave chase.

As Roman watched, she shoved her foot on the back of one bent fellow, and she launched herself into the air after Tomas. She slammed into him, and they both hit the floor with a roll. Tomas drew back his fist to hit her—

Oh, the hell no. A bellowing roar burst from Roman as he hurtled toward them. But he was too far away. If Tomas hit her...

I will make that bastard pay.

But Tomas didn't hit her. Harper easily dodged his blow and then delivered a fast elbow right to the man's throat. He gasped, choked, and his eyes doubled as he grabbed frantically for his neck.

Harper pushed to her feet. With one hand, she straightened her dress.

Roman staggered to a stop beside her. He was both incredibly impressed and a little bit confused. "The client is the bad guy?" Roman asked as he reached out a hand to steady Harper.

Tomas's frantic stare flew to him. The man tried to back away by doing some weird-ass spider crawl across the floor.

Roman shook his head. "Don't," he warned.

Tomas flipped over and shoved to his feet.

Some people never listen.

"He has the real necklace," Harper cried out.

"Yeah, and it's my turn to get him." And get him, Roman did. Roman grabbed the bastard around the side and threw him down to the floor. Then before Tomas could scramble to his feet, Roman had a knife at his throat. "She elbowed you. I'll just slice your throat if you piss me off."

Tomas immediately froze.

Actually, everyone had frozen. Roman didn't look away from his prey, but he was pretty sure he could feel every eye in the place on him.

"M-mistake," Tomas gasped.

"Oh, it was a mistake, all right," Harper declared as she crouched and began to pat down Tomas's fancy jacket. "Did you seriously think you were going to steal the necklace under Wilde's watch? I don't think so." She shoved her hand into a pocket inside his jacket.

Roman's gaze flew to her face.

Her smile stretched. Those dimples winked. Her eyes rose to meet Roman's. "Got it."

She sure as hell did. Her hand raised to reveal that she was holding the *Lover's Heart* in her palm.

I'll be damned. The sonofabitch had tried to steal the ruby from his own museum.

Everyone seemed to start talking at once. The voices were loud and blaring. Security guards and Wilde agents closed in. Roman kept his knife at Tomas's throat.

Harper studied the ruby. The light hit it, making the giant jewel gleam. She slid it against her skin, holding the chain behind her neck. "Oh, yes, definite weight difference, just like I thought." Her head tilted as she studied Tomas. "You are such an idiot. Do you have any idea how long you'll be in prison because of this?"

***

"Do you foil a lot of jewel thefts?" Roman asked as he watched Tomas get shoved into the back of a patrol car. The man was crying a little. Shouting a lot. Demanding to speak to an attorney. Claiming everything was a mistake.

Mistake, my ass.

"Not a lot, but every now and then, yes, I do manage to stop some." Harper's voice was modest. The shiver that shook her body was fierce.

Hell, she had to be freezing. They were outside in the chilled air, and she had on that little-bit-of-nothing dress. Sexy as could be, but not exactly warm and covering. Roman shrugged out of his coat and slid it around her delicate shoulders.

Surprise flashed on her face. "Are you trying to be a gentleman with me right now?"

"No."

Her lips parted, but she didn't speak.

Dammit, use more than one word! "I mean, I'm just trying to help you stay warm."

She pulled the coat a little closer. "It smells like you."

"Is that bad?"

"No." She looked away. "Not bad at all."

Eric Wilde had arrived. He was walking straight toward them. As he neared, he pointed at Harper. "You're gunning for a bonus, aren't you?"

"Absolutely."

His lips curled. "Caught him in the act, huh? Nice." His head turned and his smile faded as he glared at the man who was now cuffed in the back of the patrol car. "That prick thought he'd steal on Wilde time? I don't think so."

Yes, about the whole theft...There was something bugging Roman. "Harper, you *knew*. I mean, before you slammed the necklace into the floor, you knew it was fake?"

"I strongly suspected."

"Suspecting isn't the same thing as knowing." He cleared his throat. "If you'd been wrong..."

"I wasn't. Look, I also was suspicious as soon as he wanted me to wear it. Figured taking it out the way he was ordering would be a good time for a switch, and I was right." Her shoulders moved in a small shrug. "I'd worn a ruby almost that big before, and I knew what the weight should feel like. I went along with the ruse for a bit because I wanted us to catch him in the act. We did. Case closed." She winked at Eric. "Bonus earned."

"When did you wear a ruby that big?" The question slipped from Roman.

Her gaze slid to his. Held. "When I was briefly engaged to a crown prince."

He laughed. She didn't.

"I'm heading home. Been a busy night." She eased out of the coat. Handed it back to Roman. "And as a partner, you did not completely suck tonight."

"Thanks?" It was a question.

She didn't respond. Harper was already walking away.

He was admiring the view. He was also still stuck on one thing... "She wasn't engaged to some prince." That was just crazy.

"Uh..."

Roman's stare jumped to Eric. "Was she?"

"You know..." Eric eased back a step. "I don't feel real comfortable sharing personal information about agents."

Was that a yes?

Eric slapped his hand on Roman's shoulder. "But look at you. I'm impressed. You stopped a major theft with your new partner."

"I didn't stop jack. She did it." His attention shifted back to her. Harper was almost at her car. In a few more moments, she'd be gone from the scene.

Gone. *Hell.* He took off running.

"Roman?" Eric called.

"We fucking rode together!" Roman yelled back. Sure, he could have caught a ride with Eric. Or gotten a car to pick him up. But he wanted to ride with her.

I want to stay with her longer.

She'd surprised him. In his mind, he could still see her as she kicked off her high heels and shoved one foot on that random guy's back as she launched herself into the air. She'd had no fear. No hesitation.

She'd been hot as hell.

"Wait!" Roman shouted as he hurried toward the car. It was a sleek beauty, low to the ground and made to go fast.

Harper turned at his call.

"You're my ride," he reminded her. He was still holding his coat. He hadn't bothered to put it on. He'd been too busy chasing her.

"Yes…but am I your ride or die?"

"What?" He frowned at her.

She laughed. "Nothing. A joke. Forget it. Just get in the car."

He got in the car.

"You're so big you barely fit inside. Maybe next time," Harper said as she slid behind the wheel, "we should take *your* car."

His head turned toward her. "Next time?" Did that mean she was done trying to sever their partnership?

She nodded. "Next time."

And as they pulled away, Roman found himself smiling.

***

They had a new target.

He watched as the sports car hurtled away. Roman was inside. Roman and his mystery woman. He'd been close to the car, close enough to hear the pretty lady's teasing question...

Am I your ride or die?

Funny. They would all be finding out the answer to that question soon enough. For the woman's sake, he certainly hoped that she wouldn't have to die.

After all, she would just be the means to an end.

And that end...it was the monster known as Roman Valentino.

CHAPTER THREE

"You live *here*?" Harper let out a low whistle as she slammed her car door and took stock of the giant house in front of her. They'd driven to the gala from the office, and this was her first time to see his place. Oh, who was she kidding? It wasn't a normal house. It was a mansion. A freaking, honest-to-goodness mansion. "I think Eric is paying you way too much. And I believe I deserve a raise."

"I have family money."

"How wonderful for you." Her head cocked as she tried to figure out just how many rooms were in that massive house. "Some of us don't have families, and we have to work hard for every single dime that we get."

Silence.

Whoops. Had she just slipped up and overshared? A glance to the right showed that he was focused hard on her so, yes, she had just overshared. A lot. "I need to go. You should head into the super big house and tuck yourself in. Or, you know, get the butler to do it or something." She needed to get out of there before she rambled way too much.

Too late.

"You're not exactly driving a clunker, Harper. That sports car—"

"It's on loan from Wilde. It was part of our cover. As much as I love Trixie—"

"Trixie?"

"Yes, she's fun, so I figured she needed a fun name. As much as I love her, I have to give her back tomorrow. It's kind of a Cinderella thing. I'll be back to the pumpkin tomorrow."

He didn't head toward the mansion. Instead, he stalked slowly around the car. She could hear him coming toward her. For a moment, she considered jumping back into the vehicle. But, nah, that wasn't her style. She held her ground. Waited.

Soon, he was right in front of her. He stared at her but didn't speak. Just did that quiet, intense vibe that he worked so well. As she peered up at him, a shiver worked its way over her body.

"You're cold."

No, not really. That shiver hadn't necessarily been from the cold, but she still said, "Yes."

And once more, he put his coat around her shoulders.

"I don't need this." She tried to push it away. "I'm leaving and—"

"I wish you'd come inside."

Yes, that was a bad idea. Terrible. "Why?" Surely not for the hot and dirty sex that had just popped into her head. She couldn't help the imagery. It had been a very long dry spell, and she tended to have an over-eager imagination. *Down, girl. Down. He wants—*

"You," he said.

Her heart slammed into her chest. "Excuse me?"

"You have the wrong idea about me. About my family."

"If you're related to Eric, I figured you must have the same awesome family that he—"

"There is nothing awesome about my family. I barely knew my mother, and my father could give nightmares to serial killers."

Her lips parted. But, for once, she didn't know what to say.

"I shouldn't have told you that. Probably just scared the hell out of you." He glanced away from her. "But I'm not some spoiled asshole. I don't want you to think that's who I am."

"You didn't scare me." It took a whole lot to scare her.

"And you don't have to lie to me. I've had more than enough lies in my life, so, for whatever time this partnership lasts, maybe you could just skip giving them to me?"

"I'm not lying." She pulled his coat closer. It was warm and it held his heady, masculine scent. "I am sorry, though."

Slowly, his stare trekked back to her. "Sorry?"

"I have my own issues with money. I didn't know my mother, either. Or my father. So...I-I said something I shouldn't have to you. I'm sorry if I hurt your feelings."

He laughed.

"You're not supposed to laugh when someone apologizes to you. It's rude." Why did she keep having to instruct him on basic things?

He stepped closer to her. "You don't need to worry about hurting my feelings."

She thought that maybe she did. She also wondered if she'd been very wrong about him.

"And you told me you were engaged to a prince," Roman continued gruffly. "Seems like you can deal fine with any money issues that—"

"It was a brief engagement. He fell for me when I worked his protection detail." *Give Roman honesty. He doesn't want lies.* "You were right before. About me, I mean. I do get asked out a lot. For some reason, people get drawn to me. But nothing lasts. I learned that a long time ago. The prince? I knew from the beginning that he wasn't going to last for me." But she'd foolishly hoped for the whole happy-ending routine with him. Hadn't happened. "He was grateful to me. That's all." After him, she'd switched to preferring to guard things, not people.

Things didn't hurt you. Things didn't make you believe they cared. Things didn't leave you hurt and alone. *Jeez. Stop it already.* She was not the pity-party type. "Okay." She blew out a breath. "This night is getting way too long and maudlin. I need to go home. I need to—"

"I know the reason why people are drawn to you."

She swallowed. He was closer. So close that their bodies nearly brushed.

"You smile, and you light up a room."

"It's the dimples," she told him seriously. "People think I'm harmless and fun when they see the dimples. They are my secret weapon."

His gaze had fallen to her mouth. "I've thought the same thing."

She forced a smile. "See?" She knew her dimples would be out. There was plenty of light spilling from all around his house so he should be able to see her dimples quite clearly.

"I agree they are a weapon, but it's not just the dimples." His head lowered toward her. "It's you. It's..."

Wait. Was he about to kiss her? Did she *want* him to kiss her?

Her hands flew up and pressed to his chest. "We're partners."

"And you don't kiss partners?"

She had no rule about that at all. It hadn't exactly come up before. She knew plenty of Wilde personnel dated each other. They just had to fill out some PR form and... *"Roman."* Was she leaning onto her toes? She was.

She still didn't trust him. But she sure did wonder what his kiss would feel like. "This could be a horrible mistake."

"Sure. Worst ever." He didn't back away.

Harper tried to break the thick tension that surrounded them. "We could kiss and then you'd fall hopelessly in love with me, and we'd never be able to work a case again."

He seemed to absorb her words. Why was he being so quiet? She'd just been kidding. But—

"Or..." His voice was such a low, deep rumble when it finally emerged. "We could kiss, and the desire between us could burn out of control. You could get so turned on that you rip off my clothes, and we have sex right here. Fast, hot, dirty, make-you-scream sex."

"That's an option," Harper whispered. She couldn't remember the last time she'd had fast, hot, dirty, make-you-scream sex. Not like the offer was just given every single day and—

"Fuck."

Yes, if they kissed and ignited, she did imagine they might—

"Someone's here." His head turned toward the house. "An uninvited guest."

What? She was still rather stuck on the fast, hot, dirty—

Harper shook her head. Focused on his house. She saw that a light was now shining from the window to the left of the double front doors. That particular light hadn't been on a moment before. And the rest of his words registered.

Uninvited guest.

Tension snaked through her. Not the sexy tension of a moment before. But hard, driving tension. Adrenaline. "Someone broke into your house?"

"He has a way of showing up when I don't want him to appear." Roman took a step back. "I'm afraid the night has to end for us." He swung away.

That was it? He'd almost kissed her and now he was stalking off to confront an intruder? "No."

He stopped.

She grabbed his arm. "I'm your partner."

He looked down at her.

"That means when an intruder is in your home, I don't stand back and let you face danger alone. Jeez, man. Who have you been hanging out with?"

His gaze drifted over her face. "The wrong people, obviously."

She nodded. "Damn straight. If we're making this work, we have each other's back. That's just what happens." Kisses or no kisses. Her shoulders straightened. "So let's go in there and take care of this business right—"

"I know who is inside. He's a pain in the ass, but no threat."

"Well, still, I should come with you and—"

"No."

His answer had been kind of fast and hard. And sure, it made her super suspicious.

"You don't want to meet him." Roman shook his head. "Your life will be far better without him in it."

"But—"

"Drive safely, Harper. I'll see you at the office."

Well, damn. He'd just dismissed her. Without another word, he marched for the house.

He'd gone from nearly kissing her to walking away from her without a backward glance. All in just a few minutes. How about that?

Her chin notched up. She kept her eyes on him, and right before he slipped into his house...

OhmyGod. Did Roman just pull out a gun?

He had.

There was no way she was just going to leave her partner on his own to face whatever threat waited. If it was a *friendly* visitor, he wouldn't take a weapon inside.

Roman, I'm watching your back. Whether you want my help or not, you're getting it.

***

"A gun, Roman? Really?" The man sitting in the study let out a long sigh when Roman crept into the room. The lamp blazed from the corner. "Aren't we past that stage in our relationship? You know, the whole let's-kill-each-other phase? I thought that phase ended when I married your lovely sister."

Roman narrowed his eyes on the intruder—and his brother-in-law. Dexter "Dex" Ryan. CIA mastermind. All-around-pain-in-the-ass. "What in the hell are you doing here?"

"Checking in on a friend." Dex didn't get out of the chair, but he did put a hand over his heart. "I care, you know? I care deeply."

"You are such a jackass." But Roman holstered his weapon. He'd been about ninety-five percent sure Dex would be his visitor. When the light had flashed on, he'd gotten the signal to come inside. Someone who'd wanted to kill him wouldn't have ever so helpfully turned on the light.

"I am many things to many people." Dex grinned at him. "I was worried you'd bring the lady in, so I figured I'd better give you a signal that I was waiting here."

"She wasn't coming in." Though he'd hoped and he'd been so close to kissing—

"Not coming in? Are you sure? I mean, you two had a big date, she brought you back home, and then I did happen to peek outside, and I spied you leaning in for a kiss—"

"She's my partner at Wilde."

Dex's grin slipped. "What?"

"My partner." He knew Dex had heard him the first time. "Don't worry, she's on her way—"

"Behind you," Dex growled.

Roman's shoulders stiffened. He hadn't heard anyone approach. But when he spun around, he found Harper staring straight at him. Her right hand was raised and holding a gun. The gun wasn't pointed at him. It was angled toward Dex.

"Oh, my," Dex's amused voice rang out. "This is certainly an unexpected development. Did she just get the drop on you?"

Such an ass. Roman took a step to the side. He put his body between Harper's gun and Dex. "No," he snapped back at his brother-in-law. "She got the drop on you."

A faint line appeared between Harper's delicate eyebrows. "What's happening here?"

He needed to tread with extreme caution. "I'm...talking with a friend."

"You didn't strangle on the word 'friend' when you said it," Dex noted. "I am impressed."

Roman sucked in a deep breath. "You can put the gun down, Harper. He's no threat."

"If he's no threat, then why did *you* pull out your weapon before you came inside?"

"I am a threat." Now Dex sounded annoyed. "My entire body is a deadly weapon, and you know it, Roman. Don't you dare even pretend that I'm not—"

Roman fired a disgusted glance over his shoulder.

Dex clamped his lips together.

"An annoyance," Roman clarified as he focused back on Harper. "That's what the man is. An annoyance. But no threat."

She lowered her gun.

"That's a lovely dress you're wearing." Dex had risen and was edging closer. The floor creaked beneath his feet. "I don't believe I got your name."

"I'm—"

Roman caught her arm. Pulled her toward the door. "She's leaving, and you're forgetting her."

Harper's mouth dropped open. "Roman! What—"

He kept pulling her toward the foyer. "How did you get inside? I know I locked the door."

"Well, yes, but I picked the lock. I was worried about you, and I wanted to help."

He stopped at the double doors. Gaped at her.

"What? I'm not crazy. Someone was in your house. You went in with a weapon. A good partner wouldn't just leave you when that stuff was happening."

She'd come in to protect his back?

"You didn't introduce me," she chided.

"That's because you don't want to know him, and I don't want him to know you." The last thing he wanted was for Dex to try pulling her into some of his spy games.

Harper's gaze sharpened. "So you have a secretive frenemy in your home. Someone who made you so leery that you approached him with a gun, but it's no big deal."

Frenemy? His temples throbbed. "Yes."

"That's not suspicious behavior at all." She glanced back toward the study.

Dex stood in the doorway. His gaze was on her, and Roman did *not* like the way the other man was watching Harper. "Stop it," he ordered.

Dex merely crooked a brow.

He needed to get Harper out of there. ASAP. Roman yanked open one of the front doors. Prodded her over the threshold. "Thanks for having my back, but I'm good. Better call it a night."

"But—"

"Harper, you need to go."

Her lips thinned. "This is not the way to build trust."

He got that. "I'm sorry I ate your chocolates."

"What?"

"Good night." He shut the door. Firmly but, hell, in her face.

"Oh, man." A low whistle from Dex. "That is not going to score you points. If you plan to get her into bed, you are going to have do some serious groveling to make up for this crap."

Roman locked the doors and spun around. "Why are you screwing up my life?"

"I'm not screwing it up. I'm helping. I'm a helper."

Bullshit. Roman stomped toward him. *Hell, yes, I'll have to grovel. And buy her new chocolates.*

"Look, I just wanted to check in on you. Make sure this whole new-life thing was going okay." Dex didn't move. "You have a lot of enemies. We did our best to bury your past, but I wanted to make certain no one had found you."

"I'm ready for any threat."

"Um. Yes. If that's your story."

"What the hell does that mean?"

"It means a petite beauty in a white dress just got the drop on you. I'm worried you're losing your edge."

"Fuck off."

"I'm hearing whispers." Dex's voice turned grim.

Tension skated through Roman's body. "What?"

"Someone is looking for you. You pissed off a lot of people. Some of those people have long memories and extensive reaches."

"I thought the CIA fixed my past. You know, when they made me a dead man." The person he'd been before? He'd died. A violent, fiery death. Or at least, that was the story. And he'd switched lives. Become Roman Smith. A Wilde agent. He'd known the transition might not be exactly seamless, but for someone to already be hunting for him…

That was damn fast.

"Just stay on your toes," Dex advised him. "I have my people checking things out. But don't lower your guard." He swept by Roman and made his way for the door. "Because if you do, you'll turn around and find a woman in an evening gown holding a gun on you."

"Not funny." Not even a little bit.

"It wasn't supposed to be funny. It was supposed to be a warning. Or have you forgotten the last time you let a woman get too close?"

He *would* bring up that. Figured. "Harper isn't like that."

Dex slanted him a glance. "Oh, it's Harper?"

"She's with Wilde. I'm sure Eric has checked and triple checked her background."

"If she's going to continue working with you, I'll be checking her background, too."

His spine was ramrod straight. "Leave her alone."

Dex held up his hands. "What? I'm not torturing the woman. I'm just doing a standard background check. I'm looking out for you."

"Nothing is standard when it involves you. Leave her alone," he said again. "I mean it. Don't pull Harper into your world."

"You're the one who pulled her in. You're the one who was almost kissing her." Dex shrugged. "I'm just the one who wants to make sure she's not some double-agent who has been hired to kill you. Isn't that what friends are for? I wouldn't be a good brother-in-law if I didn't watch your sorry ass."

"Dex..."

"If she doesn't have anything to hide, it won't be a big deal." He reached for the doorknob. "And if she does have something to hide, then I'll just make certain she vanishes so that she's no threat to you."

"That shit is not funny."

"No, it isn't." Without another word, Dex left.

Fuck me.

CHAPTER FOUR

He'd kicked her out. He'd been meeting with some seriously shady guy with a gaze that had been downright scary. And Roman kicked her *out*. Just shoved her out the door as if they hadn't been about to kiss five minutes before. That was annoying. Insulting.

Maddening.

Harper marched out of her bathroom. She was wearing her favorite pair of pajamas. Soft and silky, they slid gently over her skin. She hopped into the bed. Yanked the covers up to her chin and glowered at the ceiling.

Had she really wanted Roman to kiss her? She'd never gotten involved with a partner. Sure, there were plenty of hookups at Wilde. When you were living twenty-four, seven in a high-adrenaline world, emotions tended to break past your control. And yes, she *had* fallen for that one client that time. But…

It had been a mistake. A painful one.

After that disaster, she'd decided not to ever mix her personal life and work, but then tonight, she'd been less than an inch away from pressing her mouth against Roman's and seeing how he tasted.

I bet he's delicious.

Delicious and dangerous. And what had been up with the mansion? And the creepy frenemy who'd been waiting inside and—

Her phone rang.

Her head turned on the pillow.

The phone rang again and vibrated on her nightstand. She threw her hand out and saw the caller's ID...Roman Smith. Tension snaked through her body as she reached for the phone. Her finger slid over the screen, and she put the phone to her ear. "Hello?"

"I wanted to make sure you were all right." His voice was deep and dark and ever so sexy.

She looked up at the ceiling. *It doesn't matter that he sounds sexy.* "Why wouldn't I be all right?" Her own voice was flat.

"You're mad."

"Why would I be mad?"

"Harper..."

"I'm all right." Her voice was softer. But still flat.

"I'm sorry...look, I didn't want you around that guy, okay? And if I seemed like an ass—"

"You did," she assured him.

A long sigh. "I apologize. He has a way of causing trouble. I didn't want that trouble touching you."

"You realize, of course, that everything you are saying about this mystery man just makes me more curious about him."

He cursed.

She caught herself smiling.

"Can you just forget him?" Roman asked her.

Not gonna happen. "Even more curious," she murmured.

Another curse. A fun, inventive one.

Her smile stretched. But worry nagged at her. "Is he a threat to you?" Her voice had turned very serious.

"No. I can handle him. There's just no need for him to pull you into his world. If you ever happen to be out and you see the guy coming at you, do me one favor, okay?"

"Uh, what's that?"

"Run."

She laughed.

He didn't.

"Want to tell me more?" Harper prompted into the heavy silence.

More silence.

Her hold tightened on the phone. So they were back to that, hmm? *That's rather what I thought.* "Good night, Roman."

"Wait!"

Her heart thudded into her chest.

"Are we going to talk about it?" Roman asked gruffly.

"It?" Her voice notched up.

"Yeah. It."

"You'll have to be more specific."

"We almost kissed."

"Oh. That."

"*Yes*. That."

Her gaze darted around her room. Had she just heard a tapping on her window? The wind must be picking up. "Nothing happened. So there's nothing to talk about. Now, it's late and I should—"

"I wanted to kiss you."

And I wanted to kiss you. "I need to go to sleep."

"Right. Got it. Good night…"

She exhaled. "Good night."

"Harper?"

"Yes?"

"I still want to kiss you." Soft.

And I still want to kiss you. But she didn't say those words. She ended the call. Stared down at her phone. Roman was driving her crazy. She felt the attraction. She wanted him. But…

His words slipped through her head. *If you ever happen to be out and you see the guy coming at you, do me one favor, okay?*

Run.

Roman was keeping secrets. Far too many of them. She'd always hated secrets. Mostly because they had a way of hurting innocent people.

She put the phone back on her nightstand. Plumped up her pillow. And decided that she would not think about Roman again for the rest of the night. Would not. Absolutely would *not*.

The man had better not slip into her dreams.

***

Roman stared at the phone. Yeah, one hundred percent, he'd screwed up that call with Harper. He didn't normally call women in the middle of the night, so he hadn't been sure what to say. He'd just wanted to talk to Harper.

He liked hearing her voice. Something about her voice made his chest feel warm.

He'd probably sounded like an idiot. Figured. Could he do nothing right with her?

He dropped his phone and shuffled toward the bathroom. A cold shower was in order. Maybe in the morning, he could take her some chocolates. An apology for eating the ones that had been on her desk and also a congrats gift for their museum case.

Yes, he'd take her chocolates.

Until then, hell, he'd be fucking fantasizing about her mouth.

***

A rustle woke her later. The faintest of sounds, but Harper had always been a light sleeper. Her eyes flew open and—

Something slapped over her mouth. A hard, rough, gloved hand.

"We won't hurt you," a male voice growled. "So just take it—"

She raked her nails toward where she thought his eyes would be. He screamed and stumbled back. Harper leapt from the bed. With one hand, she scooped up her phone, and with the other, she shoved at the hulking shadows that lunged for her.

In my home. In my home. She didn't know who these guys were, and she wasn't about to stand around and find out. She kicked at one attacker and leapt for her bedroom door.

But...

Someone grabbed her from behind.

"We don't want to hurt you!" It was the same growling voice.

She elbowed him as hard as she could. His hold loosened. She shot forward. Someone was blocking the hallway, so she rushed into her bathroom. Shut the door. Locked it and—

She swiped her finger over her phone's screen. She had to call Roman. He'd come and help her. She needed—

"Get away from the door!" A bellow.

She looked up. The window. She should get her ass out of the window—

The door flew open. Wood splintered because her attacker had kicked in the door.

Her eyes had adjusted to the darkness, and she could make out three forms crowding in her bathroom doorway. They closed in on her.

Harper got ready to fight like hell. They might be saying they didn't want to hurt her, but she was more than willing to hurt them.

***

Roman straightened his shoulders. He clutched the box of chocolates in one hand, and he lifted his other fist to pound against Harper's door.

He'd waited until noon before coming over. Noon on a Saturday. She should be up, right?

Except...

He didn't hear a sound from inside her house. He shifted a little to the left as he tried to peek through the curtains near the door. Her neighborhood was quiet. A kid rode his bike on the sidewalk. A lady was checking her mail. And Harper...

Wasn't home?

Well, shit. He probably should have called first. Roman knocked once more—

Just as his phone rang. It was a ring tone he'd assigned to her. A light, happy ring that he'd made hers because it had seemed to fit her and—*screw it*. He almost dropped the chocolates as he yanked out his phone. "Harper, look, I'm actually at your—"

"You're at her house, and you have chocolates," a distorted voice said. "That's really fucking sweet."

Roman's body went ice cold. He checked the phone's screen. *Definitely Harper's number*. He swallowed. No emotion was in his voice as he demanded, "Who the hell is this?"

"I'm the man who has your girlfriend. So that means I'm the man who has you by the balls. You'll do what I say. When I say it. Or I'll have to hurt the pretty Harper. Such a shame. She's got a gorgeous smile, don't you think?"

"I think..." He swallowed again. "I think if you touch her, I will kill you."

"Promises, promises." The line went dead.

A chill skated over Roman's body. Without hesitation, he lifted his foot and kicked in Harper's front door. *"Harper!"* he roared.

Part of him was afraid—very, very afraid— that he would find her dead inside. The bastard on the phone had never let him hear Harper's voice.

There had been no proof of life and that could mean...

She's already gone.

"Harper!" Roman shouted. He raced through the house. The den was undisturbed. The kitchen dark. But her bedroom. God, her bedroom...

He flipped on the lights and fully saw the chaos. The overturned furniture. The smashed lamp. And to the right, her bathroom door—splintered wood. It hung drunkenly on the hinges, as if someone had kicked it open, too. He ran into the bathroom. The window over the sink had been smashed, and, oh, no, that was blood. Blood on the glass. Blood on the sink. Spattered on the tiled floor.

His frantic gaze swung to the left. To the right. He hurried back into her bedroom. Yanked open her closet. Searched under her bed. He kept calling for her and—

He heard the creak of the floorboard behind him. Roman whirled and lifted his hands to attack.

"I want you to freeze." A young guy stood there, wearing jogging shorts and a loose hoodie. He had a gun clutched in his hands. "I'm a cop. Harper's next-door neighbor."

The red-haired fellow was shaking. His nervous gaze darted from Roman to the wreckage of the room.

This scene had to look bad. "I didn't do this." Roman kept his hands up.

"Where's Harper?"

"I don't know." *But I will find her.*

"I saw you kick in her door." The cop licked his lips. "I called for backup."

Roman took a step forward.

"Don't! Don't you move! You stand right there until backup arrives."

"Harper is missing. I need to find her." Before it was too late. Before that bastard on the phone hurt her.

But the cop shook his head. "You're not going anywhere."

***

The box of chocolates had been smashed in the den. Roman didn't even remember dropping them when he'd rushed inside. Her house had turned into a crime scene. The "backup" had arrived all too quickly.

"Tell me again why you kicked in the door," a detective said to Roman.

Roman's jaw clenched and he gritted out, "For the third time, I thought I heard her calling for help." That was his story. He didn't mention the phone call.

"And you have no idea where Harper might be? No idea—"

"*You* have no fucking idea what's at play here," Roman snarled back as he lost what was left of his control. "I'm wasting damn time. Get out of my way and let me find her, *now*." His voice was a lethal snarl.

The balding detective swallowed. "Uh…"

Eric Wilde appeared behind the fellow. He leaned in close, whispered something, and the detective suddenly told Roman, "You're free to go. If we have more questions, we'll follow-up with you."

Roman's nostrils flared. He jerked his head toward the front door, indicating that he wanted Eric to follow him. Then he hurried for the exit. Tension and fury filled every part of his body. Outside, the neighbors were gawking. Staring at the scene with wide eyes. He ignored them and went straight to his car.

Eric's hand closed around his shoulder. "What didn't you tell the cops?" His voice was low.

Roman spun to face him. "She was taken because of me."

Eric's eyes widened. "What?"

"I got a fucking call. Bastard said if I didn't do what he wanted, he'd hurt her." Darkness was closing in on Roman. So much fury. "Knew this was a bad idea. What the hell was I thinking? I can't erase my past. Dex tried to warn me. He..." His voice trailed away.

Dex. Roman shook his head. *Should have thought about that jerk first.*

Eric still gripped his shoulder. Eric's hold tightened. "Talk to me. I can't help if I don't have all the facts."

"Dex was at my house last night. He saw her." *Fuck. Fuck.* "Said he was going to run a check on her."

"I've run plenty of background checks on Harper. She's clean. She's good."

Good.

"Dex said..." Roman's heart raced, and he wanted to wrap his hands around a certain CIA mastermind's neck. "He said that she'd vanish. If she was a threat, he'd make her vanish."

Eric's lips parted. He didn't speak.

"He doesn't make idle threats." They both knew that about Dex. Eric had been pulled into Dex's web more than a few times, and he understood how the guy operated, too. Maybe the phone call had been part of some elaborate plan Dex was working. Maybe Dex was screwing with his head. The guy loved mind games. "If he took her..." Roman already had his phone out. He was one of the few people in the world who had Dex's private number.

The line rang once, twice.

"Well...happy Saturday to you," Dex answered. "We just spoke last night. Are you missing me already? That is so sweet."

"Where is she?" Roman snapped.

"Uh, your sister? You want to talk to her? You could have called *her* line, you know, not—"

"Harper. Where in the hell is Harper?"

Silence.

The kind of silence that made Roman tense even more. "You don't have her," he said.

"No." Dex's voice sharpened. "Is she missing?"

He looked back at the house. A yellow line of police tape flapped in the wind. "Yes."

"Since when?"

"I don't know. I'm at her house now. Got here at noon. She was gone. Bedroom and bathroom are trashed."

"I'm on it. I'll tap into every security camera on her block. We'll figure out where she is. Tell Eric I'll coordinate with him. We will find her."

"This isn't a game," Roman fired back. "Swear to me that you don't have her. Swear—"

"Roman, I don't have your partner, but I'll help you find her. *That* I swear."

***

When the door opened, she was going to attack.

Harper glanced around her surroundings. The room was nice—actually, more than nice. Giant bed. Huge tray of food. Fancy bottled water. An equally nice bathroom snaked to the left, attaching to her room—correction, her prison.

No windows, of course. Or, rather, the windows had been boarded up.

She'd woken in the room. Her last memory had been of three goons charging at her in her home—in her bathroom?—then she'd woken...here.

Still wearing her pajamas. Minus her phone. And alone.

But the door was going to open. Sooner or later, it had to open. And when it did...

She clutched the broken, wood post that she'd taken from the bed. When that door finally opened, she would attack.

When she'd woken up, her first order of business had been to escape. Unfortunately, she'd quickly determined she was locked in. Tight.

The second order of business? Get a weapon.

So she'd eyed the four poster bed. Turned it into a three poster.

Her hands gripped the post. Her gaze darted to the bedroom's doorknob just as she heard a faint rattle.

Showtime.

She flattened her back against the wall. Held her breath. Gripped her post tightly.

The door swung open. A man rushed inside on silent footsteps. Big, strong, wearing a black ski cap and a hulking, black coat.

She kept her mouth closed as she sprang forward and brought her weapon down toward his back.

But then he spun. As if he'd sensed her. His hand flew up. He curled his fingers around the post, stopping its attack, and, with his hold on the post, he yanked her forward. She stumbled against him and her eyes widened in stunned surprise as she realized that she was staring straight at— "Roman?"

She saw relief flash in his gaze. And then— then he was kissing her. His mouth locked on hers, and his tongue thrust into her mouth.

CHAPTER FIVE

She was safe. She was alive. And he was kissing her. Roman knew this was probably—definitely—not the right time or the right place, but the last ten hours had been a nightmare. He'd been so desperate to find her. He'd chased down lead after lead that had turned up jackshit. He'd been worried that he wouldn't locate Harper. And to see her, now...

He pulled her even closer. God, she tasted fantastic. Her body was soft and warm, and her lips were open and parted for him. He tasted and tasted and she gave a little moan in the back of her throat that drove him insane and then she—

Shoved him away. Her eyes were wide. Stark. Her lips swollen and red. "Did you...did you do this?"

This? He... "What?" His breath sawed in and out.

"You..." She shook her head. "Did you have me brought here?" She backed away from him. "What is happening?"

Wait. Harper thought he'd kidnapped her? "I'm not the bad guy." *This time.* "I'm the one who came to save you." His voice was gruff. Rough. Because her accusation had just been insulting. He'd rushed to the rescue and she'd—

She'd tried to attack him with a bed post. He'd tossed the post to the floor when he'd kissed her, and now he frowned down at it. "Nice weapon."

"What is happening, Roman?"

His gaze lifted to meet hers. "Are you hurt? Baby, did they hurt you?"

She shook her head. "No, but I tried my best to hurt them."

His chest warmed. Of course, she had. This was his Harper, after all. "We're getting out of here." The sooner he got her out of that place, the better. "Come on." He offered his hand to her.

She didn't take it. "I am not moving until I know what the hell is going on."

"You were kidnapped. I'm rescuing you. That's what's going on. The bastards who took you were going to hurt you unless I..." But his words trailed away because he was fully taking in the scene around him.

The bottled water. The...wine? Expensive wine. Chocolates. Breads. Pastries. Silken sheets. Comfortable covers. A wide selection of books on a cozy shelf. "What in the hell? What is happening?" Roman demanded.

"That was my question! My repeated question."

His attention flew back to her. "Tell me you didn't eat anything here."

"What is this? My first kidnapping? Actually, yes, it is the first time I've been kidnapped." Her tongue swiped over her lower lip. "But I know you don't just greedily gobble up the food that your abductor provides to you. I didn't touch the food. I *did* drink some of the water. But I made sure the bottle hadn't been opened. It's a glass bottle, factory sealed, or at least, it looked that way."

There were plenty of ways around seals. "We'll get the bottle checked. We'll get the whole place checked. The rest of the cavalry will be here soon, but for now, we're getting out of here." He didn't wait for her to take his hand. He took hers.

She was in her pajamas. Cute, silky red pajamas, and her feet were bare.

"They broke in while I was sleeping," she murmured.

I am going to destroy them.

"How did you find me?"

"I had some help." A lot of help. Help courtesy of Dex, and Roman would have to pay that debt back in blood. "They left you alone in the cabin. Or, at least, you were alone when I arrived. We need to get out of here before they come back."

She nodded. A quick, jerky motion. "As soon as it's safe, you'll explain everything?"

Ah...*some* things. He couldn't exactly reveal all the dark, deep details of his life to her.

"Promise?" Harper pushed.

"I'll explain what I can," he replied carefully.

"Good enough for now." Her head turned toward the doorway. "Let's go." With her free hand, she scooped up the bed post that had rolled across the floor.

They crept through the old cabin together. Located in the mountains along the Alabama/Georgia border, the cabin had taken some time to find. Back at the scene of the abduction, Dex had pulled up all the street cam footage that he could get his clever hands on.

Then it had been a matter of tracking the mystery van they'd discovered parked suspiciously near Harper's house in the middle of the night. They'd tracked and followed the van's progress, and eventually, they'd discovered it had come to this little dot of a town. After he'd found the town, Roman had started thinking like the kidnappers.

If I took her, I'd need a remote spot to keep her. If I was going to keep her and not kill her—

Harper glanced back at him. She shivered. "Why do you look that way?"

Roman immediately schooled his features. For a moment, savage fury had burned through him when he thought of what those bastards could have done to Harper. And...

I still don't know what they did.

"Never mind." She shook her head. Focused forward again. They were almost to the front door. "There's no other furniture in this place. Just in my room?"

Yes, the furniture had only been in the room used for her. The rest of the place seemed abandoned.

When they reached the main door, he went out first. Roman had his weapon ready. Snow fell lightly onto the ground. Only his vehicle was there, the rented SUV that he'd hauled ass in so that he could reach her. The other Wilde agents were checking different cabins. Dex had a crew helping in the search, too. They'd all fanned out to search possible locations.

I found her first.

"Stay behind me," he ordered.

"Really? Because I was hoping to run in front of you and make myself a big, giant target."

He stilled. Glanced back. After being abducted, she was still joking?

A shiver shook her body as he stared at her and tried to figure her—

Shit. A shiver.

Pajamas.

No shoes.

I am such an asshole.

Once more, he did a quick visual of the scene. No other vehicle. No tracks in the snow. Looked as if they were alone. Time to get the hell out of there.

He grabbed her. Scooped her up against him and cradled her against his chest.

"Roman! What are you doing?" Her question was low, barely a breath.

He was protecting her cute little feet and sharing his body warmth. He ran to the SUV. Tucked her into the passenger seat then raced around to the driver's side. Moments later, he had the engine growling to life, and he was racing away with her.

***

When something mattered to you, you didn't let it go. You fought for it. You took any risk.

You got back what had been taken.

He watched the SUV hurtle away through the night vision goggles. He'd known better than to get too close to the cabin. Roman would have spotted him.

The woman hadn't been hurt. Not so much as bruised.

But Roman had still carried her out of the cabin. Cradled her as if she was some precious, broken doll. He hadn't sent others to retrieve her. He'd come himself, even knowing he could be walking straight into a trap.

Such a mistake, Roman. You know better than to reveal what matters to your enemies.

Because when an enemy knew how to destroy you, the battle was already won.

***

Roman shouldered out of his coat as he drove and pushed it toward her. "Here. Put this on so you can warm up."

He already had the heat blasting out of the vents for her, but she eagerly took the coat. When they'd left the cabin, her veins had seemed to immediately ice. Good thing he'd carried her to the car. Otherwise, her poor toes would have been icicles. "Th-thanks." She was still shivering.

He grunted a reply.

Her eyes narrowed on him. A grunt. Seriously? Her lips parted as she prepared to tell him—

He'd dialed a number and the ringing of a phone filled the interior of the vehicle. The rings didn't last long, though, before Eric's deep voice boomed, "Tell me you found her."

She hunched deeper into the coat. It was thick and huge and she felt as if she were wearing some kind of armor with it around her. *I'm safe now. Everything is okay.*

"I've got her with me." Roman rattled off an address. "Get a team searching up there. I want tests run on the food and the drinks in the cabin. She had some of the water, and we have to make sure nothing was poisoned."

A lump rose in her throat. She choked it down.

"Every inch of the cabin should be dusted for prints. Dex will have people who can get us an immediate turn around—on any evidence, on any potential poisons, on *anything* found there."

"Was she hurt?" Eric asked, worry edging in his voice.

"*She* wasn't," Harper responded. "Though, I, um, do think I was drugged back at my place. The last thing I remember was being in my bathroom, three hulking figures coming at me, and then—nothing. Not until I woke up in the cabin."

"We're going to the closest hospital," Roman declared. "Get agents to meet us there. I'm finding out what those bastards gave to her."

She reached out and touched his hand as he gripped the wheel. "Eric is the boss," she reminded him. Had he forgotten that in the heat of the moment? "You don't give him orders—"

"I do right now," Roman responded without missing a beat. "When it comes to your safety, I'm in charge."

That was news to her. "Since when?"

"Since you were kidnapped because of me."

"What?" Her heart slammed into her chest.

"You were taken," he rasped, "because of me. That means that until I find out who kidnapped you, *I* am going to be in charge of your safety. I will be sticking to you like glue."

She didn't have a quick comeback for that bombshell. Not quick or slow. She didn't have any comeback at all.

Eric was talking. Saying something that was probably important. But she just kept hearing a mental replay of...

You were taken because of me.

"We'll meet you there. Right. Thanks."

She tuned back in to catch the tail end of the conversation. Eric hung up, and she sat in silence. The heat blasted from the vents.

"You're certain they didn't hurt you?" Roman's voice was halting.

"I don't feel hurt anywhere."

"We'll get a doctor to check you out to make sure that everything is all right. I won't leave your side. You don't have to—"

"You won't leave my side because you think my abduction was your fault?"

Snowflakes drifted against the windshield. "I don't think." His voice was grim. "I know. I was at your house, and the piece of shit who took you called me. Said that if I didn't do exactly what he said, he'd hurt you."

Deep breath. Take lots of deep breaths. "And what did he say for you to do?"

"That's just the thing. Nothing. He hung up. Didn't call back. I wasn't going to stand there with my thumb up my ass and wait for you to be sent to me in pieces."

Oh, dear Lord. "Did you say pieces? Because that was an option? Me getting cut into pieces was on the table?"

"I called in every favor I had. I found you. I didn't wait for your abductors to make a deal. Step one was finding you and getting you to safety."

She licked her lips. "What's step two?"

The tension in the vehicle seemed to ratchet up even more. "Finding the SOBs and making them pay."

***

"I want to go home." Harper's toes curled beneath the hospital sheet as she stretched the material. It was sure tucked in tightly at the bottom.

She'd been poked. Prodded. Examined. And finally given the all clear by the doctor. Harper wasn't sure how many hours had passed while she was checked and kept waiting at the hospital, but she wanted to leave.

Now, please.

She'd been fed. That was a win. At first, they'd given her green jello. She'd never realized how amazing jello could be. She'd moved up to broth after keeping down the jiggly green stuff. The warm broth had been incredibly tasty. Or maybe she'd just been incredibly hungry.

Paste would have tasted great to her.

She wasn't even sure why the doctor had been so careful with her food intake. She'd told the hospital staff—multiple times—that she would be happy starting with a whole chicken. No one had listened to her. But she *had* eventually gotten two chicken legs. Win.

She'd been patient. She'd answered question after question for the ever-watchful Roman. He never left her side, and whenever they were alone, he'd ply her with his questions.

But her being *nice* time was over. "I want to go home," she said again.

Roman shook his head. "Not happening." He reclined in the chair near her bed. He'd angled the chair so that he had a clear view of the hospital room door. What did he expect? For the bad guys to suddenly burst in and try to grab her again?

She almost snorted. Like that would happen.

The door flew open. "I'm here for Harper."

Her lips parted. It was—it was the guy from Roman's house. The one with the eyes that had made her so nervous. The frenemy. "I'm supposed to run," Harper announced.

Roman's hand flew out, and his fingers curled around her wrist. A lick of heat—the sexy, passionate kind of heat—rushed through her at his touch. Such bad timing for that heat to occur.

Roman's eyes were on the intruder, but he told Harper, "You're not going anywhere."

The man needed to learn how to make up his mind. "I distinctly recall you telling me that if I ever saw this guy again, I was supposed to run."

The mystery fellow laughed. Not some lightly amused sound, but a full-fledged thunder of laughter.

Her head tilted. She rather liked his laugh. "Who are you?" If Roman wouldn't tell her, maybe this guy would.

He grinned. "Dexter Ryan, at your service." He'd already shut the door and now he advanced toward the bed. "My friends and my enemies both call me Dex. So, you know, choose which one you'll be, then just call me Dex." He had a chart in his hands. A medical chart. Hers?

He flipped through the contents. "She's totally fine. No signs of assault. My team discovered a cloth behind the cabin that smelled faintly of chloroform, so that's probably what they used to knock her out. I spoke to her doc about that, and he said the quantity used on her wasn't enough to cause any severe issues so—"

"Someone used chloroform on me?" Harper cut in. "Like in the old movies when a white cloth is shoved over someone's face?"

Dex stopped reading through her file. "Something like that, yes. The good news is that you've been carefully examined and will have no lasting side effects."

Her gaze jumped to Roman. "He's not telling me everything."

Roman didn't reply.

A knot grew in her stomach. "Why does he have my file? Just who is he?"

"I'm someone you want on your side," Dex retorted. "I'm the man who helped lead Roman to you. I suppose that means I am the man you owe for your life."

What?

"No worries," Dex continued smoothly. "I'll find a way for you to repay that debt in due time."

"Harper owes you nothing." Roman's voice had goose bumps sliding down her arms. "You want repayment? Add it to my tab. I've already told you, she's not coming into your world."

Her gaze darted between the two men. Yes, this must be *exactly* how Alice felt when she woke up in the rabbit hole. In the rabbit hole? Or had it been down the rabbit hole? Whatever. Unlike Alice, Harper had woken in a cabin, after being *chloroformed*. And now everything seemed all topsy-turvy. "I want to go home." She had said that before. Multiple times. She felt like a broken record that no one was hearing.

"Your home isn't safe." Roman kept staring—glaring—at Dex. "But I'll take you back to my place. You'll be safe with me."

She wasn't so sure about that.

"Will she?" Dex's question was all silky. "And here some people think that being in your company is the most dangerous place *to* be."

Red flag. Lots of red flags. As if her whole *abduction* had not been a red flag.

The door swung open behind Dex. Relief flooded through Harper when she glimpsed Eric. "Finally. Someone I can trust."

From the corner of her eye, she saw Roman stiffen. Crap. She slanted him a fast look. His expression had completely locked down, and she had the crazy urge to make some kind of excuse. To say she hadn't meant her words. She'd just been grateful to spy a friendly face.

Roman *had* saved her. Come rushing to the rescue and all that. He'd had her back, exactly like a true partner would. He deserved better from her. Her hand turned so that she was holding him. She gave him a little squeeze.

"Harper." Relief filled Eric's voice. He hurried toward her. Leaned over the bed and gave her a fierce hug. "So glad you're safe."

She let go of Roman and clung to Eric for a moment. "You and me both. I was—"

Eric had been pushed away from her. By Roman. A Roman who was on his feet and glowering.

"I don't think *Piper* would like for you to be holding so tightly to Harper that way. You know Piper, your wife."

"Uh, yes. I know my wife." Eric squinted at him. "She'd be hugging Harper just as tightly if she happened to be here. Harper is like family to us both."

"Family." Disgust thickened that one word. "Right."

Eric winced. "Look, man, I didn't mean—"

Harper clapped her hands together.

All eyes flew to her.

"Hi, there." She used her dimples. "I want to know what's happening."

Dex scratched his chin. "Thought you did know. You need a recap? You were abducted. Taken from your home in the middle of the night. When Roman here brought chocolates to your place the next day—"

Her head swung toward him. "Chocolates? You brought me chocolates?"

Did a faint red stain his cheeks?

"Yeah, when Romeo..." Dex coughed. "I mean, when Roman brought you chocolates, he got a call from your abductor. So Roman broke down your front door and searched the place for you. The cops were, ah, brought in, and we all did a super-hero-type team-up..." His hand motioned toward the other men in the room. "We managed to track down your general location. The teams split up to search the cabins in the area, and Roman found you first. Now you've been checked out, and Roman is about to take you into what I imagine will be his very protective custody." He nodded. "Does that help clear things up for you?"

"No. It doesn't. I knew most of that before you started talking." She had *not* known about the chocolates. Though she shouldn't be focusing on them at the moment. They weren't as important as her abduction. "I want to know who took me."

"Don't we all," Eric groused.

"I'm not going into some kind of protective custody." Harper was definite on that one. She would not be hidden away. She swung her legs to the side of the bed. Shoved to her feet. "I'm joining the hunt for the assholes who kidnapped me." She determinedly stepped forward, intending to stride right out of the door.

She had no idea where her pajamas had gone, but Harper was sure that she'd find some helpful nurse or orderly or doctor in the hospital corridor who could point her in the direction of some scrubs. She'd get dressed and get out.

Eric side-stepped, clearing her path.

Roman didn't move, so she sidled around him.

And Dex just tilted his head and studied her before his gaze drifted over her shoulder. Dex whistled. "Hate to tell you, Harper, but I think you've giving Roman one hell of a view from the back."

She felt the draft. Realized he was right.

Dex added, "Probably Roman *and* Eric—"

"Dex, Eric..." Roman's voice was a low, lethal snarl. "Get the fuck out. I need to talk with Harper, alone. *Now*."

She whirled to face Roman—and made sure that she grabbed the back of her hospital gown and clamped it together with one hand. No way was she giving any additional shows. "I have told you this," she hissed to Roman. "You need to stop ordering your *boss* around. Long lost relative or not, he will fire your ass."

Roman quirked a brow. "You're worried about me. That's a good sign. It means you don't completely hate me right now."

"Why would I hate you?" She was legitimately confused.

He swallowed. "Because I brought this trouble to you. Because you could have been killed, and it would have been my fault."

She stared into his eyes. Saw the pain. The shadows. Harper shook her head. "You didn't kidnap me."

Eric strode for the door. "No, but he did work non-stop to find you. Never seen someone so focused."

"I'd use the word obsessed." Dex's feet shuffled away. "The man was obsessed."

The door closed behind them.

Harper's toes curled against the floor.

"I'm sorry." Roman sounded strained. "Please know that I never intended for anything like this to happen. If I'd thought it would, if I'd thought that someone would try and get to me by targeting *you*—hell, I never would have started this crazy game."

Her shoulders stiffened. "Game?"

Roman raked a hand over his face. "Wrong word. It's not a game. It was a stupid, desperate dream. One that has to stop." His hand fell. A muscle flexed along his jaw. "I'll disappear. That's what I do. But I will *not* leave until I'm certain you're safe. That means I will find the people who took you. And I will hurt them, very badly."

She rocked forward. "I'm sure you meant to say...*We* will find them, and we will turn them over to the proper authorities. You just used the wrong words again. Simple mistake."

For a moment, his expression softened. His lips tilted up. "Sweet Harper." His hand rose. The back of his knuckles slid over her cheek. "I said exactly what I meant."

Her hand flew up to curl around his wrist. "You're trying to scare me. Stop it."

"The last thing I want to do is scare you. But I'm done pretending around you. The lies didn't get me the new life I wanted. So you're going to get the real man I've always been." He leaned toward her. "Don't worry. He can get the job done. When it comes to destruction and revenge, I am a top-notch bastard."

Her gaze searched his. "I think you *are* trying to scare me," she accused. "But it won't work. I'm truly not the type of person who sits on the sidelines when things get dangerous. If that was me, then I wouldn't be working for Wilde. I wouldn't be your partner."

His eyes were on her mouth.

She wet her lips and watched his expression harden even more.

"Thought you didn't want to be my partner." Again, his head slid a little closer to hers. "You were the one who ran to Eric and begged him for a replacement."

She wanted his mouth. When they'd kissed back at that crazy cabin, her adrenaline had been about to burst out of control. Their kiss had felt electric. Consuming. Would it feel that way again? Or would she be calmer now? No more life and death emotional punch making her emotions seem extra powerful...

Making his kiss *feel* extra powerful.

Her body leaned into his. "First, I didn't run to Eric. I walked. Slowly and professionally."

"Did you?" A growl.

"And I didn't beg." She shook her head. "I just stated that we weren't working. But he said we *had* to stay together for six weeks, remember? And our six weeks aren't up."

"No, no, the time isn't up but—"

"But screw it," she whispered. "I have to know if your kiss will feel the same."

"What?" His brows shot up.

And this time, she kissed *him*.

CHAPTER SIX

She felt so good against him. Soft and warm. She smelled so sweet. And her mouth. He freaking *loved* her mouth. He loved all the things that she could do with her tongue.

Harper had let go of his wrist, and both of his hands curled around her hips as Roman yanked her even closer against him. The paper-thin gown—hell, it *was* paper—provided no shield for her. Her pebbled nipples thrust against his chest, and he wanted to feel them against his hands. In his mouth.

He wanted to tear away that gown and feast on her. He was starving, and Harper was exactly what he'd always wanted. What he'd been searching for his entire life and hadn't known. Not until she'd been taken and—

Her hands pushed against his chest. Her head pulled away from his. "Oh, no."

No? Roman stiffened. "What did I do wrong?" And how could he make it right? How could he convince Harper to stay with him?

Shit. Roman immediately shut down his wayward thoughts. Locked down his emotions. He didn't need her to stay. Well, okay, he did, but only long enough for him to catch the fools who'd taken her. When those bastards had been punished, Harper needed to get away from him. As far and as fast as she could go.

"No, it wasn't supposed to feel that way." She was out of his arms. In a blink, she'd put a good foot of space between them. Her fingers rose and pressed to her lips. "Wrong."

She didn't like his kiss? Well, fuck. He'd been turned on like mad from her kiss. Gone molten from her mouth. He'd believed that Harper had been just as aroused as he was.

"I thought the adrenaline would have died down by now." Her hand fell. "I thought I wouldn't respond as intently."

He squinted at her. "Run that by me again."

Her chin immediately notched up. "I'm not supposed to want you this much! I've had an insane twenty-four hours—thirty-six hours—however long it's been!" Her voice rose. "I'm not supposed to kiss you and immediately want to rip off all of your clothes!"

The door opened. Dex popped his head inside. Of course, it would be Dex intruding at the worst time.

"Just a friendly warning," Dex announced cheerily. "Noise travels easily in this place."

Harper's cheeks flushed. "Out," she gritted.

"Yes, ma'am." The door clicked shut.

"Uh, Harper…" Roman swallowed. "That guy—you should probably be aware of just how dangerous he is. Dex isn't the kind of man you want as an enemy." He considered the situation. "Or as a friend."

"What is he to you?" She crossed her arms over her chest.

"He's…" A pause. Roman decided to be honest. "Family. Part of a very messed-up family situation that I have."

Her eyes widened.

Roman realized he'd just revealed more to her than he had ever anticipated. But he'd already said he was going to stop pretending. Telling her the full truth was hard, though, because he was really so…

"I'm fucked up," he told her bluntly. "I have more issues than you can imagine. I like danger too much. I've done things that would give you nightmares. I've betrayed people who trusted me, and I've put enemies into the ground without a second thought."

If possible, those gorgeous eyes of hers became even wider. There was no sign of her dimples.

"I'm not some nice guy. Definitely not the kind of guy you take home to meet the parents."

"I don't have parents for you to meet," she whispered. "I don't have any family."

That hurt him. He didn't like the image of her being alone. He wanted her safe. Protected. Happy.

"I'm the kind of guy…" His voice was gruff. Grating. "I'm the kind you send when you want to make people disappear. When shit needs handling, when gunfire and explosions are lighting the night, *that's* when you send me. I know how to hurt people. How to strike them at their core. I was trained by a master, and I was trained very well." So well that he was broken inside. Bent pieces that couldn't form back into the man that he *might* have become if he'd led a different life.

"I think you're back to trying to scare me." Harper shook her head. "You need to stop that."

"I'm trying to make sure you understand who I am." His hands were fisted. "You can't—dammit, Harper, you can't kiss me. You can't tell me that you want to rip my clothes off and expect me to just laugh that shit off. In case you've missed it, I'm not exactly the laughing type."

"I did not miss that," she assured him. "It is very easy to see."

"You can't play with me."

"That seems a shame."

Was she not listening? "Harper..."

She looked down at her gown. "So, am I walking out in this? Or do you think we can find some scrubs from a friendly nurse? Because I'd like to get out of here. I'm feeling pretty exhausted. I think a kidnapping does that to a person. I also figure we've got a very long drive ahead of us."

"We're not going home right away." *Home.* Funny word. He didn't think he actually had one of those. "I want to do more searching in the area before we leave." His first instinct *had* been to haul ass out of there and get her as far away as possible. But he'd calmed down—marginally—and Eric had assured him that he'd secured a safe place for Harper to stay. "There's a cabin close by. Eric has guards stationed all around it. I'll take you there to rest."

Her delicate jaw tensed. "You're not going to dump me, then hunt while I'm sleeping."

She had it all wrong. "I don't intend to leave you at all."

"Oh."

"I told you, until these bastards are caught, we're staying together. We'll both rest up." Because he hadn't slept since she'd been taken. Something he wouldn't mention. No sense in her knowing that part. "Dex and Eric have capable team members who can begin the recon. After we've gotten some sleep, we'll start the hunt." They'd find what evidence they could, *then* he'd get Harper back to his place outside of Atlanta.

A knock tapped against the door. "Is the heart-to-heart finished?" Dex called.

For the moment. "Get your ass in here," Roman rumbled back.

The door opened. Dex came in carrying a pair of green scrubs. He offered them to Harper. "See how beneficial it can be to have me as a friend?"

She reached for the scrubs. "How are you his family?"

"Sorry, but I don't reveal secrets." Dex shrugged. He didn't sound the least bit apologetic.

Her gaze cut to Roman. "That's okay," she said to Dex, but her focus lingered on Roman. "Sooner or later, I'll learn all his secrets."

Dex laughed. "Oh, highly doubtful."

Dex was right. Roman wanted to be truthful with her but...*No, baby, you can't ever learn about all of the things I've done.* If she did, she'd fear him too much. Fear him, hate him—was it the same thing?

Her smile came slowly. The dimples dipped into her cheeks. "Sooner or later, I'll learn everything."

An ache burned in Roman's chest.

***

"For the tenth time, Eric, I'm fine." She was trying hard to be polite, and Harper more than appreciated everything that Eric had done for her, but exhaustion had her weaving on her feet. Harper just wanted to crash in the giant bed that she could see in the bedroom behind Eric. "Please tell Piper that I am good, and I will call her soon."

"Guards are stationed all around the cabin. No one is going to get inside to you, I swear it."

"Right. Guards outside and Roman..." Her gaze darted to the left. Roman stood near the fireplace. "Roman is inside to keep me company."

Roman's stare was on her. All intense and focused.

With an effort, she pulled her attention back to Eric. "You know, I think I held my own against those guys pretty well. Things are blurry, yes, but I am remembering a few more bits and pieces." That was true. "One guy kept saying he didn't want to hurt me." She shrugged. "But I was fine with hurting him. I'm pretty sure I gave him a nice, ragged scratch on the cheek."

Roman stalked toward her.

"I was going to call Roman." She could recall this now. "I'd made it to the bathroom. I had the phone in my hand. But..." Her temples throbbed. "Then I think they broke down the door."

"And took you," Eric concluded. She could see the anger in his eyes and in the faint tightening of his mouth. Eric's agents weren't just employees to him. They were friends. Practically family.

Or, in Roman's case, actual family.

She knew Eric was furious about her abduction and that he'd do everything possible to find the perps responsible. Pissing off Eric Wilde was never a good idea. Someone out there had made a serious mistake.

"You'll take care of her?" Eric asked Roman.

Harper sighed. "I'll take care of *him*. How about that?"

"Well, yes, I knew that." Eric inclined his head toward her. "But I wanted to make sure Roman wasn't going to cut out while you were asleep because he had some crazy revenge streak going."

"Oh, I've definitely got a crazy revenge streak." Roman's words were low. "But I won't be leaving Harper. To get at her, the jerks will have to face me first."

"Good to know." Eric slapped him on the shoulder. "I'm going back to the cabin where she was held. I want to search the area myself. You two rest, and I'll check in later."

Right. Rest. She was so ready to fall face-first into the bed.

Harper didn't speak again until Eric was gone and the cabin's security system had been engaged. Eric had made arrangements for clothes to be brought to the cabin, and she'd changed out of the scrubs and into a comfy pair of sweats and a black t-shirt as soon as she'd arrived. Now she rubbed her hands on the soft cotton of the sweats and said, "So, I'd imagine this place probably has about four or five bedrooms. I think I'll just take this one." She pointed to the one she'd been eyeing. The closest one. She would be crashing face-first into that bed so hard.

"That seems like a good choice."

They stared at each other.

"Okay." She could handle Roman better after sleep. "See you in a few hours."

His brow furrowed.

Harper turned and hurried into the bedroom. She pretty much jumped into the bed. The mattress was as soft and heavenly as it had looked and...

The floor creaked behind her.

Harper immediately whirled over and lunged up. Fear had her heart racing because the last time she'd been in a bed and she'd heard a creak like that, three creeps had swarmed at her.

But the dark, hulking shadows weren't coming for her this time.

Roman stood at the foot of the bed. His hands were loose at his sides, but his shoulders were tense. His expression seemed so carefully guarded. She realized he almost always seemed that way. So very guarded. And the times when that mask of his slipped, those were in the instances when she saw his stark need.

A need for her.

Her hands curled around the covers. "What are you doing?"

"Getting ready for bed." He grabbed his shirt. Yanked it over his head.

Maybe she should have kept her eyes up. On his. That might have been polite. But *he* was the one stripping in front of her, so it wasn't exactly her fault when her gaze drifted down to his chest. His abs.

Muscles. Power. She'd known he was strong. But this was different. This was sexiness. Hotness to the extreme. But there were marks on him. Scars. Faint lines that told Harper that Roman had never been some pampered rich boy. His life had been hard. Rough. Violent.

His hands were going to the snap of his jeans. This show was about to get seriously intense unless she did something. She heard herself squeak out, "Stop!"

He stilled. "I can sleep in the jeans. That's fine." He kicked away his shoes. Ditched his socks.

"Uh, Roman?" Harper cleared her throat.

He looked up.

"Why are you stripping in front of me?"

"I told you, I'll leave on the jeans. It's not a full strip."

She lifted a brow. "Why did you take off half your clothes?"

"So I could be more comfortable and sleep better."

"You mean you're sleeping...in here?"

"Yes. You picked this room, and it was a good choice. I did a survey of all the bedrooms earlier, and this one has the biggest bed. We'll both fit nicely."

Fit nicely. The images those words conjured. Images that had nothing to do with the size of the bed, but rather with their bodies. Fitting ever so well.

She cleared her throat again. Twice more. "Why do you think you're sleeping in here? I do not remember inviting you to come into this bedroom with me."

His head cocked. "I told you I was going to stay close."

They should discuss the full meaning of the word 'close' so there was no confusion. "Yes, inside the cabin is close. In the same bed, that's *intimate*."

His mask cracked. Because she was watching him so closely, Harper saw it happen. She saw the flash of hunger. Such raw need. A lust that had her heart pounding out in a double-time rhythm. Then he blinked, and Roman's guard was immediately back up.

"You don't want to be intimate with me," he said slowly.

Actually, she rather wanted that very badly.

"I won't touch you." He motioned to the bed. "You stay on your side. I'll stay on mine. I just need to make sure you're safe."

"And you have to do that by being in the same bed with me?"

A shrug. "It would make me feel better."

Was he serious? "You don't trust the guards outside? Or the security system?"

"You had a security system at your place. Those assholes still got inside. Didn't trigger anything."

True.

"And no, I don't really trust anyone else with your safety. The attack was personal, and that means I am going to *personally* make certain they don't get you again. Close for me isn't being down the hallway or being upstairs. It's not being in another room while some sonofabitch sneaks inside to take you—or to slit your throat so that I can't even hear you scream."

"Well, someone just painted a scary picture in my head." She yanked back the covers, moved to the pillow on the left, and got herself settled in all nice and snug. Harper plumped up her pillow and wiggled her shoulders.

He kept standing at the foot of the bed and watching her. "I can sleep on the floor. If that makes you feel better."

"Better?" She mulled that. "No, the idea of you spreading out on the hard floor doesn't make me feel better. You're right. The bed is plenty big." She reached out a hand and patted the empty pillow near her. "What are you waiting for?"

"Your invitation."

She'd just given it. "Get in the damn bed so I can go to sleep."

For a moment, his smile flashed. Such a brief moment. She thought that she'd imagined it. He settled in beside her, and the big, giant bed suddenly seemed to shrink.

"I won't touch you," he said. "I'll stay on this side."

"Has anyone ever told you that you have a severe protective streak?"

His head turned on the pillow so that he was staring at her. Such a close—no, *intimate*—

position. "No one has ever told me I was protective. Most people just say I'm a really cold-blooded bastard. And that I'm good at killing."

She nibbled on her lower lip.

"I shouldn't have said that last part. I scared you again."

Harper stopped nibbling. "You haven't scared me yet. I was just thinking, that's all."

"Thinking that you shouldn't be anywhere near me?"

"Thinking…" Her tone was soft. "What is it about me that puts you in protective mode? Is it just because I was taken and you believe it's your fault? That's got you all protective and antsy?" She could smell him. That crisp, masculine scent that she enjoyed far too much. "No…" Her voice turned musing. "You were all hyper protective even before the abduction. That was one of the reasons I had to go to Eric. You kept jumping in front of me and danger."

His gaze was on her.

"Why do I get the special treatment?" Harper whispered.

"Maybe because you're special." He shifted position on the bed. Leaned closer to her.

He'd said he wouldn't touch her, but it sure looked as if Roman was about to come in for a kiss. Her breath caught.

He reached behind her head. Turned off the lamp. The room immediately plunged into darkness. "Sleep well, Harper."

Her breath rushed out. He'd eased back onto his side of the bed. Her heartbeat drummed in her ears as she lay there. She was far too conscious of him next to her. Of his warmth. His size. His every breath.

"I didn't know...that you tried to call me." His voice was halting. Low.

She swallowed and closed her eyes. "You're my partner. Who else would I call?"

"Maybe that asshat you dated last week."

She rolled over, putting her back to him. "That asshat is history," she said softly. "Besides, it's not like he would come rushing to the rescue with guns blazing. Not like he'd do anything necessary to save me. Not like he's—"

You.

But she didn't say that. Barely.

Sometimes, a woman needed a man who could kick ass and take names. Harper was starting to think there might be a whole lot of advantages to having a guy who didn't say much but could sure get shit done. "Thanks for coming after me."

"Always."

His one-word reply wrapped around her like a caress.

"Just so you know," Harper murmured as sleep pulled at her. "I'd do the same for you."

***

Harper was asleep. He could hear the faint sound of her gentle breaths. She'd dozed off quickly. Her last words had slurred with sleepiness.

I'd do the same for you.

Interesting. Unsettling. He actually believed she meant what she'd said. If something happened to him, if he just vanished, Harper would come after him.

She'd think he was in danger. That he needed help. She'd fly to the rescue. Just like she'd rushed in his house when she'd thought that Dex was a threat.

He could see the curves of her body in the dark. His eyes had adjusted to the darkness easily. They always did. He wanted to reach out and touch her. To skim his fingers over her body, but he'd promised not to touch her.

With Harper, he wanted to keep his promises.

He pulled in a deep breath. Relief settled around him. Harper was safe. She was close.

His eyes slid shut, and he was finally able to sleep. His last thought?

Do not touch her. Do not...

***

When Roman opened his eyes hours later, Harper was stretched out on top of him.

CHAPTER SEVEN

Her legs straddled his hips. His dick shoved up against her sex—and, yes, the damn thing was *very* eager and erect. Her soft breasts pressed to his chest, and her head was nestled in the crook of his neck. He could feel the light stir of her breath against his skin.

His hands—greedy bastards—were clamped possessively around her hips.

Shit.

He'd broken his word. Hadn't even lasted a few hours. What had he done? Hauled her on top of him in his sleep? Harper was going to be so pissed. Maybe he could gently disengage before she opened her eyes.

But...

She felt so good. Smelled so sweet.

And her body was already tensing against his because, of course, she would be waking up at that exact moment.

Fuck me. "Uh, Harper..." Her name came out all raspy and hungry. "I can explain..." He couldn't, but he should try.

Her head slowly lifted. Her hands pushed onto the mattress on either side of him as she lifted herself up, and as she lifted her *upper* body, her lower pushed even harder against his dick.

Fuck, fuck, fuck—

"I'm on top of you." Her voice was husky.

He nodded.

Her lashes swept down. She seemed to study the scene. "On your side of the bed."

"Um."

Her lashes lifted. Her dimples made his heart stop. "That's not even one real word, Roman."

It—

He squeezed his eyes shut. "You need to get off me," he bit out. His hands released her hips as he grabbed for the covers. He fisted them in his grip. "Now."

"Well, good morning to you, too." She didn't move off him.

In fact, she seemed to push a little closer.

"Do you always wake up this way?" Harper wondered.

"No. I don't usually wake up with my dick *quite* so rock hard." Though, sure, he had plenty of morning hard-ons. What guy didn't? His eyes opened as he stared at the focus of his obsession. "But when I open my eyes and find *you* on top of me, it's not exactly a typical morning."

Her lips parted.

"So unless you want to fuck, and based on the whole no-touch rule from earlier, I'm guessing that's a no, then how about you move your ever-so-hot ass back to your side of the—"

She bent her head. Nestled her head right back in the crook of his shoulder. He felt her mouth press against his skin. A soft, sensual kiss. Her tongue licked over him.

His whole body jolted. "*Harper...*" She was playing with him? Such a bad, bad idea.

He wasn't the type to play. Especially not when all he wanted to do was *take*.

"We should really find time to sign that waiver form about relationships at Wilde," she mused. Another lick. "You know, before things get too complicated."

What the hell was she even talking about?

She bit him. A quick, sexy bite.

If possible, his dick got even bigger as it shoved against her. Her legs were spread, and he wanted *in*. "Your...side..." he grunted.

"But I think I like your side better." She pushed up again. Straddled him. "I think I like you a whole lot better than I ever expected."

He stared up at her. He had never seen a more beautiful woman. No makeup, but her skin still glowed. Her lips were plump and perfect. Her hair was a sinful, tousled mane. He wanted to sink his hands into it. Wanted his mouth to take hers.

Wanted to drive his cock into her until she screamed with pleasure.

Instead, he didn't move. He barely breathed.

Was this a dream? Dammit, was he still asleep? Would he wake soon to discover Harper curled on her side of the bed, with her back to him? That would just be his luck.

"I've felt the attraction from the beginning." Her voice was soft and sensual. "I just wasn't sure what to do about it."

The first time he'd seen her, Roman had felt as if he'd taken a punch to the gut. Eric had led him to the office he'd share with his new partner. Eric had rapped on the open door and then they'd both entered. Harper had been sitting at her desk, and she'd looked up.

Smiled.

Her dimples had done Roman in immediately.

But then she'd soon stopped smiling for him, and he'd realized men tended to fall right at her dainty feet. He'd never been the type to fall. "Don't play," he growled. "That's not who I am."

"That's not who I am, either." Her hands were now splayed on his chest. Caressing him lightly. Carefully.

"You went to sleep and told me to stay the hell away." He swallowed. "You woke up, and now you want me?"

"I wanted you before I went to sleep. I woke up, and I realized that I *still* want you. So maybe we should see where this goes." Still husky, but her voice was also hesitant. She caught her plump lower lip between her teeth.

Screw it. He could feel his control break. Could practically hear the sound of it shattering as he shot up into a sitting position. His arms locked tightly around her as he hauled her even closer. His mouth crashed onto hers. He wanted to be the one biting her lower lip. He wanted to taste her and to take. He'd warned her, he'd told her exactly who he was.

But then she'd crawled on top of him. Harper had said she wanted to see where things would go. He'd show her.

They'd go straight to hot, dirty, fantastic sex.

Her lips were open and eager on his. He thrust his tongue into her mouth and tasted her as he craved. Her mouth obsessed him. Her sweet little tongue. Those plump lips.

He caught her lower lip. Sucked it.

His fingers slid around her side. Up her rib cage. Eased toward her breast. She wasn't wearing a bra beneath the t-shirt, and when he touched her through the thin cotton, he could feel her pebbled nipple.

I want to taste it. He wanted to taste every single inch of her. That was exactly what he would do. Every single—

"Rise and shine, princess!" Dex's voice boomed out.

Roman stiffened.

See. Maybe I am dreaming. Only the hot dream just turned into a nightmare.

"Yo, princess!" Dex shouted again. "We have to talk, ASAP! Come on out!"

Dex sounded dangerously close to the bedroom door. Figured the guy had gotten inside the cabin easily. Eric would have given him the security access codes.

"Is he calling me?" Harper asked. Her breath panted. Her fingers had curled around Roman's shoulders.

"Princess!" Dex wheedled again. "Got news you'll want to hear."

"No, he's calling me," Roman groused. "Because the dumbass thinks he's funny. He's not." Grudgingly, hating every moment, Roman eased Harper to the side—then let her go completely. He rose from the bed. He still had his jeans on, and he was now sporting one majorly uncomfortable erection. Fuck. Dex had the shittiest timing. "I'll be right back."

"But—"

"I'll handle Dex." His voice was rough. Ragged. That happened when a man was close to paradise and got cock-blocked by a power-mad jerk. He stalked forward. Opened the door just a small amount and slipped out. Roman immediately shut the bedroom door behind him because he didn't want Dex glancing inside and seeing Harper.

"Oh, there you are." Dex smiled at him. "Sleeping Beauty finally wakes."

"This had better be important."

"Everything I have to say is always important. You should know that."

Roman crossed his arms over his chest and blocked the bedroom door with his body.

"Where is your lovely partner?" Dex's gaze darted to the second floor of the cabin. "Did you give her a room upstairs? Figured you had. That way, any bad guys would have to get past you on the first floor before they could get up to her."

Roman stared straight at him. "Bad guys will definitely have to get past me before they can get to her."

"So she *is* upstairs. Good. Not sure if you wanted her to hear all this intel that I have—"

"Then maybe you should have tried a quieter approach so you didn't wake her."

A shrug from Dex. "I could have been wrong. She could have been in the bedroom with you instead of upstairs."

She was with me. I had my hand on her nipple, and I was about to lick every single inch of her body.

"If she was with you, I didn't want to swing open the door and be psychologically scarred by what I saw. So, you know, the shout-out seemed like the better option." An exhale. "Now let's cut the chit-chat and get down to business. You're not fucking her which is good—actually, great news."

The hell it was.

"Antony picked up some chatter on the Dark Web. You remember my guy, Antony, don't you? Freaking tech genius. The man can do anything with tech if you just give him a little bit of time."

He remembered Antony, all right. Antony Kyle was one of Dex's top operatives at the CIA. By day, Antony ran a huge, billion-dollar gaming business with his partner, Sebastian. The company was certainly legit. But Antony also *did* use the company as a cover. It allowed him to slip in and out of different countries under the guise of doing business when he was really working secrets.

Back before Roman had entered his current, well, partnership, with Dex, he'd researched Antony. He'd wanted to learn as much as he could about the people allied with Dex. For too long, Roman had believed that Dex betrayed him. That Dex left him to die.

More lies.

Sometimes, Roman felt as if his entire life had been nothing but a giant cluster of lies.

"Uh, hello?" Dex tilted his head. "Are you with me or did you just phase out?"

Roman locked his jaw. "I remember Antony."

"Good. Great. Wonderful. That speeds things along. He picked up chatter saying that someone wanted proof of your death—"

The door opened behind Roman.

Dex's eyes widened. "So...there you are." A nod. "Not upstairs. Right there. In the same room that Roman was in."

"You are incredibly observant," Harper noted dryly. "Same room. Yes."

Dex's gaze had turned hooded. He looked at Roman. Then her. Then back to Roman. "We should continue this discussion alone." He turned on his heel. "There's a study off the dining room. Saw it when I came inside. Let's talk there."

"I want to hear what you have to say." Harper's voice was firm.

Dex stopped. Turned slowly.

Roman instinctively moved a little closer to Harper, making sure to shield her with his body.

"When I said we should continue the discussion alone, it wasn't a choice-type statement. It was an order." Dex's voice was mild. "Sorry, Harper, but you don't have the clearance for what we're going to discuss."

"I was the one kidnapped."

Dex's expression didn't change.

"Oh, come on!" Harper took an aggressive step forward, putting herself at Roman's side. "I am his partner. I want to help him!"

"Is that what you want? Truly?"

Roman frowned at Dex. "What in the hell is that supposed to mean?"

"It means sometimes, the deadliest enemies can hide behind the sweetest faces. After your last girlfriend, you should have learned that lesson."

He stiffened. "She wasn't my girlfriend." He knew what Dex was talking about. Or rather, who. Heather Madding. The woman had been a bodyguard, someone that Roman had made the mistake of almost trusting. Then she'd sold him out. Sometimes, they'd used the cover of being lovers, but they had never actually been involved.

"You have a girlfriend?" Harper asked. Her face had gone white.

"Oh, don't worry about her," Dex inserted as he waved a hand vaguely in the air. "She's dead."

Harper shook her head. Concern flooded her features. "Roman?"

"Don't worry about him, either. He's fine." Dex was still oversharing. "He didn't love her. That's why she was so eager to sell him out. The lady got pissed. Turned on him. People will betray you for all sorts of reasons. Money and vengeance, those are the two that I usually see at the top of the list." A pause. "Are those two items on *your* list, Harper?"

She wasn't looking at Dex. Her gaze was still on Roman. She stared at him with sympathy clear to see in her eyes. "I'm so sorry."

She didn't even know the full story. "Nothing for you to be sorry about."

Harper reached for his arm. Her fingers squeezed him. "You were hurt. That's enough for me."

When in the hell had anyone offered him comfort before? His body curled around her. The move was just instinctual. He wanted to be closer to Harper. She offered him everything he'd ever wanted.

"*Ahem*. Remember my order? Talking alone? I have intel to discuss with you, Roman, and again, Harper doesn't have clearance."

Roman sent him a disgusted stare. "You were spouting out plenty of information a few moments ago." *Overshare much?*

"Do you truly want her hearing everything I have to say? Once some skeletons are pulled out of the closet, you can't shove them back."

No, you couldn't. He caught Harper's hand. "I need to talk to him."

Her small nostrils flared. "You're shutting me out."

"I'm trying to protect you." He didn't want the evil from his past touching her.

"I don't remember asking for protection."

But I still want to give it to you. Roman brought her hand to his lips. Kissed her knuckles. "I'll tell you everything that I can." She wouldn't get how much of a compromise that was for him. He guarded his secrets like a dragon guarded his gold. But for Harper, he would try.

He pulled away from her. Headed toward Dex. Gave a grim nod. "The study."

The wooden floor groaned behind them. "I just have one question before you two disappear…"

They both looked back at Harper.

She smiled.

Freaking dimples. Damn.

"Why does someone want proof of Roman's death?" She pursed her lips. "Yeah, I overheard that part. Had my ear pressed to the door so I *could* overhear it." She waited. "No answer?"

Roman didn't know what the hell to say.

"I will expect a *full* answer." Her green stare focused on Roman. "Sooner or later. Though I much prefer for it to be sooner."

He swallowed.

"Go have your chat. I'll be waiting."

She sure didn't sound happy about it.

As they walked away, Dex whispered, "I think you're in trouble."

Tell me something I don't fucking know.

CHAPTER EIGHT

"I want you to be careful with Harper," Dex warned. His expression had turned inscrutable. Typical Dex. "Emotional attachments can be dangerous. Though I'm sure you learned that lesson for yourself after the way things went down with Heather."

Heather. He wasn't going to take that bait. "Emotional attachments." Roman nodded. "Right. You mean like the attachment you formed with my sister when you tricked her into working with you? When you were intending to use her against me?"

A faint hardening of the jaw was the only sign Dex gave of his displeasure. "I was intending to protect her, always. Lacey knows that."

Roman glanced toward the closed study door. They were being quiet, keeping their voices barely above a whisper, but he was still worried that Harper would hear them.

"She knows Lacey."

His gaze snapped back to Dex.

"You must have realized that by now. Lacey *did* work for Wilde before she decided to put her skills to use for my team. And Harper has been at Wilde for quite some time. It's only natural that their paths have crossed, but I'm betting you haven't brought up your sister's name to Harper even once, have you?"

No, he hadn't. "What did Antony discover?"

"Told you already. Someone is looking for proof of your death. I would have thought the teeth and the bones we left behind when we faked your death would have been proof enough that you had left the land of the living. My people did a stand-up job, but I guess there will always be folks who want more and more."

"So in this case, someone wants...what?" A bitter laugh escaped him. "My head? Think that will satisfy them?"

"That's what they used in the old days."

Roman glared at Dex.

"They did. People were real savage, bloodthirsty beasts in the past. Don't get all pissy with me just because I know history. If you hated someone back in the Middle Ages, then you lopped off the bastard's head and brought it back to your ruler as proof that you'd gotten the job done."

"No one is taking my head."

"Nah, I figure they'll just go after your heart instead."

Roman paced across the room. "Haven't you heard? I don't have one of those." But tension snaked through him. "So, Lacey, I mean..." He stumbled to a halt because he didn't know how to talk about his sister. The sister who had never been in his life, not until recently.

Their relationship was strained. Not her fault. Maybe his? Hell, he had no clue. He just knew that for most of his life, he'd been jealous as hell of her.

Their mother had kept Lacey. She'd raised her. Loved her.

While Roman had been left with a monster.

Or at least, that was the story he'd believed for so long. Until he'd actually met Lacey. Until he'd learned that she had no clue he existed. Until Dex had given him proof that Roman's mother *had* wanted him. She'd fought to get him back. But when you went up against Dex's father…

You lost.

Roman's father had killed the mother he'd longed to have in his life. His father had destroyed everything good. *He sure destroyed everything good in me.*

"Don't worry about Lacey." Suddenly, Dex's tone and expression were fierce. Deadly. "No one will touch her. I immediately sent her to a safe house with some of my best guards when I learned Antony's news."

Not many knew the true nature of Roman's relationship with Lacey. Roman wanted to keep things that way. For her safety.

"But Lacey isn't the one I was talking about here," Dex added. "You know what's happening."

Roman flexed and clenched his hands. "Spell it out for me."

"Fine. Someone caught you with your pants down. Same way I almost did a few minutes ago."

He took a lunging step toward Dex.

"Easy, tiger." Dex held up his hands. "Harper was taken because someone thinks she matters to you. The fact that you immediately raced out to find her? That proves your attachment. So does the fact that, once she was safe, you rushed her to this romantic cabin and locked her in your bedroom."

"I *didn't* lock her in—"

"No?"

"I wasn't having sex with her!"

"You sure about that?"

"Oh, for shit's sake, Dex! I think I know when I'm having sex with someone." He'd been very, very close to sex, but Dex had ruined that moment for him.

Some of the tension seemed to ease from Dex's shoulders. "Good. No sex. How about you keep things that way, hmm? You know, just be partners. Don't make things more complicated than they already are. You'll regret it if you do."

"I do not want relationship advice from you." Again, his hands flexed and clenched. "I want to know what intel Antony discovered that I can use. I want to know how someone found out I was alive. I want—"

"You are a needy bastard."

His eyes narrowed.

"Look, Antony is working undercover on the Dark Web. He's ferreting out what he can. Seems like most people in the game believe you *are* dead, if that's any consolation. Obviously, someone with power thinks differently. That person tracked you and now Harper is part of the equation, too." Dex scratched his chin. "You know, I could move her to a safe house. Until this is all over."

"Harper stays with me." Roman's immediate response.

"Yeah, okay. I am going to try and be tactful here. I don't bother being tactful very often, so I might screw up the attempt."

Roman waited.

"You were betrayed before by a woman close to you."

"I was *never* romantically involved with Heather. She was my bodyguard. I thought—"

"Are you certain you're not being set up again?" Dex cut through Roman's words.

His heartbeat was suddenly far too loud as it echoed in Roman's ears. "What is that supposed to mean?"

"It means..." A sigh. "Have you considered that Harper might have been in on this abduction? That it wasn't an abduction at all? There are *no* bruises on her. No scratches. The docs said she was perfect. No drugs in her system, but she claims not to have remembered anything—"

"I thought chloroform was found behind the cabin."

"A little bit. And doesn't that seem too convenient? Like, here you go. Ta-da. Some proof that she's a victim."

Tension knotted at the base of Roman's skull. "She is a victim."

"Antony says there is a very high price on your head. Do you think Harper would enjoy sudden wealth? I suspect she would. When I dug into her background, I discovered that she grew up in the foster care system. Bouncing around. She was almost adopted twice, but those adoptions fell through. When she was eighteen, she took off on her own. Went to Europe. Hopped around over there for a while. Even spent some time in your neck of the woods."

Roman stiffened.

"She worked all kinds of jobs during that time," Dex continued. "She was a chauffeur, an artist's model, a street performer—"

"What does this matter?" Roman wanted to know.

"Money always matters. People will do anything for money. Or for revenge." His gaze had gone hooded. "I told you that already."

"Yes, you're telling me shit I know." Roman jerked a hand through his hair. "Harper went to Europe when she was eighteen. Big deal. Lots of people do that. People backpack around. They take odd jobs. They explore. I don't see anything wrong with that. Eric has checked her out. *You* checked her, obviously. If there is something that is a giant red flag, then tell me. Spit it out." His words were coming too fast. "Otherwise, back the hell off Harper."

Dex studied him.

Roman waited. He found himself leaning forward onto the balls of his feet, like a boxer getting ready to go in swinging.

"You're very protective of her," Dex finally said.

"You're stating the obvious."

"If she'd been dead when you went in that cabin, what would you have done?"

He blanched.

Dex swore.

Roman schooled his expression. "You're asking if I would have left a bloodbath in my wake? Become a whole lot like my old man?" A rough laugh. "If you want the truth, I still intend to be like him. I will track down the people who took her, and I will make them pay."

"Then you'll vanish from her life?"

He didn't want to talk about leaving her. He'd just gotten her.

Gotten her. She wasn't a freaking prize. And she didn't belong to him. Why was he thinking that way?

"This is going to end badly, Roman. Mark my words. I tell you not to get emotionally involved and you tell me to screw myself. You know what? I think I'm going to send Antony in so he can work more with your crazy ass. I'll take a bit of a backseat. Give you some space."

Bullshit. Dex was just doing his usual routine of being the puppet master. He wanted to be behind the scenes, pulling the strings. "Just keep my sister safe, got it?"

"You are always giving orders. Doing it like you're some big, bad crime boss, and I have to jump to do your bidding. That's not who you are anymore." A deliberate pause. "Is it?"

"Of course, not."

But Dex kept staring at him.

Roman spun away. "I want to go search the cabin they held her in. If there's any kind of trail there, I'll follow it. Otherwise, Harper and I will be heading back home."

"And why go back? Why not just vanish now? You could, you know. Just go...poof."

Poof, my ass. He reached for the doorknob. "You know why." Roman spared a brief glance over his shoulder. "Harper was taken at her place in Atlanta. Our partnership started there. Obviously, I was being watched in that area—or she was. I need to retrace our steps. Something started this mess. A match to the flame. I'll find out what it was, then I will put out that fucking fire."

One way or another.

***

They'd left tracks in the snow. They'd circled the cabin multiple times, gone inside the cabin, trekked to the woods...and still found nothing.

Harper shoved her gloved hands into the deep pockets of her coat. The coat and gloves had both come courtesy of Eric. Some Wilde agents were still scouting out the scene. But everyone seemed to be turning up the same results.

Nothing.

"It's weird," Harper finally said. She wanted to break the silence. Silence had never been her friend. As a kid, she'd been a chatterbox. Or at least, that was what one foster mom had told her. The truth was...when she talked, Harper just didn't feel so alone. "It's like they just abandoned me here. Why go to all the trouble of taking me...only to disappear? When I woke up, I was alone. It seems as if they dumped me here and vanished."

Roman's stare was directed toward the distance. On the slopes of the mountains. "They didn't vanish. They were watching."

"There aren't any security cameras in the cabin. Not inside or out. The place has been thoroughly swept—"

He waved toward the slopes. "Probably had someone stationed right there. He saw me rush in for you and reported back."

She squinted into the distance. "So...what? They just let you take me? Didn't care about ransom? Didn't care about anything?"

"They got what they wanted."

She shivered. "What was that?"

"Proof I'd do anything for you." He turned away.

Her gloved hand flew out and curled around his arm. "Whoa. Whoa, hold up. You don't get to say something dramatic like that and then just turn away."

He looked down at her hand.

She didn't move her hand. She kept holding on. Tightly. "You and I haven't been together very long. You wouldn't do *anything*—"

He faced her. His eyes seemed to blaze as he said, "Be assured, I would. I don't take very kindly to someone wanting to hurt my partner."

She shifted closer to him. "Did I say thank you?"

His brows rose.

"When you rushed in to save me?" A wince. "Before I tried to hit you with that wooden post? Or maybe after? Did I thank you for working so hard to find me?"

"You don't need to thank me. Not when it's—"

"It's not your fault, so don't say that it is. You didn't take me. You're not responsible for what other people do." She stared into his eyes. "Thank you."

"Harper…"

She rose onto her toes and brushed a kiss over his lips. "No one has ever been willing to risk so much for me." He overwhelmed her. He made her start to hope. "I would do the same for you," she vowed.

"Harper…" He growled her name, and she loved that growl.

Another quick kiss, one that had her heart racing far too fast. She pushed against him, eased back a little, and flattened her hand over his chest. "When we're alone, I can't wait to—"

She stopped. Stared at her hand.

At the red dot in the middle of her hand.

"Harper?"

She didn't hesitate. Harper shoved against him as hard as she could. He slipped on the snow and fell back, right before a bullet slammed into the side of the cabin—inches away from where he'd been.

CHAPTER NINE

The snow cushioned his fall. One moment, Harper had been kissing him, then she'd pulled away. She'd been in the process of making him what sounded like a very awesome promise—

Then she'd shoved at him with surprising force. He'd slipped on the snow and fallen on his ass.

He saw the wood explode near the side of the cabin even as he heard Harper suddenly scream, "Shooter!"

Then she was scrambling down and diving over him. Wait, hold the hell up. *Over him?* She thought she was going to use her sexy body as some kind of shield for him?

Fuck, no, she wasn't. His arms locked around her, and he rolled, fast. Snow kicked up around them as he got her *under* his body.

"What are you doing?" she snapped. "You need to—"

"Don't even think about it, sweetheart. You stay down. You stay covered."

"You're giving orders." A hiss. "You know that's one of our issues."

"Yes, and it's not changing." He could hear voices. The other agents were springing into action and giving chase. "Stay down." He looked at the damaged side of the cabin. Then turned his head toward the north. *Shooter.* "You need more shelter," he told her.

"Uh, *we* need more shelter. Technically, maybe even you, not me. Because the red dot was on your chest, not mine."

He blinked at her. "Did you just save my life?"

"That's what partners are for."

"You could have been shot." His voice had turned guttural. He'd also pulled out his weapon. He was crouched, staying low, and finally off her body, but he was still shielding her. They were near the edge of the cabin, and part of another agent's vehicle was in front of them. Not the perfect cover, and that was why he was waiting for the moment when he could get Harper to a more secure spot.

"I work for Wilde. Getting shot is a risk of the job."

She didn't even sound mildly worried. She should be. "You shouldn't risk anything for me."

"Agree to disagree." She had her own weapon at the ready as she sidled closer to him. "Are we going to sit here all day or are we planning to join the hunt for the shooter?"

"You need to stay down. Stay safe. Stay covered."

"It's like you've never met me." She brushed a quick kiss over his cheek. "This bastard kidnapped me *and* just took a shot at you. Hell, no, I'm not staying down. But you stay here. You stay safe. You stay covered."

Even with the cold surrounding him, he felt the warmth of her brief kiss slide all the way through his body. And then he realized—

Shit. She was running away. Staying covered. Staying alert. *But heading for the shooter.*

Without him?

No way. He rushed after her. *"Harper."*

***

The shooter had gotten away. They'd found his tracks. Both footprints and tire tracks from an ATV. But by the time they'd gotten up to the ridge where he'd taken the shot, the perp had been long gone.

Roman had been less than thrilled. And that was a severe understatement.

They'd finished searching the area. Turned up nothing useful. With every moment that passed, Roman had grown even more grim. A darkness clung to him. A tension and rage that vibrated just beneath the surface. By the time they returned to their "secure" cabin—the one Eric had acquired for them—Harper was pretty sure that Roman was about to explode.

The door shut behind them when they entered the cabin. The other Wilde agents remained outside. Only she and Roman were in the home. They'd rest for a while. Eric had a private plane scheduled to come and pick them up. Soon, they'd be out of that place and back in Atlanta.

Roman didn't say a word as they both stripped out of their coats and boots. Harper pulled off her socks, and her cold toes curled against the wooden floor.

Carefully, Roman put down his weapon. He stared at the gun as it rested on the table. Harper had already set her own weapon there when she'd slipped inside. She waited for him to speak, then realized...nope. This was Roman. He'd be silent for hours.

"Want to tell me who is gunning for you?" Harper asked. A shiver slid over her. She reached for the remote and turned on the gas fireplace.

"No." He stopped staring at his gun and moved his focus to his hands.

Her eyes narrowed. "We're past this. Way past it." She tossed down the remote. The flames had flared all nice and bright. Harper stalked toward him. "We don't do one-word answers. Especially not when your life is on the line." She caught his hands. "Who is after you?"

He swallowed. Lifted his head. "You don't have time for that list." His eyes *burned*. Rage. Fear?

Her hold tightened on him. "You've got that many enemies?"

"You shouldn't be near me."

She inched closer. "Why not?"

"Because when you're close to me, you become the target. That bullet could have hit *you*."

"The shooter wasn't aiming for me." She'd thought about this plenty. "I'm just the tool that was used."

His brow furrowed.

"You already know this." She was sure of it. "I'm what they used to draw you out. They took me and they left me in the cabin to see if you'd come for your partner. You did, and now they have you out here. Isolated. Vulnerable. Or at least, that's what they think. They're idiots because I doubt that you're ever vulnerable." She was rambling. "Eric knows having you here is dangerous, too. That's why he's getting that plane ready for us. The sooner we're out of here, the sooner we can get back in a controlled environment. This whole town could be a trap and we don't want to play into their hands any longer than necessary—"

"You're wrong." Low. Deep. Rough.

She was still holding onto his hands. Or rather, onto his wrists. Thick, strong wrists. "What am I wrong about?" She couldn't look away from his eyes. His gaze still burned with a dark fire, but the fear and rage were gone. Something else stared back at her from his eyes.

Need. Lust.

"They didn't want to see if I'd come after my partner. They wanted to see if I would come running after *you*."

"Uh, yes." Wasn't that what she'd just said?

"*You*."

He seemed to be stuck on that part. "Roman—"

"How the hell did you do it?" Angry.

"Excuse me?"

"It hasn't been long at all. No one else has gotten close."

"Close to what?"

His head lowered. "Close to making me lose my mind."

"That...that wasn't my intention." She let go of his wrists.

But he grabbed her. Curled his hands around her hips and yanked her against him. "I knew you were trouble the first time I saw you. Fucking Eric telling me that I was going to love you even before we met. Then I walked into the office. Saw *you*. Have barely been able to see anything else."

Her heart slammed into her chest.

"I didn't just come after my partner. I came after you. The woman I can't get out of my head. The woman who obsesses me. The woman I need way too much." Each word seemed torn from him.

She stared into his eyes. Waited for more.

He didn't say another word.

Harper found herself starting to smile at him. For Roman, he'd sure as hell just said plenty.

"No." A snarl from him. "Don't you do it. You don't get how close to the edge I am right now. I'm barely holding onto my control. That bullet was too close. You were *taken*. Don't you smile at me. Don't give me the dimples because I will be—"

Too late. She'd smiled fully at him. It wasn't something she'd intended to do, but Roman had said that he needed her, and she needed him and her smile had just appeared.

"Lost," Roman rasped. "That's what I am. That's what I think we both are, now."

"Then be lost with me." She tipped back her head. Wanted his mouth. Waited for it. "Be with me."

His lips locked onto hers. There was need in his kiss. Passion. A lust that burned soul deep. There was anger. Fear. So many things.

But the lust—the desire? That was the strongest.

Her hands curled around his neck as she pulled him even closer. He was kissing her with a wild, reckless fury, and she loved it. She wasn't holding back. For the first time in a very, very long while, Harper was letting go completely.

They could crash and burn. But, oh, she had a feeling the ride would be worth it.

His mouth was desperate on hers. His tongue thrust past her lips, tasted her, and had a moan pulling from her throat. She rubbed her body against his. He was hard and strong and warm. The flames were dancing in the fireplace near her, but all of the heat in the room seemed to be coming from him. Harper rubbed against him. The clothes were in the way. They needed to go.

Her hands trailed down his body. Went to the waistband of his jeans. Fumbled with the belt and the snap.

His mouth tore from hers. "You're sure?"

"I want you." She could hear the hunger in her own voice. "Right now." She'd never felt this way about someone before. Maybe it was the adrenaline. Maybe it wouldn't last. She didn't care. She was grabbing tight—enjoying the ride. There weren't second chances. She knew that. The red dot on Roman's chest had proven that to her today.

Take what you want.
Hold tight while you can.

He lifted her into his arms. The move was sudden and fast, and it distracted Harper from her attempt to get Roman out of his jeans. He kissed her as he carried her, and in a flash of time, Harper found herself back in the bedroom. He lowered her onto the floor near the bed.

And he started stripping.

She should probably have stripped, too. But Harper just took a moment to enjoy the view. Making a memory, that was what she was doing. Memorizing every single inch of him. She didn't want to forget this moment. Not ever.

Wide shoulders. Tanned chest. Abs forever. He'd already taken off his belt. Now his hands were at the snap of his jeans. But he'd stopped. Why had he stopped?

"You still have all of your clothes on, Harper," he rumbled.

"Right." She nodded. Motioned to him. "I was enjoying the view. And then, you know, I thought you could help rip my clothes off me or something."

His eyes widened.

"Is that not a good plan?" she asked with a blink.

"It's a fucking perfect plan."

She smiled.

"*Fucking lost.*"

He ditched the jeans and his underwear, and wow—Roman was built. Long and thick and his cock bobbed straight toward her.

He reached for her shirt. "Your turn."

Hers? Yes. Right. "Strip away. Tear away. Whatever. Just get me naked."

Her shirt flew across the room. Her jeans hit the floor. Her bra? Gone. As for her panties, Harper was pretty sure she heard those tear. She was still standing up, and his wicked fingers went right between her thighs. He shoved the cotton fabric of her underwear to the side, and that was when she heard the sound of it tearing, but his fingers were sliding over her sex—her already eager and wet sex—so she didn't care at all about what happened to her panties.

She bit her lower lip and rose onto her toes as he stroked her. Her hands clamped around his arms as she tried to balance herself. He thrust one finger into her, and she gasped. Her body was hyper aware. Hyper aroused. When a second finger joined the first and his thumb began rubbing back and forth over her clit, she was pretty sure that her eyes just wanted to roll back into her head. It was a good thing she had a death grip on him because Harper didn't think that her balance was going to last long at all.

She also thought that she would be coming in about five, four, three, two—

He pulled his hand away.

She almost screamed at him. Harper knew she glared.

"On the bed," he growled.

Her breath heaved in and out. And she couldn't help but ask, "My side or yours?"

His gaze hardened. "Harper..."

She laughed. Crazy, because she wanted him so much her whole body trembled, but laughter spilled from her lips. "Kidding." She kissed him. Tasted him. Teased him with her tongue and nipped his lower lip. The man was positively bitable.

He lifted her up. Put her in the middle of the bed and followed her down. Her legs spread and he slid his hips right between them. His mouth went to her neck. He kissed her throat. Licked. Sucked a little and had her arching toward him.

"You need a condom," she told him. "And you need to get inside me."

"Not just yet."

"*What?*"

He kissed his way down her body. Caught one nipple in his mouth. Licked. Sucked.

She grabbed the bedding and fisted it. "I am so ready. Right now."

"Bet you can be readier."

Was that a thing? Readier? She felt plenty ready, thank you very much. So ready that her whole body seemed to be vibrating. She wanted him. Right then and there. Why wait longer? They both needed this.

But he was licking her other breast. Flicking his tongue over her nipple and her hips were arching eagerly toward him. Her heart thundered out of control. Her release was so close...

His mouth feathered over her stomach. On down. *Down.*

He kissed her core. Licked her. Thrust those two long, strong fingers into her even as he caressed her with his mouth, and there was no holding back. Harper didn't even try. She just exploded. The pleasure crashed through her whole body, and she cried out his name as she squeezed her eyes shut. Every muscle went tense as the climax rocked through her. So good. So incredibly good.

Another lick and he pulled away. She heard the rustle of the foil packet, and Harper opened her eyes to see him rolling on the condom. Round two. She was still catching her breath and hearing the thunder of her heartbeat from round one.

He looked up at her. Savage need. Primitive lust.

Her tongue swiped over her lower lip.

There was no more talking or teasing. He settled between her legs. His cock pushed at the entrance to her body, but he didn't thrust inside. Not yet. He reached for her hands.

She was still fisting the covers. She let go, and her hands turned to curl with his. When their hands were locked, then he drove inside her. All the way. So deep that he seemed to be a part of her. Her legs curled around his hips. His name whispered from her. She felt full. Stretched. Her body was still sensitive from the first orgasm, and for a moment, she was almost afraid to move.

He kissed her. A careful, tender kiss. It seemed odd because the emotions firing in the air between them weren't tender. Everything felt primal. Fierce.

But the tender kiss relaxed her. Had her body melting into his and suddenly, she wasn't afraid to move. She wanted to move. Needed to move. Was so eager for the thrust of his hips against her.

He withdrew. Pressed so slowly inside. He was being careful.

Sweet.

His mouth slipped from hers. His head lifted. She licked his neck. Kissed him. Moved her head toward his shoulder. Gave him a sensual bite.

He growled in response.

His thrusts got harder. Rougher.

The need spiraled ever higher. No more teasing. No more play. The bed rocked beneath them. She held on as tightly as she could. She'd just come, but she was already barreling toward another release. Her body met his, thrust for thrust. She squeezed her inner muscles around him and loved his savage curse.

She wanted to drive him insane. Wanted to give him as much wild, uncontrolled pleasure as he'd given to her but—

Her body was tensing again. Flooding with feeling. The pleasure hit her without warning. A muscle-jerking climax that shook her entire body.

His thrusts became even faster. "Hell, yes. You feel so good around me. *So good.*" Deep. Hard. Over and over.

Then he was coming. He jerked against her. Pleasure washed over his face and darkened his eyes even more. Her heels dug into his ass. She arched toward him and didn't want to let go.

How have I missed out on this? Aftershocks still pulsed through her body. Little zings of pleasure that made her breath catch. The mad thunder of her heartbeat filled her ears. *Bam. Bam. Bam.* Their hands were still linked. Their bodies, too. And, already he was, um...

Yep, getting hard again.

Wow. *Yes, please. More. Lots and lots more.*

But Roman stared down at her. His expression had turned unreadable. A muscle flexed along his jaw as he slowly withdrew from her. She wanted to cling to him, but she forced her hands to let his go.

He padded toward the bathroom. Going to ditch the condom, of course. They'd had sex on top of the covers, but while he was gone, she shimmied and dove under them. Not that she had a problem with nudity. Harper totally didn't. But she was feeling all kinds of weirdly vulnerable. And shaky. And still after-shocky. And like she'd just had the best sex of her whole life.

Because she had.

Harper had never enjoyed playing games. Games just got people hurt, and she wasn't particularly in to the whole mind-screw scene. So she saw no reason to hold back. She wanted to be completely honest with Roman, and she hoped that he'd be the same way with her, too.

He'd just reached the bathroom door when she told him, "That was great."

He stopped. His shoulders tensed.

She craned her head to get a view of his ass. *Oh, so nice.*

Roman peered back at her.

"Better than great," she added and couldn't help her grin. "The best I've ever had, in fact."

His lips thinned. His eyes went flat and hard.

That wasn't the reaction she'd expected. Come to think of it, she wasn't sure what she had expected. She'd just been happy and wanted to tell him how she felt.

Without a word, he disappeared into the bathroom. She heard water running. Some of her happy glow started to fade. So maybe she hadn't been the best he'd ever had. Not like she'd wanted him to say that back or anything.

Such a lie. Of course, him saying it back would have been awesome. But maybe she'd just been having fantastic, body-shaking sex while he'd only been having average fun. Or, dear Lord, below-average fun?

She yanked the covers up to her eyes. No, over her eyes.

The floor squeaked. He was coming back. Well, okay, better make *sure* it was him because with the week she was having, it could be the kidnappers again and wouldn't that be just her luck? Harper shoved down the covers. A little bit.

Roman stood at the side of the bed. His head had tilted to the left. "Were you just hiding from me?"

"No. Absolutely not. I was cold so I was covering up."

He stared at her.

"That's a lie," she allowed. "I was hiding. You looked pissy, and I'm sorry if I—"

"You don't have a fucking thing to be sorry for." He sat on the edge of the bed. Put his hands on either side of her body. Caged her. "I'm the asshole who got so damn jealous he could barely see."

She squinted at him. "Why on earth would you be jealous?" Had he missed the best ever portion of her speech?

"Because I don't want to think of you with anyone else. I don't want to think that you almost married some dumbass prince. Or that just in the time I've known you, I've seen men trip over their own freaking feet to catch your attention. I don't want to think that when I leave, you'll move on and forget me."

Back up. She sat up. Almost slammed her head into his. Grabbed his hand. "When you leave? What are you talking about?"

He stared into her eyes. "Let me be clear."

"Okay. Be clear." *Leave?* Her heart squeezed even as a voice in her head whispered... *You know they always leave. Get attached to things, not people.*

"You are my best ever. Nothing could have stopped me from being with you in this bed. You fucking destroyed me. Sinking into you was like sinking into heaven. I came so hard that I thought I'd lost my mind."

Her lips began to—

"Can't handle those right now," he muttered. Roman bent forward and pressed a kiss to her lips. "I'm a jealous bastard," he added. Another kiss. Slower. More sensual. "I don't want to think of anyone else with you."

"Not like I want visuals of you with your exes, either," Harper informed him crisply. Just so they were both on the same page. "I don't want to hold back with you. I want to tell you how I feel. I want to be honest."

His right hand lifted, and he brushed a lock of her hair away from her cheek. "You want honesty from me?"

"It would be fabulous, yes."

"I want you again."

"I want you again, too."

"I was worried you might be sore. I lost control at the end, and I'm scared I was too rough."

"I don't remember you being rough. I remember you being awesome."

His expression hardened. "Your honesty is going to make things hard."

"Why?"

"Because when you say stuff like that…" His head dipped toward hers once more. "It makes me want you even more."

"Oh, I get it." She kissed him. Teasingly thrust her tongue past his lips. Savored him and pulled back to murmur, "When you say things are hard, you're talking about your dick."

He stared at her a moment. Blinked. Then…laughed.

A deep, warm, booming laugh escaped from him. It was such a happy sound that Harper wanted to hear it over and over again. And she kept thinking…*So that's what he sounds like when he's happy.* But before she could say anything else, his mouth took hers again. The laughter had faded, but she could have sworn that she tasted the joy in his kiss. His mouth was absolute magic on hers, and Harper even thought that she heard bells ringing.

Hold up. She *did* hear bells ringing. Her hands pressed to his chest. "Phone," Harper gasped against his mouth.

His head lifted. He frowned.

"My replacement phone." The phone Eric had given her because Harper had zero clue where her old phone was. Her kidnappers had taken it.

Wilde tech agents were trying to use their magic to track it. "It's ringing." From somewhere on the floor.

A furrow appeared between Roman's brows, but he rummaged around and found the phone. He tossed it to her.

Eric's number filled the screen. *Eric*. She took the call and immediately put it on speaker. "What did you learn?" Her voice was breathless. Way too husky.

"Harper, you okay?"

"Fine. Wh-what's up?" Fine for someone who was naked and who'd just been about to have more great sex.

"Your ride will be pulling up any moment. Look, ah, is Roman there?"

Her eyes were on Roman. "He's right beside me." Technically on the bed with her. "And you're on speaker."

Silence.

Well, that was odd.

"What's wrong?" Harper pushed.

"Dex is sending one of his men to be on the plane with you. Said Roman already knows the guy so he'll vouch for him on sight. Full disclosure, I know the fellow, too. Our paths have crossed a few times but I didn't exactly expect this development, so I'm not sure how I feel about this shit." Frustration boiled in his words. "I can't shake the feeling that I'm walking blind here."

Wasn't that how she'd felt when she was first partnered with Roman? Like she was in the dark and missing something?

"Antony," Roman growled.

Um, who was Antony?

"That's him," Eric agreed.

So everyone was in the know but her. Check.

"He'll be at the door within five minutes," Eric said. "You'll be in the air in thirty. When you get back to Atlanta, Wilde will be focusing all available resources on this case."

All available resources? Alarm flickered through her. "We have a lot of cases going, Eric."

"*You* were taken, Harper. One of our own. That doesn't happen on my watch. Every available resource will be used, hell, even the resources that aren't under my domain. That's why I'm letting Dex send Antony in on this. I want him close to you two, and I want him directing the tech team."

So this mystery Antony guy was a techie. Wait…when she'd been doing her level best to eavesdrop on Dex and Roman, hadn't she heard Dex mention an Antony? He'd been the one searching the Dark Web…right?

"I heard about the shooting, Roman," Eric continued grimly.

Roman's gaze never left Harper's face. "Then you know Harper saved my ass."

"You did the same for me," she whispered. He'd rushed into the cabin to save her. Pushing him away from a bullet had been the least she could do.

"You're family." Eric's voice was flat. "No one attacks my family. First Harper and now you. When we're all back in Atlanta, I want to know everything, you understand me? Everything. If I don't know, then I can't help you."

So Eric *was* in the dark. He'd joined the club with her. Interesting.

"Are you coming on the flight with us?" Harper wanted to know. They could all clear the air on the plane.

"No. I've got a second flight for me. I want to do a little more checking out here. Priority one is to get you both home."

Roman's gaze finally cut away from hers.

"Stay safe," Eric ordered.

"You, too." She ended the call. Her hold tightened on the phone. "I want to know everything, too. You get that, don't you?"

He swallowed. Didn't meet her eyes.

"I'm not afraid of whatever is in your past. Your past doesn't matter to me."

His stare lifted. Held hers. "It does to me."

"Roman..."

"We should get dressed. Sounds like our ride will be here damn fast." He rose and paced away from her. His back seemed extra tense. He grabbed his jeans. Hauled them on.

"Do you think I won't like you any longer if I find out that you did something bad in your past?" She pulled the sheet with her as she climbed from the bed. "Roman, that's not how I work. Everyone makes mistakes."

He swung toward her. "Bad doesn't even begin to cover the things I've done." His gaze was hungry, possessive, as it swept over her. "Shouldn't have touched you."

Oh, he had so better not start singing that song.

"But I couldn't help myself."

That was better. A little bit. "Roman—"

She heard a sharp pounding. A knock? It was coming from the main door. "Someone's fast," Harper murmured.

Roman hauled a sweatshirt over his head. "I'll make sure it's him. You get dressed."

"Why are you always giving orders?" She shook her head. "Partnership. That's what we have. And I'm *still* the senior partner."

Roman stopped his march out of the bedroom. He frowned, glanced at her, and said, "Will you please get dressed? Because if Antony sees you wearing only a sheet, I'll have to kick his ass."

"That sounds a bit over the top."

A shrug.

The pounding came again.

"With you, I'm finding that I am a bit over the top." His gaze blazed. "Maybe more than a bit." He cleared his throat. "It's time for us to get the hell out of here." He strode away.

She stood there, clutching her sheet. Her thighs were still a bit trembly. Her sex a little quivery. Goose bumps covered her arms as she glanced back at the bed.

They'd gone straight from amazing sex to...getting the hell out of there.

Harper sucked in a deep breath. Let it out. And dropped her sheet. If he could switch things up so fast, then so could she. Not like she had a choice. Bad guys were after them, and, as Eric had said, it was time to go home.

CHAPTER TEN

He'd checked to make sure that Antony was his visitor even before he opened the door. Doing anything else would have been a serious amateur move. Roman also made sure he kept his weapon at the ready as he allowed Dex's agent to enter the cabin.

"I was wondering about the reception I'd receive." Light glinted off the lenses of Antony Kyle's glasses. His thick hair was tousled from the wind, and faint flecks of snow dotted his coat. "Figured you wouldn't exactly greet me with open arms, but is the gun necessary? I mean, there are Wilde agents outside. They checked me out before letting me on the doorstep."

Roman shoved the door closed behind Antony. "It's necessary." He assessed the other man. Tall, fit, with sharp, intelligent eyes. No nervous movements. Just stillness. Poise. Roman had never worked on a case with Antony Kyle before, but their paths had crossed. Antony had been on Dex's side and Roman...had not.

Because for too long, I thought Dex sold me out. I thought he left me to die. He'd only recently learned the truth. Basically, when his worst enemy had become his brother-in-law. But that was another story, for another day.

"We're going to be working closely on this one. Perhaps we should just let the past die and carry forward?" Antony suggested.

"I don't exactly have a grudge against you."

A sigh of relief slipped from Antony. "That's great to know. Because I was afraid that, you know, since I was the one who helped Dex to hook up with your sister that you might be pissed about—"

Roman took a fast step toward him. "You did what?"

Behind the glasses, Antony's eyes widened. "And you didn't know that. I see. Got it. Let's just pretend I did not say anything about that part, hmmm?"

Hell, no, he wouldn't pretend that shit.

"Ahem. Where is Harper Crane?" Antony peered down at his watch. "Because I've been told we need to have wings up in thirty minutes."

"She's getting dressed." He tucked the gun into the waistband of his jeans. "She'll be out when she's done."

When Antony looked up at him, he was frowning again. "You *did* get the last update from Dex, didn't you?" Antony asked.

"What last update?"

"He told me that he came by. Talked to you. Told you what I'd discovered."

"Yeah." Roman glanced over his shoulder. The bedroom door was still shut. "You've been digging on the Dark Web. Some asshole wants proof that I'm dead. Probably my head or some shit like that."

The door opened. Harper stood there, with her hair tousled, her lips plump and red, and a faint pink glowing in her cheeks. She'd dressed in tight jeans, knee-high boots, and a thick, flowing red sweater.

She looked absolutely gorgeous, and for a moment, he simply stared at her.

"Oh, screw me," Antony muttered. "He *would* leave this part out."

Roman hauled his gaze off Harper. It took a serious effort. "What are you talking about?"

Antony pulled off his glasses. Began to clean the lenses on his shirt. "Nothing. We'll update later." He offered a smile to Harper as she crossed the room. "Hi, I'm Antony—"

"Kyle," Harper finished. Surprise flashed on her face. "You're Antony Kyle. You're the hot tech guy."

Hot tech? Roman's brows rose. "Excuse me?" She thought Antony was hot? Roman's jaw locked. *And she's saying that crap in front of me?*

Harper waved toward Antony. "I read an article about him last week. His company is on the Hot Tech 20 List."

Ah. Okay. So his company was hot. Harper had not been referring to her personal interest in Antony. Of course, she hadn't.

"What are you doing here?" Harper asked. She paused next to Roman. Her shoulder brushed against his arm.

"I'm helping with the case. I owed a friend a favor, so I said I'd do some tech digging."

Antony's answer was part truth and part lie.

"My presence here is strictly confidential," Antony continued. "Eric Wilde assured me that you were not a security risk. That you would not share my involvement with anyone." He slid his glasses back on his nose.

"Absolutely. You can count on me." Harper smiled.

Fuck.

Roman instinctively shook his head.

But it was too late. Antony had blinked. His gaze dropped to her mouth. Lingered on the—

"Nope," Roman interrupted. He waved a hand between them. "Don't be disarmed. Don't fall for them. She is not available, and Harper is not looking to hook up right now. Focus on the case, and we'll all be happy."

Both Harper and Antony gaped at him.

Antony was the first to speak. "Buddy, we *are* focusing on the case. And I'm not disarmed by anything." A hint of steel had entered his voice.

Harper stared at Roman as if he'd lost his mind.

Hell, he felt like he *was* losing him mind, at least where she was concerned. When had he ever been possessive or jealous like this? The answer was immediate. *Never.* But with Harper, he wasn't responding normally. Nothing about the situation or how he felt was normal.

He still seemed to be in overdrive. The fear that she was going to be taken from him kept pounding through his mind and body. The sooner the threat to her had been eliminated, the better.

***

Harper settled in her seat on the private plane. She bent her head as she locked her seatbelt, and her hair slid over her face.

Roman took a step toward her. He intended to sit in the chair opposite hers.

But Antony's hand curled around his shoulder. "We need to talk. *Immediately.*"

He shrugged. "Fine. Let's talk as soon as this plane is in the air."

Antony cut a glance at Harper. "Not around her." His voice was low. Carrying only to Roman's ears.

He was way over the spy games. "Let me guess. Dex told you she didn't have clearance, so you had to watch what you said around her."

"Not like you're telling her your secrets, so don't give me that BS response," Antony snapped right back, voice still barely above a whisper. He leaned closer to Roman. "You don't understand what you're doing with her."

I have a pretty good idea.

"You're going to hurt her. Badly. As soon as we can be alone, we have to talk. Damn Dex—he should have told you before it was too late."

What in the hell was that dark warning supposed to be about? Roman turned his head and met Antony's stare. "I will never hurt her." A vow. Hurting Harper was the last thing that Roman ever intended to do. She was like a breath of fresh air in his life. The woman made him *laugh,* for shit's sake. All he wanted to do was protect her.

Not like he had a ton of experience protecting something good. But he was trying. As hard as he could.

He was screwing up, yes, as evidenced by his whole *Harper isn't available* routine. But he didn't want to lose her. He'd never had anything good. Not until her.

I want to keep her safe.

Pity darkened Antony's eyes. Pity? "I'm afraid it's too late for that." He spared a glance for Harper. "Just try to keep your distance, okay?"

"If you've got something to say, spit it out right now. Don't give me cryptic warnings. I don't go for that crap."

Harper looked up. Her stare met Roman's.

Some of the tension slid from his shoulders. Hurt her? Never.

But Antony seemed even more agitated as he warned, "You don't want this kind of bombshell delivered in front of her. Just keep your hands off her, okay? Try, man. *Try.*"

The pilot called out to him, and Antony hurried toward the cockpit.

Roman took the seat opposite Harper. Settled in. Buckled up.

"What was that about?" Harper asked as she tilted her head. "Looked all intent and whispery."

"I'm not sure."

Her brows rose.

"I'm not." Unease had settled in his gut. "Guy told me that we have to talk—alone—very soon." He paused. "You know I wouldn't hurt you. I mean, you understand I would never do anything to cause you pain?"

Yet hadn't he, already? Because she was his partner, Harper had been pulled into his nightmare. Was that what Antony had meant? That he was putting Harper in harm's way just by being close to her?

"I know." Her gaze was steady. "You don't need to tell me that."

His breath eased out. He glanced out the window. They'd be taking off very soon.

"But you do need to tell me what the heck you were doing back at the cabin. Warning Antony away from me? What was that about?"

Roman winced. "I'm...possessive with you."

"I did notice that."

"I apologize." His voice was stilted. "I don't exactly do a whole lot of relationships." So he had no clue how to navigate things with her.

"Pro tip," Harper told him cheerfully. "Don't speak for your partner. You don't need to warn others away from me. I'm not interested in other men. I'm only interested in you."

His gaze swung back to her.

Harper leaned toward him. "I want to know you. Good, bad, everything. All your secrets. You tell me yours, and I'll tell you mine."

He could not look away from her gorgeous eyes. "Harper—"

"Prepare for lift-off," Antony called out. "Time to get this baby into the air."

***

A limo was waiting for them at the airport. A long, sleek ride courtesy of Wilde. As they headed toward the vehicle, Harper stayed at Roman's side. He saw her gaze cut around the area, and he knew she was searching for threats.

He was doing the same thing.

The plane ride had been short. Tense. Harper wanted his secrets, and he was actually thinking about giving them to her. It was just a little hard to start that conversation. It could go something like...

So, my dad was a sadistic killer, and he raised me to be just like him.

Or maybe...

I used to work for the CIA. But then I thought my best friend sold me out and left me to die, so I went rogue. I've been living in the darkness for so long that I almost forgot what the light was like.

Or the always popular...

I had to fake my own death to start a new life because I've got so many enemies gunning for me. I've left fire and destruction in my wake and I—

Harper stopped. So did he.

Antony kept right on strolling past them toward the limo.

"He's going with us?" Harper asked. Her head turned toward Roman. "He's coming with us back to your place?"

"Hurry up," Antony chided. "Standing in the open just puts targets on you."

Roman curled his arm around Harper's shoulders. "This is not a permanent situation."

Antony was already at the back of the limo. His stare took in Roman's arm. Harper's body. He shook his head. "Did you even *try* to follow my advice? Like, for half a second, did you try?"

"Look, asshole, I—"

"Harper, this is your ride." Antony gestured toward the open limo door. "We'll meet you at Roman's house."

"Excuse me?" Harper demanded.

"What?" Roman shook his head. "No, no, Harper stays with me. She—"

"Yes, yes, I get that you have a very strong attachment to Ms. Crane, but we have to talk, confidentially, and we will be following her in the next vehicle." He pointed in the distance, to a black SUV that waited near a chain-length fence. "This is non-negotiable. She rides in the limo. We ride behind her. We *must* talk."

"She is *staying* with me," Roman snarled back.

"Non-negotiable," Antony fired. "I know you understand what the word means—"

"Oh, just stop it." Harper shook her head and climbed into the limo. "Roman, I'll see you at your place. Go get your confidential briefing." She pointed to Antony. "And *you*...do your tech work, dig into my life, and get me cleared enough so that this bullshit doesn't happen again, got me? I want to know everything that's happening." She settled against the leather seat. "Utter bullshit."

Antony appeared bemused as he gazed inside at her. He shook his head. "Yes, ma'am." He slammed the door.

Roman's hands fisted. "I wanted to stay at her side."

"Yes, yes, I got that." Antony was already hurrying toward the SUV. "But we'll have her in sight at all times if you just haul ass with me."

Roman hauled ass. Got in the SUV. He noticed an armed guard a few feet away. The man inclined his head to Antony.

The limo pulled away. Moments later, the SUV was on the road and following closely behind the limo. "The vehicle has been swept. We're clear to talk here," Antony informed him. "No one else will know what we're talking about."

So this was his briefing? His gaze remained on the limo's taillights. Light rain pelted against the windshield. The wipers flew back and forth. Back and—

"I can't believe Dex didn't tell you. I mean, he assured me that he'd warn you. That he'd tell you to be careful with Harper."

Roman's hands flattened over his thighs. "We're not back to this crap, are we?"

"Just what crap would that be?"

"Harper isn't going to betray me."

"You sound awfully certain of that for a man who only recently met the woman. I believe you've been her partner for approximately one week?"

Roman's jaw locked.

"And didn't your last, ah, female companion turn on you and—"

"Heather Madding wasn't a female companion. We weren't involved. She was a paid bodyguard. And, yes, she turned on me." He'd been involved in an abduction of his own. Maybe that was why things with Harper had freaked him out so much. *No, I was freaked out because it was*

Harper. He cleared his throat. "Thanks so much for asking. No need to keep throwing the past in my face. I'm good. She's dead." Flat. "And Harper is nothing like her."

"Because you're so sure of Harper already. So certain she's this good, trustworthy person."

"Don't play games with me." The limo was turning up ahead. "You have something to say, spit it out. If you've found intel in her background that I need to know about, tell me."

"*Dex* was supposed to tell you."

They turned to follow the limo.

"The only shit Dex told me was to be careful with Harper. He said to not get my ass emotionally involved." Roman's voice roughened. "Don't worry. I'm not exactly the falling-in-love type." Ice burned in his chest. "So go back to the spy master and tell him I'm good."

They stopped at a light. "Yes, um, you sound super good. The best."

Roman slanted a glance at him. "You're not funny."

"She won't love you back," Antony mumbled.

"Excuse me?" That ice in his chest was growing thicker.

"Not that I'm saying you're falling in love with her or anything. Because I'm not saying that. But if you did, she won't love you back."

"You're pissing me off, Antony."

The light changed. The limo drove forward.

"She can't," Antony continued doggedly. "I'm sorry, but because of what happened to her—"

The limo ignited. The back of the limo exploded into a ball of flames, and the vehicle flew forward. The back tires flipped into the air, and the whole vehicle seemed to spin. When the limo landed, it was upside down, and flames were pouring from the rear.

Roman heard a loud roar. Didn't even realize he was making the sound.

"Oh, Jesus," Antony breathed. "That car should have been checked. It should have been clear. Roman, Roman, I am so sor—"

He was out of the SUV. Racing toward the wreckage. And screaming Harper's name over and over again.

CHAPTER ELEVEN

He ran straight for the flames. Harper was in there, and he had to get her out. He *would* get her out. She was going to be all right. She had to be. He'd get to her. *"Harper!"*

Someone tackled him. Launched right at him and sent Roman slamming into the pavement. He took his attacker down with him. They rolled, and he grabbed for the knife he'd put in his boot after getting off that plane—

"Roman. It's me."

He blinked. He was raising his knife...toward Harper's throat?

Harper?

His Harper?

"Baby?" he gasped.

She yanked the knife out of his hand. "You can't just run out in the open when people are gunning for you."

The limo was burning behind her. Gawking men and women were spilling onto the street. Other cars had braked so the road was a sea of red lights. And flames. Lots of flames.

He ignored everything but her. "You're...okay?"

She hauled him to his feet. "We're getting the hell out of here." She shoved him back toward the SUV.

He stumbled. Turned. Caught her hand. No, caught *her*. He pulled her into his arms, lifted her against his chest, and raced with her back to the waiting SUV. They ran right by a gaping Antony.

"The driver is okay," Harper said as she curled one arm around Roman's neck. "I got him out and left him near the light post. We should call an ambulance for him, though, just in case."

Roman put her in the passenger side of the SUV. Paused to stare down at her. "You're okay."

"Yes. Fine. Maybe a few scratches." She scrunched her adorable nose. "Maybe some singed hair, but I'm good. Now can you get in the car and drive—actually, no, scratch that. I'm driving." She hopped over the console and settled in the driver's seat. *"Come on."*

He came his ass on and jumped into the passenger seat.

Antony ran toward them, waving his hands. "Wait! Wait for me!"

"Do we have to wait on him?" Harper asked.

Harper. Alive. Safe.

Roman leaned toward her. Curled his hand under her chin. Turned her head toward him and kissed her. Frantic. Hard. *She's alive.*

The back door slammed as Antony hurried into the backseat. "Oh, yeah. Great job of keeping a distance. Way to listen to me."

Roman raised his head. Then he glared back at Antony. "You almost got her killed!"

"Let's talk about this after we're away from this place," Harper directed.

Roman's focus shifted back to the road in front of them. Quite the crowd had gathered. And the limo was still burning.

"Don't worry, I can get us out of here. Just make sure you're buckled up, would you?" Harper's voice was mild.

Roman's hand lowered toward the seat belt even as Harper took off. She didn't head down the crowded street. She whipped the SUV to the left, shot down the lane like a bat out of hell, then proceeded to drive like a winning race car driver through the streets. Left, right, she turned fast and kept her laser-like focus on the road ahead of her. He was pretty sure she hit ninety at one point, maybe a whole lot more.

"Um, Harper," came Antony's slightly nervous voice from the backseat. "You are aware of the speed limit—"

"And since you're the tech guy who probably dug into my background extensively before meeting me, you are aware that I was trained to drive by one of the best race car drivers in Italy. I can handle my speed. Handle myself. And keep you two safe." She never took her eyes off the road. Her hands were loose around the wheel, and her posture was perfect. "Priority one is to get the hell away from here. I want Roman secured at his house immediately. So why don't you just settle down back there, Antony? Or, you know what? Do something useful. Make sure an ambulance is one the way for the limo driver."

Roman heard Antony calling for an ambulance, though he was sure the people back at the scene had already called for help. A moment later, he also heard Antony talking to someone—Eric? Dex?—and giving an update on what had happened.

"You're alive," Roman said. Obvious, yes. And...his voice was too rough.

"Did you think I wouldn't be?" Harper wanted to know. "Try having some faith in me."

It wasn't about faith. It was about fear. "The car exploded. It flipped into the air. The flames were in the *back*." That nightmare scene was playing through his head over and over again.

"Yes, they were in the back. Good thing I was riding up front. Actually..." She bit her lower lip. "I was the one driving."

"What? But—but you got in the back." He could not take his eyes off her profile.

From the back seat, Antony coughed. "I saw you get in the back, too," he said. "What did you do, lower the privacy screen and crawl through?"

She whipped to the right. "No, I didn't crawl through the privacy screen. While you two were heading for the SUV, I decided to just move up front. I walked up there, all normal-like, I assure you. It had been a while since I drove a limo, and I was tense and didn't feel like sitting alone in the back, so I asked the driver if I could take over. He let me, and now I'm alive. Wins all around." The words were flippant, but her voice was flat.

Roman wanted to haul her into his arms. Never let go. Instead, he forced himself to look back to Antony. "Why the hell wasn't that limo checked for a bomb?"

"It was. Dex had agents at the airport. Undercover, you know? They screened the car."

"Then they did a really shitty job of that screen." *If* the agents hadn't been bought off.

"I'm on it," Antony assured him. "Already texted Dex. We'll figure out what happened."

"I am not impressed," Harper declared. "Dex and his agents have me feeling very underwhelmed."

"I'll be sure to tell him that," Antony mumbled.

"You do that," she urged.

Roman had been checking the road around them for a tail. Actually, he'd been getting his dumb ass in gear so he could make sure Harper stayed safe. Hard because he was so focused on just her.

Flames. Fear. Harper.

He couldn't remember ever being so scared. Not even when he'd been tortured. When he'd been sure he was moments away from death. This was all different—because it was her.

"I expected more from the CIA," Harper added. "Such a letdown."

Silence. Then Antony laughed. "What?"

"I am not in the mood for more secrets. CIA." She shot a fast glance into the rearview mirror. "You think I don't get who Dex works for? Who you work for?"

"He works for Dex," Roman told her.

"Your accent is good, Roman. Generally, you sound very American. But every now and then...when you're stressed or, you know...like really, really involved in something..."

What did she mean...*really, really involved in—*

"Your accent slips. You stop sounding quite so American. Go a little more guttural. Rougher. I'd say Eastern European."

Roman's lips parted, but he didn't speak. He couldn't. He'd fucked up. He hadn't even realized it.

Really, really involved in...

"Sex," Harper told him helpfully. "You lost the American accent during sex. Guess it's hard to focus on holding a mask then, hmm?"

When he had sex with her, yes, it was hard to focus on anything else but the extreme pleasure he felt.

"Since you're so chummy with Dex and the man has all this classified BS that he likes to spout, it wasn't hard to put the pieces together. When we first met, I thought you were former military, but I was wrong. You're a former spy."

Still not exactly the truth. Not a full lie, either, though.

"Please, don't confirm or deny. You can both sit there in silence. Do you. Be fabulous. But, you know, considering that I was just in a car that caught on fire and *flipped*, I think I should at least get the courtesy of *something*. It was quite stressful for the flames to be at my back while broken glass and metal chunks were all around me, and I had to haul Travis out of the driver's side window."

Roman's heart shoved too fast against his chest. "You do deserve an explanation." Hell, yes, she did. "You'll get one." They were almost to his home.

"Um, Roman..." Antony's voice sounded strangled. "I don't know about that being the best idea. We still need to have that private talk of ours."

"*She almost died.*" And he'd almost lost everything. His mind. His heart. Hell, he had no soul. That was long gone. "We all know that bomb was meant for me." Must have been a bomb. "They thought I'd be in the back with her. They thought they'd take me out." His enemies hadn't cared if Harper died, too.

"Why are these people after you? Why are they working so hard to get to you? Do you have secrets on them? Intel? What?" Harper's questions were rapid-fire.

Once more, his gaze swept the area for attackers. "They want to kill me," he replied simply. "Because I'm the bad guy, sweetheart. I'm the bastard. I hurt them, and now, they want to hurt me."

"That's...not true." Her voice was halting.

He knew she *wanted* his words to be a lie. And wasn't that why he hadn't wanted her to learn who he really was? "I'm afraid that it is."

He was bad. Evil. Just like his father.

***

"This is insanity." Antony shut the door to Roman's study. Harper was upstairs, changing out of her torn and smoky clothes.

Because she was in a damn fire. An explosion.

She didn't have extra clothes at his place, but he was sure the folks at Wilde would be sending more over to her. When they'd arrived, two agents had been guarding the perimeter of his house.

Eric had installed the security system himself. It was supposed to be the most secure system in the world. Better than Fort Knox. No one should get to Harper while she was there.

And while she's safe, I will destroy those bastards.

"Are you even listening to me?" Antony yanked at the collar of his shirt. His glasses were off-kilter on his nose.

"No," Roman replied honestly. "I'm not." He gripped the back of the chair in front of him. "I keep seeing the car explode. I keep thinking about Harper and I—"

"She's not going to stay with you."

His hold tightened. "I'm not asking you for love life advice."

Antony hurried toward him. "I don't know how long we have before she's done changing, and this isn't how I wanted to say things. Just blurting isn't my style." He winced. "I am also very much not good at this emotional stuff. I tend to avoid entanglements whenever possible. Emotions are messy."

Roman just stared at him.

"I get that you think you need to come clean with her. But you can't tell her who you really are. Who your father was. She'll hate you when she learns the truth. She'll run *from* you. That will just make protecting her harder right now. The people after you have latched onto her. They want to use her against you, obviously. So we need to keep her close."

"I intend to keep her close." His knuckles had turned white. "I already told her that I was the one who'd done bad things. She didn't run then. Harper isn't the running type. She isn't—"

"She went to Europe when she turned eighteen."

"Yes, yes, I know that—Dex told me."

"Dex left out big pieces." Antony yanked off his glasses. "Who the hell knows why? He needs to stop the games."

"*Why* did she go to Europe?"

"She wanted to visit her dad's grave. Her mom met him when she was a college student. Got swept off her feet by a dark and dangerous stranger. He...he was killed right in front of Harper's mother. Gunned down in the street."

"Fuck."

"Harper's mother came back home. Had Harper but...she gave her up. The mother's family was afraid of what had happened in Europe. Afraid that trouble would come after them."

"Because of the baby?"

"Because it was a mess." Antony put his glasses back on. "Because Harper's father was a spy. He tried to recruit her mom, too. Fell in love while he was seducing her. Tried to get out and just got dead when his cover was blown. Harper's mother *was* being hunted. She knew it, and that's why she ran home to the US. She had her baby in the hospital and disappeared. Maybe she thought she'd come back for the baby later, I don't know. But there was no later. She didn't go back. She kept running. Invented a whole new life for herself. One that didn't include Harper."

Smiling Harper. Harper who could light up a room.

A life that didn't include her? It would be dark. Cold. Empty.

"Her mother died when Harper was seventeen. Heart attack. When Harper turned eighteen and started looking for her parents, they were both gone." Grim. "So she headed to Europe. She didn't know her father was a spy back when her parents met. I still don't think she knows."

He hated the pain she must have felt. And, damn, but he could understand. He and Harper were so much more alike than he'd realized. But while he'd turned cold and hard, she'd stayed warm. Caring. *Good.*

Roman's mother had never been in his life. She'd run from his bastard of a father. He'd always wanted to find her, but by the time he'd had the chance, it had been too late. She'd been killed—

"You're not getting what I'm saying, Roman. Her father was a spy."

"Yeah, so are you. So was I. Harper won't turn from me because of—"

"He was gunned down in the street to send a message."

"I heard you." Was Harper done changing? He craned to look around Antony.

"By your father."

"What?" He'd misheard. He must have misheard. There was no way—

"All evidence uncovered by the CIA indicates that *your* father was the shooter. He was amassing quite a bit of power in those days, he could have hired the hit out to someone, but our intel indicates he chose to do the job himself. He wanted to send a message. No matter how high he rose, if you turned on him, he would come for you." Antony shook his head. "I'm sorry. Dex should have told you not to get involved with her. It won't end well. When she finds out the truth—"

A light knock rapped at the door. Then, "I'm coming in. No more secrets." Harper swung open the door. Stood on the threshold, wearing one of Roman's shirts. A blue dress shirt that she'd rolled up to her elbows. The bottom of the shirt fell below her thighs. She looked delicate and sexy and—

A million miles out of my reach.

Roman knew Antony was right. When Harper found out the truth, she would hate him. She'd grown up without a family...*Because my family destroyed hers.*

"Roman?" Her eyes widened. Then she was immediately rushing straight to him. Her hands rose and pressed to his chest. "What's wrong? What's happened?"

He could not tell her. There was no way he could open his mouth and say, *"Sorry, sweetheart. I just found out that my dad killed yours. Shot him in the street. Your mother was terrified so she ran. You lost everything because of my family."*

Harper wouldn't just run away. She'd hate him.

Normally, he didn't mind hate. Didn't really care how others felt about him. But she was different.

When Roman didn't answer, Harper's head whipped toward Antony. "What did you do to him?"

"Me?" Antony's eyes widened. "I didn't do a thing to him!"

"Obviously, you did something. The man looks like he just lost his best friend!"

Roman's chest burned. Why the hell wasn't his mask in place? How was she seeing through him so easily? What the fuck was happening to him?

And he hadn't lost his best friend...had he? He didn't have a best friend. He didn't let people close.

Except Harper was close. Harper was touching him. Warming him. Glaring because she wanted to protect him.

Lost a best friend? No. *I think I lost even more than that.*

"Tell me what you said to him," Harper directed. "Tell me right now. I could kick your ass for upsetting Roman."

"It's been a real upsetting day for everyone." Antony shuffled toward the bar in the corner, but he didn't touch the drinks there. "The driver is resting comfortably in the hospital, by the way. Thought you might like that update."

"Glad to hear it." Her hands still pressed to Roman's chest. "But I want to hear a whole lot more, too." She looked back at Roman. Her right hand rose. Curled against his jaw. She stared into his eyes, and her own gaze narrowed. "No. Don't do that."

He backed away from her. Had to do it. "Do what?"

"Block me out. When I came into this room, I *saw* you. Don't go throwing up your walls now. It's far too late for that."

It was too late. He should have never touched her. "I'm sorry."

"Damn right, you should be." A firm nod. "We're in this together." Her hands fell away—only—only for her right hand to reach for his. Her fingers curled around his. She held his hand. "We're a team. A partner has your back. Always. I'll have yours. You'll have mine."

Roman stared down at their joined hands.

"Now I want to know everything," Harper ordered. "Tell me exactly what we're dealing with here, and don't even *think* of leaving anything out."

CHAPTER TWELVE

"Dex has given approval for you to receive certain information," Antony allowed as he began to pace. "And your cooperation on this case is certainly appreciated."

"So glad to be appreciated," Harper replied breezily. Like it didn't matter. Like she was totally fine and cool and handled near-death experiences every single day.

Lie. Lie. Lie. She wasn't fine. She wasn't in control. In fact, if she hadn't been holding so tightly to Roman, Harper was afraid that she might have shattered into a million pieces. She could still feel the flames on her skin. At first, when she'd been driving the limo, Harper hadn't even known what was happening. She and Travis had been listening to the radio. Talking. Small talk. The kind of talk that you forgot later because it doesn't matter. Then the car had been flying. It had hurtled forward, and Travis had started screaming.

They'd slammed into the pavement. The car's alarm had begun blaring. The seatbelt had bit into her shoulder, and the air bags had deployed. It had taken a moment for the fire to register, and when it had, she'd worried about a secondary explosion. Had the gas line already been hit? Did they only have moments before they were burned alive?

She'd dragged Travis out and heard the bellow of her own name. When she'd whipped around, Roman had been running toward the wreckage. She didn't even remember racing toward him. She'd only known that she had to keep him safe.

"I was a spy." Roman's voice was halting.

Her hold tightened on him. "Tell me something I don't know."

He blanched. For a second, she could have sworn that something very much resembling agony flashed across his face before he rasped, "I'd rather not."

"Yes, well, you don't have lots of options." She moved even closer to him and lowered her voice as she said, "I don't care, Roman. I don't care about the past. I get that you must have taken dangerous jobs. That you made enemies. I'm not going to back away from this. I can handle whatever happened in your past."

A muscle flexed along his jaw. "Baby, I've done things that would give you nightmares."

She kept right on holding his stare. "Why are you trying to make me think you're the villain?"

"Because I am."

"Not to me."

His gaze cut away from her. Landed on Antony. "Tell her what she needs to know." Clipped. Angry. Roman pulled away from Harper. Paced across the room. A fire blazed in the massive hearth, and Roman gazed into the flames as if they were the most fascinating things on the face of the earth. His back was turned to Harper.

She wrapped her arms around her stomach. She felt as if he'd shut her out, and she didn't like the feeling. Not one bit.

"So..." Antony took a few hesitant steps toward her. "Roman was recruited by Dex years ago. Roman had lots of European connections that were valuable, so for a time he worked, um...in a sense, I suppose you could think of him as a double agent."

Roman was still staring into the fire.

"Only eventually, his role with the CIA was discovered. He was captured. His captors demanded that Dex surrender himself in exchange for Roman. Dex has a lot of power. Far more than you probably realize."

She just waited.

"The exchange didn't go as planned." Antony winced. "In fact, I'd say it went very badly."

"I'm going to need more than that." Harper took a step toward the fire.

I can still feel the flames. Hear the crunch of metal.

She froze.

Antony quietly revealed, "Dex went for the exchange, only instead of giving up Roman, the bastards shot Dex and threw him in a river."

Her breath heaved out.

"I didn't know that Dex had shown up for me." Roman's voice was low. "They tortured me. The hours bled together, and all I knew was that no one would come for me. I'd been betrayed by the one friend I thought I had."

She hurried toward him and ignored the flickering flames in the fire. Her hand reached out and curled around his shoulder. "You are not alone, Roman."

He stiffened beneath her touch. "I don't deserve you."

If possible, his words had been even lower. Even rougher. She wasn't sure—had she even heard him correctly? "Roman?"

He turned toward her. "I don't," he rumbled. "But how the hell am I supposed to let you go?"

"I am not going anywhere. We are in this together." Why couldn't he get that?

His expression was fierce. So much longing filled his gaze.

"Ahem." Antony had crept closer. "I'll speed up the recap, how about that?"

She did not take her eyes off Roman.

"Roman parted ways with the agency after that. Went, um—"

"Rogue," Roman said flatly.

"Yes, went that. Caused lots of international drama. Made more enemies. But, also, I think…covertly did some good."

Roman's head whipped toward Antony. "Shut the fuck up."

"Oh, what?" Antony straightened his shoulders. "Did you think I wouldn't find out about that stuff? Tech is my world. I tracked the donations you made. The medical supply drops. The relief packages. Guess you were trying to buy yourself some forgiveness? Is that the way it worked in your—"

"I can break your entire face in five seconds flat."

Antony blinked. "Maybe, but that's not the kind of shit *good* guys do, am I right?"

"Never said I was good."

"But I don't buy all the hype about you being bad, either. Figure a lot of that was just flash for show. You had to have some nice window dressing or else who would believe the cover you were pushing?" Antony's head tilted. "How many syndicates have you shut down? How many targets did you take out of commission once you went freelance? And isn't that really the reason you have a target on your back? You destroyed them, and now one of your enemies—someone who was left in the ashes you left behind—that person wants to destroy you."

Roman's nostrils flared. "You talk too much."

"I was just updating the lady. And I'm done talking now. Unless, of course..." He shrugged. "There's more you want me to reveal to her? I could go on—"

"Why don't you go and get the hell out of here for now?" Roman's order was curt. Hard. "We need to crash. I'll connect with you tomorrow."

Antony saluted. "Will do. Wanted to go take a look at the limo's remains anyway. And, I *am* supposed to be in town looking at real estate for a second Shark Gaming location. So...I have lots to do. Don't worry about me." He turned on his heel. Headed for the door. "I can stay busy."

"Fabulous," Roman said.

They didn't speak again, not until Antony was gone. Harper rocked onto the balls of her feet and made sure her gaze didn't drift to the flickering flames. "Roman…"

He eased away from her. "You have to be exhausted. There are plenty of bedrooms. Choose whichever one you want."

She'd already chosen the room when she changed. "I'm sorry."

His head whipped toward her. "What?"

"I'm so sorry for what you went through when you were captured. It must have been hell."

His Adam's apple bobbed as Roman swallowed. "Doesn't matter now. That's all over."

"I'm still sorry for you pain, and if you want to talk, I'm here."

He whirled away. "Talk. Yeah, pretty sure there's been enough of the whole *talk* thing for tonight."

She wanted to reach for him again, but each time she reached out, Harper felt as if he pulled away. She was missing something. "Is there more?"

His broad shoulders stiffened. "More?"

"You seem different. Like something happened. Like…" Her voice trailed away before she said…*Like you're trying to put walls between us.*

He strode toward the desk. "Oh, a few things happened. You were in the car that exploded right in front of me. I thought I was watching while you died. You know, because of me. Because I foolishly thought I could bury the past, but there are some bodies that crawl back out of the ground no matter what you do."

She didn't move. Her feet now felt rooted to the spot. "You didn't make the limo catch on fire, Roman."

His eyes glittered. "What if you hadn't gotten in the front?"

"I don't like the 'what if' game."

"Too damn bad because—"

"I played it too much when I was a kid. What if my parents had wanted me? What if they hadn't given me up? What if I had a real family? What if, what if..." She blew out a hard breath. "What ifs don't change anything. They just twist you up and make you doubt what you do have. Make you wish or worry. I stopped playing with them long ago. I just focus on *what is*. Not what if. Life is better that way."

His hands fisted.

"I can tell you what is, if you'd like."

He didn't speak. Typical Roman.

"I'm alive. You're alive. The attackers missed us both, and we're going to come back at them harder and stronger. That's *what is* happening. I'm here with you. We're safe. Another *what is*. Those are the things that matter. I have you, and you have me." Her chin lifted. "And it's not your fault. I'm a Wilde agent. Because of my job, I take risks. I understand danger. If I wasn't prepared for a threat, I would have finished my art studies degree years ago, and I'd be spending my days blissfully painting."

He shook his head. "What?"

"Painting. I'm quite good, actually. Never even realized I had talent for it until I was working as a model for an artist." She was rambling.

Distracting him a little. No, no, that wasn't what she was doing. She was trying to be fair to him. His past had just been laid bare before her. Wasn't it only fair that he deserved her secrets, too? "When I was eighteen, I took my life savings, and I boarded a plane. I flew to Europe. I had found out that my father died there, you see. Before I was born. I had this crazy idea about meeting his family. Figured...he didn't give me up. He didn't have a choice, you know? He died. My mother—she was the one who left me at the hospital." By the time Harper had found out about her mother's identity, she'd been dead, too.

"Harper..." Roman took a halting step toward her.

"My life savings turned out to only be enough to *get* me to Europe. I landed in Paris and had to figure out how to earn enough money to survive." She wrinkled her nose. "This probably seems insane to you. That I just rushed off that way. But there was nothing for me here, so I just...I went." Her lips pressed together. "There are lots of affordable youth hostels near Paris. I stayed at some of those. Found out that one of the museums paid money for models. So I just—I went to see what that was about. Turns out, I could sit still for hours and be a pretty good model." It had been oddly peaceful. "I met this great lady. Marguerite Valeux. She was doing a sketch one day, and she asked if I wanted to go from being the model to becoming the artist. And the next thing I knew..." Harper laughed. It was a happy memory. "She was teaching me everything she knew. And I loved painting and it was wonderful, and Marguerite was almost like the grandmother I'd never had and..." She stopped.

"What is it?"

An exhale. *Get attached to things, not people.* "She was sick. I didn't know. She didn't want anyone to know. I went in to check on her one day, and she was gone." The pain flashed inside of her. "But she told her nephew about me. He was the race car driver. I think I told you about him before? He took me under his wing." Another faint laugh. "I became the driver for a driver. During that time, I realized that I liked to learn new things. I'd never had the opportunity before. Never been encouraged. This was different. There was no stopping me. So I learned everything that I could."

"Did you learn about your father?"

She rubbed her finger across her right cheek. Strange. It felt wet. "There was nothing to learn. Despite my efforts, I couldn't find a record of his family. I located his grave. Nothing more. It was like—like he didn't have a past. Like I didn't have one." Her lips curled down. "I realized then that the past can't matter. What happened before—you have to let it go."

"If only it were that fucking easy," he muttered.

Her spine stiffened. "I never said it was easy. I said you can't let it matter. You can't let it hold you back from taking what you want."

His gaze seemed to burn with intensity as it locked on her.

"The past doesn't define us," Harper continued somewhat unsteadily. There was just something about the way he was staring at her. Need. Desperation. Hope? She took a careful step toward him. "We define ourselves."

He closed the distance between them. Reached out for her, but stopped. His hands hung in the air between them. "Do you really believe that?"

"Would I say it if it wasn't true?"

His hands fell to his sides. "People say a lot of shit. It's easy to say stuff, but when you get the cold, hard facts in front of you, things are different."

"I'm saying what I mean. I don't care about the past. I care about the here and the now." *I care about you.* Far more than she had expected.

His eyelids flickered. "I...I care about you."

Harper's breath caught. It was as if he'd just read her mind. "Then—"

"That's not a good thing, baby. It's a very dangerous thing, or haven't you realized that yet? There have been two attacks on you so far. Three, if you count just how close you were to me when the bullet was fired at that godforsaken cabin. By being near me, you are in harm's way. That's not what I want for you."

"What do you want?"

His hand lifted. Trailed over her cheek. "For you to smile when you see me. For you to light up the whole damn room because you're so happy. I want you to be happy every day of your life." His hand pulled away. "But if you're with me, that won't happen."

"You act like I can't handle danger. We've covered this." Determination hardened her voice.

"Wilde agent, remember? Death and danger are part of the package deal there."

"You should get some rest. You have to be exhausted."

"No more so than you."

"I didn't crawl out of a burning car."

She shrugged.

"You are so fucking beautiful." His voice was rough. "And I will never deserve you."

"Well, sure, probably not." She'd forced her own tone to be lighter. She wanted to chase the shadows from his gaze. "But you can try. You can just turn everything around right now. You have this obsession with the past. I say it doesn't matter. I say the here and now matters. But if you want to prove that you deserve me, fine. You can do it." She put her hands on his chest. Leaned onto her toes. "Want to know how?"

"Yes." Ragged. Desperate.

"Be a good man. Do what's right."

"I'm trying…"

"And don't hold back with me. Never hold back with me. Because I want you, Roman. This thing between us? I've never felt this way about anyone else. It's kind of ripping me apart inside and putting me back together in a whole new way." That probably made zero sense. "You want to deserve me? Put me first. I'll put you first. Let's take care of each other. Let's *trust* each other." Because she hadn't trusted him at the beginning.

It wasn't the beginning any longer.

She waited. She wanted his response. She needed him to—

"I can't give you what you need." Pain knifed through his words. "I am so sorry."

The same pain seemed to slice into her heart. *Don't get attached to—*

Forget it. Too late. She was already attached to Roman.

Harper kissed him. Pressed her lips to his in a soft, tender kiss.

Tension hardened his entire body.

"I think you can," she whispered against his mouth. "Turns out, I have some faith in you." Then she slipped away. She'd done her part. The rest—well, the rest would come. Harper turned from him and headed for the door.

"Harper!"

Her steps faltered. Did he even realize how much emotion was in his voice? She glanced back at him. Saw the torment on his face. Poor baby. He was stumbling around, and he had no clue how to deal with the way he felt.

She'd help him. "Yes?"

"Where are you going?"

"To bed. You're right. I am exhausted."

A jerky nod. "You...you said you picked a room already?"

"Yes, I did." Her gaze savored him a moment more. "Sweet dreams, Roman."

He swallowed. "Sweet dreams, Harper."

***

Roman's steps were slow as he made his way to his bedroom. All he wanted to do was go to Harper. To hold her, to—

Antony is right. She'll run from me. When she learned what his father had done, Harper wouldn't smile when she saw him. That gorgeous smile of hers wouldn't light up a room. Instead, he'd see fear on her face. Anger. Hate?

Roman didn't want that. Even from the grave, his father was reaching out to destroy him. To destroy the most precious thing that Roman had ever treasured. *Harper.*

His hand curled around the doorknob. He wondered which room Harper had taken. The whole house was secure, so he didn't have to go and bunk with her like he'd done in the mountains. But...

He wanted to. He wanted to find her. To slip into bed with her. To pull Harper in his arms and hold her tight.

The fucking limo exploded.

He shoved open the door. Growled with rage as he stomped inside and—

"Jeez, you could wake the dead," Harper called out sleepily.

Roman froze. "You're...in my room."

"Yes, very observant."

He staggered forward. Turned on the lamp on the nightstand. Soft light immediately formed a small glow around them. "You're in my bed."

"Again, your observational skills are top notch. No wonder you're on track to be a lead Wilde agent."

"*Why* are you in my bed?"

She brushed back a lock of hair as she rolled toward him. "Because you said I could pick my room. And I did."

"This is *my* room."

"And I want to be with you. So I picked this room."

He realized she was holding a little too tightly to the covers.

"Unless..." Her voice shook the smallest bit. "Unless you don't want me here."

She was afraid.

Harper sat up. Stared at him with the amazing eyes that he'd never forget. "If you don't want me," her chin lifted, "I can certainly find another bed."

His breath was coming too fast. Too hard.

Her shoulders squared, and Harper reached out to him. She caught his hand in hers. "I can leave. I can—"

"Don't run." Ragged.

"Um, I was going to walk. With dignity and grace and perfect poise." She bit her lip. "Not run. Why would I run from you?"

"Don't leave." Shit, he was barely managing to speak. Emotions were choking him. He'd never had to deal with this mess until he met her.

Her hold tightened. "I won't go anywhere."

That was it. There was no more control. She was touching him, staring up at him so tenderly. She was in his bed. And he wanted her.

Let her go? How the fuck was he supposed to do that?

His mouth took hers with a ravenous need. So much for his good intentions. But as he'd tried to warn Harper, he'd never been particularly good, anyway.

CHAPTER THIRTEEN

He was kissing her like he a man possessed. With so much need and raw desire. And she loved it. A moan built in Harper's throat. Both of her hands curled around him, and she yanked Roman down onto the bed with her.

Her heart raced in her chest as her body squirmed beneath his. The adrenaline rush from the explosion still had her feeling shaky and revved up, and his kiss? Oh, it was revving her up even more.

When she'd crawled into bed, she'd made sure to only be wearing his shirt. No underwear. Now she wanted to yank the shirt out of the way and strip him, too.

Would the sex be as good this time? She had the feeling it would be even better.

"Need to go slow…" He tore his mouth from hers and kissed a fiery path down her neck. "Need to be careful with you."

Harper arched her neck toward his mouth. "I think…" Her nails bit into his shoulders. "You meant to say…you need me desperately. You want to take me right, ah, now." Her breath hitched when he licked a particularly sensitive spot. "And if you have to wait, you just might go insane."

His body stiffened. His head rose. His glittering eyes captured hers. "I need you desperately."

She could feel that need. Long and thick and hard and shoving against his jeans. Shoving between her spread thighs.

"I want to take you right now."

Her hips pushed against him. A nice, what-are-you-waiting-for move.

"If I have to wait..." His voice was guttural and deep and sexy as hell. "I will lose my mind."

Perfect. "Get out of those clothes."

They both started yanking and shoving and soon he was naked. But their bodies had twisted, and she wound up on top of him, a position that worked out perfectly for Harper. She pushed him back and straddled his hips. Her sex slid over his cock.

"Fuck." His nostrils flared. "You don't have on underwear."

"Good of you to notice."

"Did you..." His teeth clenched—she'd just done another sensual glide, and Harper was glad he appreciated her skill. His voice was more growl than anything else as he gritted, "Did you...were you wearing panties when you were downstairs and Antony was there? Dammit, tell me that you *were* wearing—"

She shimmied her way down his body. He wasn't quite at the edge enough for her, not yet. When she'd said she wanted him to nearly lose his mind from need, she'd meant those words. Wasn't it only fair that they both suffer from the same madness? Harper thought so. She put her mouth on him. Took the broad head of his cock between her open lips.

"Harper."

That was what she wanted. A savage desire that stripped everything else away. She decided to see just how far she could push him. She licked. Sucked. Got lost in enjoying the way he tasted as her mouth moved and stroked over him. Lips and tongue and—

She was on her back. He was looming above her. His expression? *Savage.* Exactly what she wanted.

"Can't. Wait."

"I don't want you to wait." She leaned up. Nipped his lip. "By the way, a condom's on the nightstand. I found a box in the bathroom, so I thought I'd be helpful and move one close to—"

He got that condom on, and his cock shoved at the entrance of her body. "How the hell will I ever let you go?"

"Don't. Hold on tighter." Words torn from her.

He sank deep. Thrust hard. Control was gone. Hers. His. There was only consuming need. Their bodies heaved together. Her nails raked down his back. Every glide and thrust had her gasping. His hand slid between them. He strummed her clit as he drove into her. Again and again and the orgasm that ripped through her whole body made her scream.

So good. No, amazing. The pleasure hummed and rolled and kept her shuddering beneath him. His thrusts quickened, and her legs locked tightly around him.

He was beautiful. In a primitive, sex god kind of way. When Roman's release hit him and the pleasure swept across his face...

She smiled up at him. Smiled and held on even tighter.

Sex with Roman wasn't like sex with anyone else. Because he was special. Different.

With care, he withdrew from her. Padded to the bathroom. She heard the running of water as she slowly stretched in the bed. She still had on the shirt. *His* shirt. Harper laughed. They hadn't even gotten around to taking it off.

"What's funny?"

Roman was at the side of the bed. He bent and carefully pressed a warm cloth between her legs. Wasn't that sweet? Her hand slid over his cheek. She liked the rasp of stubble against her fingers. "Next time, I can't forget to take off the shirt."

He pulled away the cloth. Ditched it. Then lingered by the bed. "You're planning for a next time?"

Another yawn. The adrenaline crash was sweeping through her. "Of course." She settled comfortably amid the covers. "Aren't you?"

He didn't slide onto the mattress.

Uncertainty trickled through Harper. "Do you want me to go find another room?" Careful. No emotion.

"No."

Okay.

He stared down at her. She waited for more from him.

The seconds ticked past. Then..."I don't want you to leave."

Was that so hard? She patted the pillow beside her. "I won't go anywhere."

"Promise?"

"Roman, the only place I'm going is to sleep. Right here. In this bed, with you."

He slid into the bed. Lay stiffly beside her.

A sigh eased from Harper as she moved closer to him. "Will this make you feel better?" She put her head on his chest. Right over his steady, strong heartbeat. "This way, you can make sure I don't leave. You can put that muscled arm of yours around me and hold me all night."

His arm came up. Settled around her.

Her eyes drifted closed. "Better?" she asked sleepily.

His hold tightened. "Much."

That was good. Sleep tugged at her.

"You…you do make me feel better."

"Glad," her slurred response. She fell asleep with her head over Roman's heart.

***

He'd made a mistake. Sure, during the course of his life, Roman had made more than his share of bad decisions, but this time, he had a clusterfuck on his hands.

Sex with Harper.

She was asleep in the bed. Curled against him. Exactly where he wanted her to be. She felt good against him. Right. As if she belonged…

Belonged to me.

But that was *wrong*. Harper wasn't his. This was just temporary. It was…sex? Partners with benefits? It was—hell, he didn't know what *it* was. Roman only knew that it was the best thing he'd ever had. The connection with Harper was unlike anything he'd experienced before.

His head turned. His lips brushed her temple. "Don't hate me." Low. Rasping.

But...

She would learn the truth. Secrets had a way of bubbling to the surface. When Harper learned his truth, her truth, she wouldn't want to curl trustingly against him while she slept.

Instead, she'd probably want to kill him.

***

"Are you planning to sleep all day or do you want to join me for some hunting?"

Roman cracked open one eye. Of course, the chipper voice belonged to Harper. The chipper, perky, and far too awake voice. He opened his other eye.

She perched on the end of the bed. Looking cute as could be—and fully dressed.

Her hair was sleek and stylish. Light makeup covered her features. And she wore a pair of black pants and a gray sweater.

"Where did you get the clothes?" he mumbled as he sat up. He rubbed a hand over his jaw. His growing beard felt like sandpaper against his fingers.

"Antony brought them."

Roman stiffened. "When?"

"About an hour ago. Before we had breakfast."

"You had breakfast with Antony."

"Yes. The man can make some mean pancakes." Her head tilted. "What's wrong?"

"You…I didn't hear you leave the room. Or come back in."

She leaned forward. Winked. "That's because I tip-toed."

No, she didn't get it. He always stayed on guard. He usually slept lightly, rousing at the faintest sound.

Harper laughed and rose from the bed. "Don't look so stressed. It was just me. I can slip in and out…look, if you must know my deep, dark secrets…"

I want to know all of your secrets. But I'm terrified of you learning mine.

"I have training." She'd maneuvered to the side of the bed closest to him. "Back in my traveling days, I even joined a circus for a while. Don't get too impressed, but I had a high-wire act."

"You're kidding."

"Nope. I was actually quite good. Had a fabulous stage name. Want to hear it?"

"Yes," he responded cautiously, completely fascinated by her.

"High-wire Harper."

He blinked.

"Okay, fine, it wasn't fabulous, but it got the point across. I stayed with the group for a while. Learned lots of tricks." An incline of her head. "In fact, it's my high-wire training that helps me to case museums so well. Most of the people who are trying to get past security systems in museums and art galleries have to be pretty dang agile. Because of my training, I can think like they do. Can see how they maneuver through tight spots and even drop down from the ceilings so they don't set off the pressure security indicators on the floors."

"I thought you were a thief."

Her brows rose. "Excuse me?"

"Eric once told me...he said that you had a background that made you uniquely suited for the job you did. I thought he meant you were a former thief."

She laughed. "No. Sorry to disappoint you."

"There isn't a single thing about you that is a disappointment."

Her eyes widened. "You just gave me a compliment."

"I just told you the truth."

Harper nibbled on her lower lip. "Did Eric tell you anything else about my past?"

"No, he said *you'd* tell me. When you trusted me."

"He was right." She turned on her heel. Made her way for the door. "You get that I just showed my trust, don't you? By telling you about Highwire Harper? Next time, it will be your turn."

He shook his head, but she didn't see him. She was already gone.

***

The scene was damn cozy, and Roman didn't like it. Not one bit. When he entered *his* kitchen, Harper and Antony had their heads bent together.

A half-eaten plate of cinnamon rolls rested between them. There was no sign of pancakes. He figured they must have eaten them all. Tall coffee mugs were within reach for both of them, and Harper and Antony were whispering together. Nodding.

Way too cozy.

"Am I interrupting?"

Antony cut him a sharp glance. Didn't jump, though, so the guy must have known that Roman was there. *You just didn't bother moving away from Harper.* He still hadn't moved away from Harper.

As for Harper, she beamed at Roman. "Finally!" Harper scooped one of the cinnamon rolls off the plate. "I was saving this for you, and believe me, it was extremely hard." She hurried toward him and lifted the cinnamon roll to his mouth.

He stared at the roll. Then at her.

"Antony's greedy," she continued as she patiently held up the offering. "He wanted to eat all the cinnamon rolls. I told him this one was yours."

His gaze slid to Antony. "Mine," Roman said flatly but he really wasn't talking about the damn rolls.

Antony's inclined head said he got the message.

Roman took a bite of the offered roll. He let his tongue lick lightly over Harper's fingertips. "Delicious."

A faint red flushed her cheeks. "So glad you think so."

Another bite. Another lick.

"Ah, you can hold it." The red was darker in her cheeks. "I've got some things to run by you."

He took the cinnamon roll. The freaking thing was surprisingly good. No wonder Antony had been trying to take them all.

"We have a plan of attack," Harper announced as she clasped her hands together. "We're backtracking. You weren't at Wilde for long. So we are going to start with our most recent case—Tomas the would-be thief—and work back from there. Because whoever is after us, he struck right *after* Tomas was taken into custody. Maybe the two things are connected."

Roman finished off the cinnamon roll. "I didn't know Tomas until that case."

"Yes, but that doesn't mean he wasn't familiar with you," Antony pointed out. "You were rather infamous in certain circles. If the guy was selling off art on the black market, then he's probably had dealings with some rather shady people. You know, the kind of people you attract." A pause. "The kind of people who also want you dead."

True enough.

"He's in jail, but I have a friend at the PD who can get us in to see him." Harper's eyes gleamed with excitement. "Layla is a homicide detective, but she has some serious pull. We'll be able to have a one-on-one talk with him, no problem."

Roman rubbed the back of his neck. "He'd need a partner."

Harper's brows rose. "Excuse me?"

"It's never a one-person operation. When this much money is on the line, there's always a partner. You need someone to watch your back. We got Tomas..." And if he hadn't been so distracted by Harper and her abduction, he would have focused on this sooner. "But what about his partner?"

She looked over at Antony, then back at Roman. "There was no sign of anyone else's involvement. He was the one with the ruby that night."

"But someone could have helped him get it. Someone who would have been able to work the security at the museum. Someone who would have run interference while he made the switch." Roman kept considering the options. "Tomas was locked up, so he couldn't send out the goons after you. If he was working with a partner, the partner would have been the one to hire the thugs and get them to—"

"If this *is* about Tomas, we could be looking at it all wrong." She bit her lower lip. "Maybe it's not about your past after all, Roman. Maybe it's about me. You. What we did. Together." She paced to the counter and picked up her coffee. She sipped it and then said, "Maybe Tomas did have a partner, and that partner was pissed because we stopped the theft. I was the one to first go after Tomas, so for payback, the partner took me. Perhaps the plan was to punish us both." Her eyes widened as she looked at Roman. "That's why you were called after I was taken! That's why you were pulled in. The partner wants to punish us for messing up his plans!"

Roman peered over at Antony.

Antony shook his head. "No, sorry, Harper, I hate to burst your bubble, but the word on the Dark Web is that Roman is the target. Someone knows he's still alive, and that person wants him taken out. You were the means to that end. The lure to get him to show his weakness."

Her delicate jaw firmed. "I'm still talking to Tomas. As soon as possible. I think he has intel to give us." She put down her mug. "Ready when you are, Roman."

"One issue that you haven't fully worked out...what if Tomas won't talk to you?" Antony asked. "You *are* responsible for him currently being behind bars."

She waved that away as she strolled for the door. "He brought that on himself."

Antony didn't look convinced. "Oh, I'm sure he sees it that way, too."

Her brows lifted as she threw a glance back at him. "You think he'll hold a grudge?"

"Yes, a thousand times, yes, I do think the man you both got locked away will hold a grudge."

Harper turned her attention to Roman.

He shrugged. Hell, yes, he thought the man would also be holding a grudge. But... "If he wants any kind of deal, he'll talk."

"Whoa! Wait a minute!" Antony scrambled forward. "You don't work for *any* government agency any longer. You have zero authority to make deals. I don't even have the authority to make deals with this guy. He's just a regular criminal. Not some international spy!"

Roman took Harper's hand. "Fine, but he doesn't know that."

"Shit." Antony grimaced. "This is a bad plan. I hope you know that."

Harper didn't look away from Roman. "Let's do this."

CHAPTER FOURTEEN

"Sorry, but you're not going to be able to talk to him, not without the guy's lawyer present." Detective Layla Lopez had paused beside a closed door. Her thick, dark hair was twisted into a loose bun. She wore a light blue suit—one that looked both professional and feminine on her. No jewelry, except for the very large diamond ring on her left hand.

"That's new," Harper noted with raised brows. She pointed at the mega diamond. "Did you forget to tell one of your closest friends something very, very important?"

Layla lifted her hand. "What? This thing?"

"Don't tease, Layla."

"It's just...a loaner."

Behind Harper, Roman was silent. She'd introduced him to the detective a few moments before. Layla was the rising star in the homicide department, but she had pull everywhere at the PD. Harper had hoped Layla could get them in to chat with Tomas but...

But I have been momentarily distracted by the fact that one of my best friends may have gotten engaged without telling me. "Kendrick." Harper knew Layla had been spending a *lot* of time with the criminal defense attorney, but she hadn't realized they'd grown quite so close.

Layla nodded. "Yes. Tomas hired Kendrick Shaw to represent him."

"No, no, that wasn't what I—" Harper stopped. "Wait, what? Say that stuff again."

"Kendrick is waiting inside for you. I told him that it would be to his client's advantage to take this meeting, so he hauled ass down here to get things set up." She looked at the ring. "I shouldn't be wearing this here. I don't know what I was thinking." She started to pull it off.

Harper caught her hand and leaned in close. "What's going on?"

Layla swallowed. Her gaze darted over Harper's shoulder toward Roman. Then back to Harper. "Nothing. We'll talk later. I heard about the kidnapping. You have a whole hell of a lot more to deal with right now than my drama."

Harper squeezed her hand. "It's not drama. It's you." Layla was the most drama-free person Harper had ever met.

Layla eased a little closer to Harper. "I told Kendrick I'd think about the proposal. He told me to keep the ring while I did. That maybe I'd start to like how it felt." She wiggled her fingers. "I like it." Her gaze rose. Held Harper's. "I like him."

"Then tell the man yes," Harper encouraged her.

"He defends criminals. I lock them up. He's been a player for years, and I—"

The door opened. Kendrick Shaw stood there. As always, he was dressed to impress. Handsome, tall, lean, Kendrick had been known to have the ability to charm even the most cold-hearted of judges or jurors. In a courtroom, every prosecutor cursed him while every client praised him.

"My ears were burning," Kendrick murmured as his gaze took in Harper and her grip on Layla. "Thought I'd better see what was causing the fire." He smiled at Harper. "Good to see you again, Harper." The smile dimmed a little as concern lit his dark eyes. "Heard about what happened. Glad you're okay."

"You and me both." She'd noticed that Layla's shoulders had stiffened. Harper had also taken note of the fact that Kendrick had sidled closer to Layla.

Kendrick raised one brow as he took in the silent Roman. "Who's the new friend?"

She let go of Layla and moved back a step toward Roman. "He is my partner. Roman Smith," she put a hand on his chest, "this is Kendrick Shaw."

Kendrick inclined his head. Seemed to assess Roman.

She had the feeling Roman was doing the same assessment. Tension thickened the air. Men. "Thanks for agreeing to let us see your client. We'll only need to speak with him for a few moments." Maybe. Hopefully. She squared her shoulders. "We'll be right back out as soon as we're done." Harper strode for the interrogation room.

Kendrick stepped into her path. "That's adorable."

Harper shrugged.

"Nice try, Harper. You know that isn't how things work. I'll be in the room. The entire time," he emphasized.

"Great." She offered him a high-wattage grin. "Then you can make certain your client cooperates."

"My client is being framed."

She snorted. "Right. Like he didn't have the ruby *in his coat* when I tackled him."

Kendrick swiped a hand over the lower part of his face. Harper was pretty sure he was trying to hide a smile. "I did hear about the tackle."

"Good. Then you heard that he had the stolen ruby in his possession at the time I took him down. That means the man has zero defense."

"Don't be so sure…"

She was sure. "His cooperation would help things for him. Tomas could sure use a deal right about now."

Kendrick's hand fell. "We both know you don't have the authority to make any deals. Unless…have I missed something? Is Wilde now working with the DA?" He blinked innocently.

Layla sighed. "Kendrick, get them in the room."

"Of course, my love."

Layla's shoulders became even straighter.

"I meant, of course, Detective Lopez," Kendrick corrected smoothly. "But I want to be very clear on this…no subterfuge will be used on my client. You can't pretend there is a deal for him when nothing is on the table."

"Nothing?" Harper's chin angled up. "My partner has a great many connections."

"Does he now." Not a question. Once more, Kendrick assessed a silent Roman.

"If Tomas answers our questions, then Roman might be willing to use those connections." Harper kept her voice casual. "It would really just depend on the answers that Tomas gives."

"Uh, huh." Kendrick's gaze sharpened. "You know, I don't think your partner has actually said one word during this whole conversation."

"He's the strong, silent type...who still gets shit done." She tapped one foot. "Can we get this show rolling? I do have other plans for the day."

Kendrick waved toward interrogation. "Absolutely, but be warned, I will advise my client against answering any questions that would incriminate him."

"I have been warned." She hurried into the room. The museum manager waited at a table. A bit of scruff lined his jaw, his eyes were surrounded by dark shadows, and the jail uniform appeared quite garish on him.

When Tomas saw her, he jumped to his feet. "Keep her away from me!"

Harper gasped. "That is hurtful. Especially when I am here to help you."

"I'm *in* here because of you!" He glared. Then his glare jerked to Kendrick as the lawyer entered the room. "I thought you'd have me out on bail! I thought—"

"Working on the situation," Kendrick allowed with a shrug. "You need to have some patience. Even I can't work miracles. Despite what you may have heard."

"Oh, shit!" Tomas's eyes doubled in size. "He's here, too? You let him in?" Tomas pointed at Roman. "What kind of lawyer are you?"

"The kind that is getting annoyed." Kendrick propped his shoulders against a nearby wall as annoyance slid across his handsome features. "Sit down, Tomas. Let's make this blessedly brief."

Layla hadn't followed them into the room. Harper figured she was watching on the other side of the one-way mirror. A young cop waited in the corner, and the cop's sharp gaze remained on Tomas as he slowly sat back down.

"Harper and...Mr. Smith, I believe it was?" Kendrick drawled. "They have questions for you."

Tomas opened his mouth—

"I am here, of course," Kendrick continued with a droll wave of his hand, "to make sure that you receive full legal representation. I don't want you to speak out of turn to them."

"Maybe I don't want to speak to them at all!" Spittle flew from Tomas's mouth.

"Too bad." Harper flattened her palms on the table and leaned toward him. "Unless you want to go down for kidnapping."

"What?" Tomas blanched.

Kendrick sighed. "Here we go. Harper, don't throw out big statements like that. Don't—"

"You have a partner," Harper said. She could feel the weight of Roman's stare on her. "Name the partner."

"Why the hell would I do that?" Tomas snarled.

Ah. So there *was* a partner. His answer had just confirmed it for her. "You should do that because your partner is trying to pull you into a murder."

Tomas's jaw nearly hit the table.

"Stop right there," Kendrick ordered before Tomas could speak. "Harper, if you're going to pull this BS, you might as well walk out of the door this instant. You're wasting my time and disappointing me and—"

"No." Roman's voice. Low. Lethal.

She looked back to see Kendrick blink.

"He speaks," Kendrick drawled.

"Harper disappoints no one," Roman growled.

"Noting that right now." Kendrick nodded. "Anything else I should be aware of?"

"Yes." Harper turned back to Tomas. "Since you were arrested, Tomas, there have been several attempts on Roman's life. On my life. Your partner didn't like that we stopped the theft, so he reached out for some payback? Is that what happened?"

Tomas paled. "I-I had *nothing* to do with any attempts on you—or him! I've been locked up since that night! If someone is going after you two, it's probably just someone else you pissed off. Has nothing to do with me!"

She glanced at her nails. "Cooperation is key. Roman knows so many people. So many folks who would like to help him." She flickered her gaze to Tomas. "You should be someone who wants to help him, too. You should want to be on his good side."

"Harper," Kendrick warned. "The ice is thin. It will break. You'll fall."

She huffed out a breath as she kept her attention on a sweating Tomas. "Your partner is leaving you to take the full fall. How is that a good plan? Are you going to let him get away while you stay locked up?"

She saw the flash of anger on Tomas's face. *Nope.* He wasn't going to let that happen. But the man also wasn't talking. His lips had clamped tightly together. Great. Maybe it was time for her to tag out on this one. Harper pushed away from the table. Turned on her heel.

"We're done already?" Kendrick glanced at his watch. "Excellent. I have a meeting with a judge—"

"Your turn," Harper told Roman.

His features immediately tightened. It was interesting to watch. He'd looked hard and dangerous a moment before, but at her words, a change swept over him. Subtle at first. His lips thinned. His eyes became narrower. His jaw harder. His shoulders somehow looked broader, and when he stalked toward the table, Harper could have sworn that a chill swept the room.

Tomas stiffened. "What does he want?"

Roman stopped at the edge of the table. "Do you know who I am?"

"You're her partner. Roman Smith."

Silence. Then Roman asked again, "Do you know who I am?"

"Ahem." From Kendrick. "Asked and answered. My client—"

"Because if you knew who I really was, you'd be shitting yourself right now."

Harper's brows shot up.

"You would know that I don't give a damn that your lawyer is standing behind me. Because, you see, I could kill you before he even took a step forward."

"This interview is *over*," Kendrick thundered.

"You don't want me for an enemy, Tomas. That's a fatal mistake. Because I do have lots of connections. Only they are not just with people in the government. They're with folks who spend all their time behind bars. People who don't have trouble doling out some pain."

"Harper." Kendrick was beside her. His voice snapped like a whip as he snarled, "He's threatening my client. We are *done*."

Tomas was sweating buckets. Maybe crying?

"Do you like pain, Tomas?" Roman asked. "I hope so."

Chill bumps rose over her arms. That voice—she'd never heard Roman sound quite like that. It was almost as if a stranger was talking. Not Roman. Not *her* Roman.

Tagging out had not been the best idea ever. Roman was taking the "bad cop" role to a whole new level.

The door opened. Layla stood there. Appeared way less than pleased.

Tomas's whole body had started to shake as he stared up at Roman.

"Time to go," Layla announced.

Still, Roman didn't move. But he did say, "Rhonda sends her regards."

Fear flashed across Tomas's face.

Who the heck was Rhonda? Harper grabbed Roman's arm. "They're kicking us out." He felt like steel beneath her grip. "Come on. He's not talking."

She pulled on Roman's arm, and he followed her lead. But just as they reached the door—

"I swear," Tomas's voice was shaking just as much as his body had been, "I didn't send anyone after you two. It was supposed to be easy. All I had to do was walk out with the ruby. She was going to take it. That's *it*."

"She?" Harper looked back.

But Tomas had clamped his lips together. Fear blazed in his eyes, but the man just shook his head.

"Not another word," Kendrick ordered. "Until there is a *real* deal on the table. Harper, if you want to know more, then I need something worthwhile. Not threats. Not bullshit."

Roman's head turned toward him. "I don't make threats, and I don't deal in bullshit." Without another word, he stalked out. Harper was right with him.

Her heart was racing. Her palms felt sweaty. As soon as the door shut behind them, Harper hauled Roman toward the corner a few feet away. "What was that about?" Harper's voice was hushed. Trembly. "Did you just *threaten* to kill Tomas?"

"Like I said, I don't make threats." His gaze was still flat and hard. The lethal edge to his expression remained, and as she stared at him...

No, no, she was *not* afraid of Roman. Harper caught his hand in hers. "I know you're upset about everything that has happened. But the good guys don't get to go inside and threaten the criminals. It looks exciting and dramatic on TV shows, but in the real world, you can't threaten to get some prisoners behind bars to beat the hell out of Tomas so that he'll talk to you."

He slid closer to her. "Oh, you're still stuck on thinking that?"

The fire in his eyes... "Thinking what?"

"That I'm good. Figured you knew better."

Her hand tightened on his. "Don't you even try to play me right now. I'm not Tomas. I'm not going to buy your scary routine."

"It isn't a routine." His voice rumbled at her. "If that bastard is involved in *your* kidnapping, he deserves to be scared. If he was involved in the attacks that almost took your life, he'll beg and scream before I'm done with him."

She pulled her lower lip between her teeth.

Roman's head lowered toward her. "Looks to me," he whispered, "like you're getting scared."

Is that what he thought? "Roman—"

"What in the hell was that?" Layla demanded as she stormed toward them. "And how did you know his mother was named Rhonda?"

Wait. Tomas's mother was Rhonda?

"You can't threaten someone in police custody," Layla continued curtly. "You can't—"

Roman straightened and turned toward her. "When you review the video footage, you'll see that I never actually threatened him. I was very, very careful with my words."

Harper replayed the scene in her mind.

"I talked about things that could happen, not things that would. After all, I'm not psychic."

Harper realized that while they'd been in interrogation, Roman had been very careful regarding the placement of his body. As she walked through the scene once more, the images were stronger in her mind. *He made sure to never face the camera recording the interrogation.*

"Now, if you'll excuse us," he added. "Harper and I have places to be."

They were still holding hands. He turned for the hallway and carefully pulled Harper with him.

"Nope." Layla moved in front of him. "Who's the partner?"

"Harper is my partner," he replied seriously.

Her lips thinned. Layla shot a hard look at Harper. "Love the new guy." Her tone said she did not. "So warm and friendly. Totally your type." When she was mad, Layla had a tendency to say the opposite of what she meant.

Harper winced.

"Who is working with Tomas?" Layla pushed.

"What makes you think we know?" Roman asked with a shrug.

"Because you left interrogation. A man like you doesn't just give up. You keep fighting until you get what you want."

Kendrick had exited the interrogation room. He was hurrying toward them.

"We know what you do, detective. Tomas was working with a woman. Now Tomas is in jail, and she's not." Roman stared steadily back at Layla.

Harper's mind spun with possibilities. She wanted to get to the museum. Review video footage. Talk to the staff. Her gut said the partner was an inside man—or, rather, woman. Time was wasting. "We'll be sure to call as soon as we get a good lead," Harper assured Layla. "Thanks for your help today, and, ah, good luck with trying out the ring. Personally, I think it's a great fit."

She wanted Roman gone before Kendrick got any closer. She and Roman double-timed it toward the elevator, they slipped inside and then—

Kendrick strode onto the elevator with them. The doors slid shut. Seemingly taking his time, Kendrick turned to face them. Then casually hit the emergency stop button.

Roman took a step forward, positioning his body just the slightest bit in front of Harper's. A totally unnecessary move. Kendrick wasn't a threat.

Was he?

"You're not a former cop. You don't have the polish for a Fed. I could see you as former CIA. Those agents use fear as their weapon of choice all the time." Kendrick crossed his arms over his chest. "But if I didn't know better, I'd go for mob boss. You know, because you have that whole I'll-destroy-you-and-everyone-you-love vibe happening."

Roman stared back at him.

"Silent again, huh?" Kendrick blew out a breath. "I get it, okay? Harper was pulled into the fray. You're involved with her. The danger to her pissed you off, and now you're out for blood, but you're handling your shit wrong. You have to control your emotions, not let them control you."

"I am in control."

"You sure? Because it didn't look that way to me. To me it looked like—"

"If I weren't in control, your client wouldn't have been breathing when I left that room. Like I said before, I don't make threats. If I'd wanted him dead, he would have been before you could even take a step."

Kendrick's stare jumped toward Harper. "Where did Wilde find him?"

She wasn't about to tell him that his guesses before hadn't been far off the target.

"I don't need anyone to tell me how to handle my shit," Roman continued. "But thanks."

Kendrick's lips twitched. "I don't know if I should be scared of you or if I should take you out for a drink." His face sobered. "I'll talk to my client. If there is someone else out there pulling the strings, someone who has tried to kill you both, then it's in his best interest to talk. Dead bodies lead to longer prison terms."

Uh, yes, yes, they did.

"Besides, I like Harper. It pissed me off, too, that she was targeted." Kendrick tapped the button to restart the elevator. A good move because if they'd stayed there much longer, Harper was afraid that the cops in the building would have mounted a rescue mission.

The elevator descended in silence. When they reached the bottom floor, Kendrick motioned for them to head out first. As Harper passed him, he whispered, "You sure you know what you're doing with him?"

Her head turned so she could meet his dark stare. "I trust my partner."

"And I trust my instincts," he replied softly. "Watch yourself with him."

CHAPTER FIFTEEN

"So...that got intense." Harper finally spoke as they pulled up at the museum. Roman's hands tightened around the wheel. She'd been uncharacteristically silent during the drive, and he hadn't been sure how to break the wall that surrounded her.

He'd caught the lawyer's last words to her. *Watch yourself with him.*

As if he'd ever do anything to hurt Harper. As if—

Oh, wait. Yes, I fucking am doing something to hurt her. I'm sleeping with her and not telling her that my father killed hers. That my father destroyed Harper's family before she even had a chance to be born.

He killed the engine. Sat there a moment. "You don't need to be afraid of me."

"I almost was."

His head whipped toward her.

"Back at the PD, when you went at Tomas, for a moment there, I felt like I was looking at a stranger."

Not a stranger. The man he'd been before he met Harper. Before he'd gotten his sister Lacey in his life. Before he'd realized that Dex hadn't betrayed him and left him for dead.

"But then I realized that was just your game face. Obviously, we were doing a round of good cop, bad cop."

"Obviously." His voice was gruff.

"I'd thought I was playing the role of bad cop, but you stepped it up. Like, way, way up."

No, he hadn't. "Harper..."

"How did you know his mother's name?"

"Got Antony to dig it up for me. To text me the info."

"Right. Makes sense. Not like you'd really ever target an enemy's family."

He looked away. "I want to see the security footage."

"And while you do that, I want to see Charity." She shoved open her door.

Roman grabbed the keys and followed her.

"Charity's his assistant." Harper reminded him as they made their way to the museum's entrance. "She'll know details about his personal life. She'll be able to give us access to his calendar, tell us about any recent meetings he's held, you know, that kind of thing. I don't think you two officially met, but I was chatting with her when you approached me at the gala."

He remembered the other woman. Dark hair. Deep-set, golden eyes. Red dress.

"Security first," he said. "Then we'll talk to her, together."

Her sigh was long and frustrated. "Are you still doing that thing where you won't let me out of your sight?"

He swung into her path. "Yes."

"Roman, I can take care of myself. I've told you that like a dozen times."

"Kendrick wasn't too far off."

Her lips parted.

"My control is thread bare. And something happening to you? Another attack? Some bastard taking you again? It will cut that thread." She didn't understand how important she was to him. "I got you into this mess. Someone saw how much I wanted you. Because of that, you're in danger."

"We've been over this, too." Her voice had gone breathy. So fucking sexy. "Not your fault. The only people to blame are the ones who committed the crime. Not you."

His chest burned.

"Stop blaming yourself." She strode up the stairs. "It's not like you're responsible for every bad thing that's ever happened to me."

Fuck me. "What if I was?" Shit. No, he hadn't said that. He—

She whirled to face him. "What?"

He had said the words out loud. Roman swallowed. He tried to figure out what to say.

But Harper took his hands in hers. "You're good, Roman."

No, he wasn't.

"You've a very good thing that has happened to me. I don't know who made you think that you were so bad, but you're good for me. You make me feel safe. You make me feel like I can count on you. Like if I got kidnapped, you'd rip the world apart looking for me." A faint smile teased her lips. "Oh, wait, you did that already."

How could she make a joke? How could she not see what he was? "Harper…"

She rose onto her toes and pressed a tender kiss to his lips. "I see good when I look at you."

His chest burned. His throat ached.

"Now come on, good guy, let's go get this job finished."

***

The security footage had been useless. The guards had already turned copies over to the cops, and Roman made sure that he sent them to Wilde, too. While Roman hadn't found anything useful on them, he hoped Eric and his team would have more luck.

"A partner?" Charity Hall bounced forward onto her feet. "You mean, like an accomplice? Tomas had someone helping him with the theft?" Her eyes were huge.

Yes, they meant exactly like an accomplice. Roman crossed his arms over his chest. "Know someone like that?" He barely kept the edge of suspicion out of his voice. As far as he was concerned, he was staring at suspect number one. Charity Hall had access, she had the knowledge needed to be in on the heist, and she seemed to be the person who worked the closest with Tomas.

"Why is he looking at me like that?" Charity whispered with a side glance at Harper.

"Um…" Harper began.

"Because I think you're the accomplice," Roman told her flatly.

Charity's eyes went even bigger and became saucers. She took a giant step back.

"Tact." Harper sighed. "Have some tact, Roman." She faced Charity. "I have to agree with him that the optics aren't the best here. I'm sure you get that. You work closely with Tomas. You have access at the museum. You know all about the security schematics."

"I'm not a thief!" Her hand pressed to her chest. "I love this job! I love working here! I would never do anything to jeopardize my position at the museum."

"Your position." Roman nodded. "About that...are you due for a promotion now that Tomas is out of the way?"

"I-I have been offered his position." Her gaze darted from Roman to Harper. "But I deserve that spot. I've worked my ass off for it! *And* I didn't try to steal from the place! Tomas wasn't qualified. He should never have gotten the job to begin with, but he knew the right people, and they slid him into place."

"Bet those right people are regretting that decision now," Harper noted.

"They are." Charity drew in a steadying breath. "That's why they offered me his position. Look, the attempted theft was a PR nightmare. I have my hands full trying to reassure everyone connected to the museum that things are going to be okay." Her eyes gleamed. "I am not a thief. I don't steal what belongs to other people."

She seemed sincere. But Roman knew how deceptive appearances could be. "You understand that the authorities—and Wilde—are going to dig into your financials. If you've been selling off other pieces here at the museum and replacing them with fakes…" Just like Tomas had been attempting to do with the ruby. "Then the truth will come out. They'll lock you up."

Her hands had fisted. "No one is locking me up. I haven't taken anything."

Harper closed in on the other woman. Her fingers curled comfortingly around Charity's shoulder. "Tomas admitted that he had a partner, and I suspect that he will be offering up that partner's name in exchange for a deal."

Suspect? They knew—

"If you have anything to say, you need to speak before he does."

Oh, that was a good move by Harper. Applying not-so-subtle timing pressure.

But Charity shook her head. "It's not me." A tear leaked down her cheek. "The cops will want to check everything, you know. All the pieces here. Each item will have to be authenticated, and what do you think will happen if they discover more thefts? And there probably are more." Her shoulders slumped. "Not like it could be Tomas's first time at this."

No, Roman doubted it had been the man's first time. He'd probably started small with little pieces that wouldn't attract much attention. Then he'd built up to more expensive selections as his confidence grew.

Roman glanced at his watch. "I have a friend coming who will be accessing the museum's computer system. He should be arriving any moment."

"But—but the police—" Charity sputtered.

"He's better than the police. But don't worry, he'll have approval for everything that he does." Antony would come in with any warrants or anything else needed, courtesy of Dex's magic. Dex would be pulling all the strings needed in order to get them access to every inch of the facility. Roman figured the man must make daily deals with the devil for all the power he possessed.

Or maybe Dex just was the devil. Hard to say for sure.

"Your friend can have full access to my computer. To anything I can give to him." Charity exhaled slowly. "I don't have anything to hide. The sooner you prove my innocence, the better."

Again, she sounded sincere. Looked sincere, too.

Charity swiped away a tear. "If you'll excuse me, I have work to do. Please continue your search. When your friend arrives, just send him to my office." She rushed past them.

Roman watched her depart in silence. Then he looked over at Harper. "Thoughts?"

"I think it's hard when you like someone but you also suspect the person may be involved in a crime." She raked a hand through her hair. "People wear masks, you know? Always pretending to be someone they're not. It's hard to see the truth." She took slow steps toward him.

"What do you see with me?" Shit, no, he hadn't meant to ask that. What was his deal today? Talking too much was not normally his problem.

Her gaze gently swept over his face. "I see a man who makes me feel safe." Her hands closed around his shoulders. She pushed up onto her toes. Her lips skimmed his. Too brief. Too light.

His fingers locked around the curve of her hips. He held her close. "Harper, don't tease."

"I wouldn't. Not with you." Another light kiss. But she eased back. "What do you see when you look at me?"

Everything I always wanted.

He looked at her, and hell, it was stupid but he could see them sitting on a couch together. Watching movies. Laughing. He could see himself having breakfast with her. Her offering him a cinnamon roll. He could see a magical Christmas because he'd bet a million dollars Harper went crazy for the holiday. She'd want a huge tree, and he'd get it for her just because he wanted to see her—

No. He stopped the thought. Dammit. He was doing it again. Fucking dreams. Dreams had no place in his life. Hadn't he learned that before? When he'd been younger and he'd yearned for a family—for the mother and sister that hadn't been in his life? But his father had told him—had shown him—again and again, that foolish dreams only made a man weak. Roman couldn't afford to be weak.

When the bastards involved are caught, I leave. He had to disappear. There was no happy ending in this for him. No fucking Christmas tree with Harper.

"Is it that bad?" Harper asked, a little catch in her voice.

He let her go. Put a bit of distance between them. "I see a beautiful, smart, talented woman. The same thing everyone else sees." He turned away. "We should go look—"

"I'd hope you'd see more."

Roman swallowed. "Being beautiful, smart, and talented isn't enough?"

"That's not what I meant. I want you to see—" But she stopped.

Don't. Don't you do it. Don't—Hell. He spun around. "What do you want me to see?"

"More," she said.

"I don't follow." He did. He was such a liar.

Roman thought she realized it. Because Harper nodded. Squared her shoulders. "I'm going to stay with Charity. I don't want her to be involved, but I also don't want to be wearing blinders. I'll ask her more questions and see where that goes." She shuffled past him.

He caught her wrist. "Harper..."

"Don't worry. I won't leave the building. I'll be perfectly safe." She didn't meet his gaze as she pulled away. Then in the next moment, she was gone.

He didn't call after her to tell Harper that she was more. That she had been, from the first moment he saw her. He stood there, lost in thought. Wishing so much that he could be someone else. Someone she might love.

"Seriously?" Antony filled the doorway. Only he looked different. No glasses. Baseball cap. Scruffy beard. Fake beard? No one would recognize him as the tech giant of the world.

"What the hell are you doing?" Antony wanted to know. "I swear, you're all moony-looking."

His jaw tightened. "Always a pleasure to see you."

"I don't think you mean that."

Roman waited.

"Just point me at the tech," Antony muttered.

***

"Were you scared?" Charity's voice was careful.

Harper raised her brows.

"When you were kidnapped," Charity rushed to add. "I would have been terrified. I, um, heard some of the Wilde agents talking the day after it happened. They were back here, doing more sweeps. I was so glad when I saw you today. Well, until I realized you thought I was some super criminal."

They were standing in front of the ruby. It waited behind a giant pane of glass. Two armed guards held positions just a few feet away.

"I'm surprised the ruby is still here," Harper said as she walked slowly around the exhibit. "Would have thought the owners would yank it right away."

"Actually, they wanted to," Charity admitted. "But the head of the museum assured them guards would stay with the piece twenty-four seven." She waved to the men. "Because of the attempted theft, interest in the piece has skyrocketed. We're going to do several promotional projects in the coming weeks, and we think the ruby will draw in more visitors than we've ever had before."

Harper absorbed this news. "So the theft—sorry, attempted theft—turned out to be a good thing for the museum." She had to add, "And for you."

"I told you, I'm not a thief." Charity bit her lip. "I'll cooperate in every way, all right? I can tell you the names of the women Tomas has dated. I can give you his schedule for the last year. I can give you *my* schedule. I'm not the bad guy here."

Harper's gaze slid back to the ruby. "It really is quite beautiful."

"Danger and desire."

Her attention snapped to Charity.

The other woman rolled one shoulder. "Guess the curse was true for you, wasn't it? You got the danger. And judging by the way you looked at your partner—and the way I saw him look at you—the desire is there, too."

"I never wore the real ruby," Harper reminded her. "So the curse didn't work. Besides, I don't believe in curses."

"What do you believe in?"

"People."

"People can let you down." Charity's voice was low. "They can trick you. Look what Tomas did."

"Not all people are like that." She heard voices—Roman's voice. Antony's. Then the two men headed into the exhibit space. Roman's gaze immediately locked on Harper.

"There it is again." Charity stepped closer to her. "Danger and desire."

That's just Roman. A mix of both.

"I have something that I think you should see," Charity added quietly. "While they get to work on the tech, will you come down to storage with me? There are two big items down there—big as in they are worth a great deal of money."

"And you think they might be forgeries."

"I think it's where we should start looking."

Harper nodded. "Lead the way."

***

Antony's fingers flew over the keyboard. He'd brought his own laptop with him, and he'd gone straight to the control room at the museum. He had warrants, lots of official-looking papers, and the man was already hunched over and going to town.

"When you see something suspicious, tell me," Roman directed as he leaned over Antony's shoulder.

"Dude, I've got something to tell you right now. Stop hovering." Antony hunched forward a little more. "I can't do my job with you breathing down my neck. Don't you have a sexy partner to go and tail or something?"

"I thought you wanted me keeping my hands off her."

"Yes, we both know that bridge has been burned." His fingers kept typing. More and more boxes of text popped up on the screen before him. "Well, well. Someone *has* been tip-toeing around the parts of the web you aren't supposed to see."

Roman's muscles tensed. "Here? Tomas was using one of the computers here to make his deals?"

"Someone was. I said *someone*. I did not name anyone specifically because I don't have that intel yet."

"Eric said the cops had already searched—"

"You are looking at a master. I can find anything. Anyone. I can—"

"Yes, you are the tech shit, now just *tell* me and stop bragging."

"You are breathing down my neck even worse now. Like, I feel your breath on my skin, and it is creeping me out. Back up."

Roman eased back.

"Seriously, you eased back like a whole friggin' inch. Go find Harper. Do your recon work or whatever with her. I have this, and I don't exactly like working with a buddy. I'm more of a lone wolf."

"Oh, yeah, you're a wolf."

Antony slanted him a dirty look.

"Your fake beard is coming off a little. Press it back down." Roman turned away. "Call me the instant you track down our perp."

"Just go find Harper."

He took two steps. Halted. "Why are you so focused on Harper?" Roman looked back.

Antony's fingers had paused over the keyboard.

"And why did you get here so quickly?" Now he was more than suspicious. He was worried.

"Okay. First, don't be mad."

He grabbed Antony's chair and spun him around.

"Shit, you are already mad."

"Spit it out."

"So, uh, I picked up a little more chatter today."

"Chatter about *what?*"

"Someone offered 50K to take out Valentino's heart."

Valentino. The mention of Roman's real last name made his blood ice. "So someone wants to kill me. We already knew that—"

"I don't think they meant to literally take the heart out of your chest. I think—I think they want to target Harper."

He couldn't breathe. "You knew this shit when you walked in and you didn't tell me immediately?"

"Dex has extra eyes on the museum. The guards here—hell, I think he even has undercover teams working with them. He said he had everything covered, for you to stay cool. Told me the best way for you to be cool was not to tell you but I mean...I thought she'd be with you. Thought you'd have her at your side and since she's not here, I'm getting worried—"

Roman whirled for the door.

"You didn't let me tell you the second thing! Harper knows! Dex texted her. She's aware of the threat, and she's probably trying to draw out the perp so she can end this for you—"

Roman didn't hear the rest. He was already racing out of the room.

***

Charity typed in the security code that would allow them to access the ground-floor storage area. "The world is full of people who pretend to be something they aren't." Her voice was low. Sad. "I had an old friend who found that out a while back. Now I'm hit with the same news. Tomas was going to destroy everything that mattered to me." The door opened. "Come on. The pieces I'm most worried about are near the far-right wall."

Harper's steps were slow as she followed the other woman inside. Tension snaked through her body, but she wasn't about to let Charity see how she really felt. She'd gotten the text warning from Dex. He'd told her to be on high alert at the museum. And now Charity was leading her to a dark, deserted area?

The whole thing screamed set-up.

"This room is climate controlled. The video feed runs constantly." Charity pointed to a camera.

Except there was no little red light glowing on the camera. The little red light had glowed on every other camera at the facility. Every camera that was the exact same type.

"Tomas would be able to get in here." Charity paused near two large crates. She shoved her hand into one.

"You'd be able to get access, too," Harper said. "I'm disappointed."

Charity's head turned toward her. "Disappointed? Why?"

"Because I didn't want you to be the perp."

Charity laughed. "I'm not. How many times do I have to tell you that?" She lifted her hand, revealing a Mayan statue. "Beautiful, isn't it?"

Harper barely glanced at the statue. "What else is in the crate?"

"This statue is worth fifty thousand dollars." Charity peered down at it. "So gorgeous."

Harper eased closer to her.

"You never answered my question, you know," Charity said without looking up.

"Which question was that?"

"When you were taken, were you scared?"

Harper's fingers slipped inside her purse. Curled around the gun that waited inside. "Yes."

The overhead lights flickered.

Charity's head snapped back. "That's strange."

"Is it?"

There was a scratching sound. Like claws against wood. Charity bumped into Harper as they both turned to look at a tall, Egyptian sarcophagus.

"Do you have rats?" Harper asked softly.

"No. No way are there rats in here." Charity's fingers had gone so tight around the statue that her knuckles were white.

The scratching continued. Got louder. A thumping followed the scratching.

The lights flickered again.

The front of the sarcophagus flew open, and someone in black—black clothes, black ski mask—leapt out. A knife gleamed in the assailant's gloved hand. Charity screamed and swung out with the statue. It shattered when it hit the assailant's outstretched arm.

The knife clattered to the floor. The attacker shoved Charity out of the way and scrambled for the fallen knife.

Charity started screaming again. Over and over. The lights were flickering once more. Harper raised her gun. Took aim. "Drop it," she ordered.

The attacker lunged for her.

Harper fired.

CHAPTER SIXTEEN

He found her because of the gunshot. Harper hadn't been in Charity's office, and he'd been searching for her. *The woman wouldn't answer her phone!* But he headed to the ground floor, he heard the gunshot, and when he raced down to the end of the narrow hallway and into the room that waited...

Harper stood over a figure in black. The figure was hunched on the floor, holding her shoulder, and cursing.

"What did you think would happen?" Harper snapped down at the injured person. "When you came at me with a knife, did you think I was just going to stand there and let you stab me? I *told* you to drop the weapon. If you'd listened, you wouldn't be bleeding all over the floor right now."

She was okay. His breath heaved in and out. Harper was safe. Alive.

Charity ran toward him. Her cheeks were flushed a bright red. "She jumped out of the sarcophagus!"

He frowned at her. He'd been ninety-five percent sure Charity was the perp.

"The lights started flickering." Charity was breathless. "She came out. I hit her with a statue—it was fake, Harper, did you notice that?" Her head swiveled around so she was looking at

Harper. "It's plaster or something." Her focus swung back to Roman. "Anyway, she was running for Harper, but Harper *shot* her!"

His gaze flew back to Harper. Harper reached down and yanked the ski mask off the still cursing perp.

Blonde hair immediately tumbled onto the woman's shoulders. She glared up at Harper.

"I know you," Harper said slowly. A faint line appeared between her brows as she studied the bleeding woman. "You're one of the interns. I saw your picture when I was doing research for the ruby exhibit."

The blonde cried, "He's locked up because of you! You did this! Tomas and I should have been on our way to Mexico, but you screwed everything up! And you *shot* me!"

Harper kept her weapon aimed at the woman, but she glanced back at Roman. "Looks like we found his accomplice."

"I *told* you," Charity huffed. "I'm not a thief."

***

"Tomas was sleeping with the intern." Antony poured himself a drink. "That seems about right."

They were back at Roman's place. The intern—Francesca Wallace—had been taken into custody. Unlike Tomas, she wasn't staying quiet. She was telling her story to anyone who would listen. Loudly telling it.

Roman had listened. And just gotten more pissed off.

Francesca and Tomas had planned to run away together. When Tomas had gotten taken down, Francesca had been desperate. So desperate that she'd broken into the storage room with the intent to make off with some of the museum's older pieces. But, according to Francesca, she'd been interrupted by Charity and Harper.

Then she'd gotten her ass shot.

"She's not the one we're after," Roman said as he stared into the fire. Harper was seated on the couch behind him. Quiet. She'd been quiet all evening. Very unlike her.

"Um, she confessed to being Tomas's partner," Antony pointed out.

Antony. Roman was still pissed as hell at him.

"That means she *is* guilty and belongs in jail," Antony continued. "And I tracked the Dark Web activity to Tomas's system. Guy thought he was encrypted and protected, but no one can block me. He was making deals left and right on there."

"But he wasn't the one who arranged my kidnapping," Harper noted softly.

Finally. Roman spun toward her. He didn't like silence from Harper. He needed her talking. He needed her—hell, he just needed her. He'd been waiting desperately for Harper to break her silence and speak.

"I'm still working on that aspect." Antony's fake beard was gone. He'd ditched his ball cap and battered jeans. He was back in khakis. A black sweater. Wearing his glasses. "As well as the, uh, hit on you, Harper. You know, the whole taking Roman's heart thing."

Her gaze slid to Roman. "His heart. Right."

Roman's heartbeat seemed to pound far too fast.

Her stare flickered toward Antony. "Thanks so much," she said drily. "Glad we're looking into that. I'd hate for us to be ignoring it."

Antony winced. "No one has accepted the job, if that makes you feel better. And it disappeared an hour ago. That should mean it was canceled."

Bullshit. Roman thought it meant that the job *had* been taken.

Harper's lips pursed. "Is it like a help wanted ad or something? You post what you need and stuff gets done? Stuff like, oh, murder and kidnapping?"

"It's not a billboard. Or a newspaper. You're talking going deep and dark. Into places that most people would never know existed. The Feds do their best to monitor the Dark Web. So do a dozen or so cyber units that normal folks don't even realize are working for Uncle Sam. But this shit is insidious. The people running things are *good* at what they do."

"Better than you?" Harper questioned quietly.

"No." His shoulders straightened. "No one is better than me. That's just insulting."

"Good to know," she murmured.

"That's why I will get them. I know my shit. I know—" He broke off because his phone was ringing. He pulled it out of his pocket. Frowned at the screen. "Sorry. I have to take this." He paced toward the door. His finger swiped over the screen. "Ella, what's happened?" Concern sharpened his voice.

Roman's gaze dipped to Harper. She'd curled her legs under her body as she sat on the couch. She looked small. Delicate. He found himself being pulled closer to her.

"I—what?" Antony raked a hand through his hair. "I'm not hurt. No, no, you absolutely do not need to fly down here. Wait. You're on the company jet? Are you shitting me right now?" He spun back toward Roman.

Roman cocked his head as he studied Antony.

"I'm *fine*." Antony sounded far from fine, and he was double-timing his pacing. "I'm looking at a facility down here because you know I want a second factory and one just outside of Atlanta will be prime for me." A pause. "Yes. It was an accident. No, I wasn't the target. I don't know how that video got online."

What video?

"I'm *your* boss," Antony growled. "I get that you are my head of security, but I'm safe. I don't need you flying down to—" He broke off and lowered the phone. He frowned at it. "She hung up on me."

"She?" Harper prompted.

He kept staring at the phone. "My head of security. She's flipping out because there's some clip of the limo explosion circulating on social media." His lips thinned. "Dex is usually better at getting shit like that taken down."

"Dex and his limitless powers." Harper didn't look or sound impressed.

"Apparently, in the clip, I'm running toward the limo. Now Ella is upset because she thinks I was the target of the bombing." He tightened his hold on the phone. "She's on my jet. On her way *down* here. How the hell am I supposed to do tech work for you two when Ella is here? She doesn't know a damn thing about what I do with Dex."

"Maybe you should tell her." Harper unwound her legs and rose. "Secrets aren't ever a good thing."

Antony's gaze cut to Roman, then went back to Harper. "Oh?"

"If she's your head of security, then aren't you making her job about a million times harder by *not* telling her that you're some super spy? She thinks she's looking after you—"

"She's supposed to look after the company," he corrected. "You know, trade secrets and what not."

"From what I've read, you are the company. You and your partner, Sebastian. If someone takes you, then they get all of your gaming technology. She doesn't know you're risking yourself constantly playing spy."

Antony shoved the phone into his pocket. "I'm not playing at anything."

"Wrong word choice." Harper rolled back her shoulders. "But you do agree that you are making things harder on her. How can she protect you—sorry, the company—if she doesn't have all the facts?"

"She *can't* know the facts." Antony was adamant. "I'm successful at what I do for Dex because only a select number of people know the depths of my true involvement. If word gets out…" He exhaled. "Then I won't be able to get the job done."

"You don't trust her." Harper nodded. "I see. Perhaps you should have said that at the beginning. But, if you don't trust her, why on earth would you make the woman your head of security?"

"I do trust her!" The words blasted from him.

"No, you don't." What could have been pity flashed in her eyes. "Because when you truly trust someone, you give them all your secrets." Her stare slid to Roman. Lingered.

His stomach knotted. He had too many secrets. He couldn't give them to her. If he did—

"Roman," Harper said and there was a wealth of emotion in his name. "We need to talk. Alone."

Did she know? That was his first thought. Had she somehow learned the truth? He realized he wasn't even breathing. Shit. What was wrong with him? Of course, she didn't know.

Antony was making a beeline for the door. "I've got damage control of my own to do." He grabbed the doorknob. Hauled the door open. Stopped. His head turned toward Harper. "Have you ever considered that some folks keep secrets because they want to protect the people who matter to them? Sometimes, secrets hurt people. They destroy. I think I can see that truth a lot better now." His stare drifted to Roman. "Good luck," he mouthed.

Then he was gone.

Roman headed toward the bar. "Want a drink?"

"No."

He reached for a bottle of whiskey. Stared at the amber liquid. "Then what do you want?"

"I want to tell you my secret."

His hold tightened on the bottle. "You tell me yours, then I'll tell you mine? That how this will work?"

"Something like that."

He put the bottle back down. "I can't tell you everything." Antony had been right. Secrets hurt people. They destroyed. The last thing Roman ever wanted was to destroy Harper.

"You don't have to tell me everything. Just the important parts. I'll tell you my important parts."

Slowly, he turned toward her.

"Ready for the biggest secret I have?"

"Baby?" No, no, he wasn't ready.

She took a fast step toward him. "I'm falling in love with you."

Roman blinked. Shook his head. He was sure that he'd misheard. There was no way—no way in the world—that Harper had just told him—

She took several more quick steps and stopped in front of him. "I am falling in love with you," she said clearly. "The more time we spend together, the stronger my feelings grow. I didn't expect this. I didn't expect you."

"Harper..."

"I don't get attached to people." Her shoulders straightened. "I even have a little rule I follow. It's... 'Get attached to things, not people.' Because people leave you. They abandon you. They die. They disappear when you need them the most, and you're left alone."

His hand lifted toward her cheek. His knuckles slid over her silken skin. "You should never be alone."

"When I'm with you, I break my rule. I got attached to you without even trying, and I feel like you and I—we're stronger when we're together. I feel like...Roman, I think we're something special. I think we could be amazing. I don't want to hold back with you any longer. I want to tell you how I feel. I don't want to be afraid that I'll lose you. I want to enjoy what we have." A soft release of her breath. "I want you to know...that I love you."

The drumming of his heartbeat was even louder. All he wanted—fuck, it was to say the words back to her. To tell Harper that...

God, yes, I love you, too.

Because he did. He'd been falling for her from the very beginning. Helplessly, completely. Her smile had bewitched him. Her wit freaking enchanted him. He would never, ever forget how glorious she'd looked when she'd launched herself into the air and tackled Tomas at the museum. She was a fighter. A warrior.

I want her. I want to stay with her. I want to live with her. Have kids with her. Have—

No. No. "I am a selfish bastard."

Her delicate brows climbed. "That's...not exactly what I was hoping you'd say."

"It's who I am." Every instinct he had demanded that he grab Harper. Hold her tight. *Never let go.* She didn't need to know the truth. She was saying she loved him. He could keep his worst secret to his dying day, and she didn't need to know. He could make her happy. He was sure of it. He could...

His hand slid from her cheek.

"Is this about that Heather woman?" Harper's voice trembled. "I didn't want to push you about her. I know things were bad, but I thought you'd tell me when you—"

He knew she'd overheard plenty about Heather. "I was never romantically involved with Heather Madding. She was my bodyguard."

"You're more than capable of guarding yourself," Harper pointed out.

"In some situations, it paid to have extra eyes. We often used the cover of being a couple. It provided us with an additional level of security. But what I didn't realize was that she had developed feelings for me. Heather had convinced herself that she loved me."

Harper took a slow step back. "Convinced herself? You don't think she actually did love you?"

I don't think there is a whole fucking lot to love. "I didn't return her feelings. She didn't like that. Got angry and sold me out. In the end, she died. I lived." His voice sounded too clipped. Too cold.

Harper's hand rose and pressed to his chest. "I would never do that to you, Roman. We are partners. I have your back. You have mine. Whether you love me or not, it doesn't change the fact that I would do anything to protect you. How you feel doesn't change what I—"

"I can change everything." The words just poured out. As soon as they did, Roman knew there would be no stopping.

I am a selfish bastard.

Those words had been true.

But with Harper, for Harper...

This one time, he wouldn't be. He wouldn't lie. He wouldn't keep the truth from her. He'd tell her everything because Harper deserved everything.

"I-I don't understand."

"You know my real name isn't Roman Smith."

A glint of humor lit her eyes. "Of course, Roman, that's been obvious from day one."

"My last name is Valentino. My father was Gideon Valentino."

The humor died.

"Recognize the name?" Her hand was still on his chest. It seemed to brand him. "Most people have at least heard of him. Hard not to have picked up on one or two news stories about the prick."

"I've heard of him." Soft.

"He wasn't exactly a kind man."

"I think that's an understatement." She moved *closer*.

Closer? Why? "What are you doing?" he rumbled.

She wrapped her arms around him. "Hugging you."

He was stiff and hard in her embrace. "Why?" *Don't, baby, don't. Don't touch me. I don't deserve you.*

"Because I can't imagine what life must have been like for you when you were younger. Because I am so very sorry for the pain you have known, and I wish I could make things better for you."

His arms ached because they wanted to rise and wrap around her. He wanted to hold her so badly. *Never, ever let go.* And his arms did start to rise. The temptation was too great—

Selfish bastard. Give her more. Tell her—"He killed your father."

At first, she didn't move. Just kept right on holding Roman. He wondered if he'd even managed to say the words out loud. Maybe he hadn't. Maybe they had only been spoken in his mind, and if that was the case—

Her head lifted. She stared at him with wide, confused eyes. "What?"

"My father…killed yours." Why was his voice so cold? Why was he cold? Ice seemed to encase his entire body. Every single inch. Except where she touched him.

But she was pulling back. Gazing at him with growing pain and shock on her beautiful face. "That's not true."

"Yes." *I wish it wasn't. I wish…*

Like his wishes mattered for any damn thing.

"How do you know?" While his voice was cold, hers was shaking. Strained.

"Antony told me. He uncovered intel. My father…" *Tell her.* "He learned your dad was a spy. He shot him in the street in order to send a message. He liked sending messages, and, hell, he just liked killing people."

She jerked back.

He didn't reach for her.

"Antony told you?" Harper shook her head. "When?"

"Does it matter?"

"Yes, yes, it matters. How long have you known that your father killed mine?" She put her hand over her heart. "Did you know when we made love?"

He shouldn't have touched her after he learned the truth. He knew it. The limo had exploded, and he'd kept imagining what his life would have been like if Harper hadn't gotten out. If she hadn't survived. When he'd been kissing her in his bedroom, when she'd been wanting him so much...*I lost control.* He swallowed. "I am a selfish bastard."

"Stop telling me that!" Harper's voice rose.

He looked away.

"Why? Why did you do this to me?"

His gaze slid back to her. A tear trailed down her cheek. "Don't."

"Don't? Don't what?"

"Please don't cry." He lifted his hand to wipe away her tear drop.

She flinched away from him.

His hand fell.

Harper spun from him. Rushed for the door.

He took a step after her. Stopped. He'd known this would happen. Antony had warned him. Roman had realized the truth himself. When Harper discovered the man Roman truly was...she would leave.

But she couldn't go. Not just yet. It wasn't safe. She could be in danger if she left his house.

Danger. I have to protect her. She can't leave yet. He broke from his stillness and raced across the room. His hand slammed down on the door just as she was hauling it open. His body was behind hers, curving around her, and his hand held the door shut. "I get that you hate me."

She didn't say a word.

"I get that you want to run as far from me as you possibly can, but we haven't found the kidnappers. You're still at risk. You have to stay here until it's safe."

Her body trembled.

His head was bending toward hers. Her sweet scent filled his nostrils. He wanted to pull her close—

"Is that all you have to say to me?" Harper asked in a voice that made his heart squeeze.

He'd told her his father had killed hers. "Isn't that enough?"

She whirled toward him. Dammit, there were more tears gleaming in her eyes. The sight hurt more than any knife to the ribs ever could.

"It's not," she whispered. "Not even close."

He caged her with his body. Wanted her with his very soul.

"I'm sorry. Please stay." A desperate plea. "Until it's safe. Then you don't have to leave me. I'll disappear from your life. That was always the plan."

She flinched. "You are such a bastard."

"Told you that, I—"

"Get away from me."

He backed up. One step. Two. "When it's safe, I will get out of your life. You won't have to see me again."

Her lower lip trembled.

I am so sorry, baby.

She turned away from him. Opened the door.

"As soon as you're safe," he added, and his voice was ragged. "The intern isn't the one we're after. There are bigger players involved. People want me dead because I am too much my father's son. I followed in his footsteps. I've done things that would give you nightmares. I've…" A rough inhale. "If you'd known who I was from the beginning, you would have never let me get close."

Her shoulders were stiff. "Are you done? That the last thing you want to say?"

"I…" Roman clamped his lips together. What was he supposed to do? Shout out that he loved her? She couldn't even look at him.

"Back to being strong and silent. Right. Got it." Without another glance, Harper walked away.

I love you. Words he wanted to say, but couldn't. Because for once—*for once*—he was not going to be selfish. He had told her the truth. He was letting her go even though it was ripping out his heart.

He'd known from the beginning that she was too good for him.

What he hadn't known? Just how much it would hurt when she walked away.

CHAPTER SEVENTEEN

"Harper, some Wilde agents are down at the museum, and they have more forgeries they would like you to—" Antony broke off as he lowered his phone. "What happened?"

She was crying. Crying gave her headaches and made her face splotchy so she *hated* to cry. Through her tears, she glared at him. "Weren't you supposed to be handling your head of security?"

"Yes, um, but I got a phone call from the museum..." He brought the phone to his ear and said, "We'll be there as soon as possible, okay?" Antony hung up the phone. "What happened?"

"Don't you know?"

He took a step back. "He told you."

"Yes, he *told* me. His father killed mine." She wrapped her arms around her stomach. She hurt so much. "I told Roman that I loved him, and in return, he said, surprise, sweetheart, my dad killed yours."

"Uh..." Antony winced. "That's really what he said?"

"Fuck off, Antony, it was close enough." She stormed past him. Every part of her ached. Her dad? That was what had happened to him? And Roman—God, she'd never told a man that she loved him before. Roman had been the first. The only. She hadn't even told the prince that she loved him!

Antony's hand closed around her shoulder.

She immediately stilled. "Don't."

"I'm sorry."

"Move the hand or the fingers will get broken."

He moved the hand. "Roman didn't know. Not until recently. When I told him, it was like I could see something dying in the man's eyes. He knew it would hurt you to discover the truth. Hurting you was the last thing he wanted."

She spun toward him. "And what did he want?"

Antony swallowed. "I think he wanted you. But his bastard of a father reached out from the grave and made sure that didn't happen, didn't he?"

She couldn't think straight. She'd been asking Roman to tell her more. Practically begging him to just say—

I love you. I'm not my father. I love you. I—

But he hadn't said that. He'd gone silent on her.

"He made Roman's life hell. Can you imagine what it must have been like growing up with a monster for a father? Most of the world assumes Gideon Valentino's son is just as fucked up as the father is."

She swiped at the tears on her cheeks.

"But you know that's not true, don't you, Harper?" Soft. Sad. Pointed.

"Antony, I'm pissed at you. You could have told me, too."

"He killed Roman's mother. That's classified intel, but I'm giving it to you."

"*What?*"

"Roman is pushing you away. You get that, don't you? Because he's part of that whole group that thinks the son is just as fucked up as the father. Roman bought the hype. Then he fell for you. I could see it the first time I found you two together. He's caught up in you, and he thinks that's dangerous—Roman thinks *he* is dangerous to you. So he's pushing you away."

Doing a damn good job of it. "He doesn't love me."

"How do you know?"

"Because he didn't say it. I told him…" Her lips clamped together. *Take it easy. Get your control back.* "I've been over this with you. I gave Roman my heart, and he told me his father had—" She could not say it again. Would not. Her temples were pounding, and nausea rolled in her stomach. "He said he always planned to leave." That part was a knife twisting in her gut. "He was never going to stay with me."

Get attached to—

She shut down the thought. She'd been afraid of being hurt. She *was* hurt. "The past is the past." She wanted to scream. To rage. But one thing that she *knew*… "Roman would have been a kid when my father died. A toddler. He didn't—he had *nothing* to do with what happened to my dad. That crime isn't on him. And I am so sorry for what happened to his mother. I hate what Roman's life must have been like." She pulled in a breath. "But he doesn't want me, Antony. He doesn't want us to be together, and I can't fight for something that he doesn't want."

"Harper, I think you're—"

"You said more forgeries have been found at the museum? I'd better go take a look at them." She had to get out of there.

"Harper, you know Roman won't like you going alone."

"Who said I was going alone? I thought you were coming with me. Didn't you just say to whoever was on the phone that 'we'd' be there soon?"

He blinked. "Oh, yeah. Right. Okay, just let me tell Roman, would you?"

She looked back at the closed door. "He won't say anything," she whispered.

"What?"

"I'll wait for you at the front door. I want to get my gun." Better to be safe than...

God, it hurts.

Her gaze darted back just in time to see Antony knock on Roman's closed door.

***

A soft knock rapped against the door. For a moment, wild hope surged inside of Roman. Harper was coming back to him? She was—

The door opened. Antony popped his head inside.

The hope died a swift death. "What the hell do you want?"

Antony grimaced. "Harper and I are going back to the museum. Got a call from some of the

Wilde agents there. More forgeries have been found. Charity suspects some of the other jewels are fakes, too, and she thought Harper might want to look at them."

"I can come, too."

"About that..." Antony slipped inside. "I think Harper is looking for a little space."

He thought she might be looking for a lot of space. "Don't let her out of your sight."

"That goes without saying. You'll have guards here, too. They're patrolling the perimeter, courtesy of Eric and Dex."

Roman turned to stare back into the fire. "Take care of Harper."

Silence, then... "I get why you did it."

"I doubt it."

"You could have kept the truth to yourself."

"Secrets have a way of working to the surface."

"This secret was buried deep. I knew about it. You knew. Dex. That was it."

The flames danced. When the limo had exploded, the fire hadn't danced. It had raged. It had licked at the sky. "It's time for my relationship with Harper to end. *That's* why I told her."

He heard the inhale of a sudden breath.

Fuck. No, no, don't be—

He turned, slowly. Antony hadn't shut the damn door. Harper stood there, just behind Antony. She stared at Roman—

Hell, the same way most people did. Like he was the enemy. A monster. Evil.

"Time for things to end." She nodded. "Understood. Sorry if I made you uncomfortable with my confession."

She was apologizing for making *him* uncomfortable? After what he'd done? Roman lurched toward her.

Her gaze cut from his. "I'm not waiting any longer, Antony. I'm leaving now. Come with me. Don't. Whatever." Ice dripped from her words.

Baby, please, please, look at me.

Her stare swung to Roman. "I will not be coming back. Consider us ended."

She didn't storm away. Didn't run. She simply turned and walked out.

He took another lurching step.

Antony moved into his path. "I am so fucking sorry. I thought she said she'd be waiting at the front for me!" The faint lines near his eyes seemed deeper. "I can help fix this, I swear it."

There was no fixing this.

"She doesn't care about your dad!" Antony spoke quickly. "Well, I mean, obviously, she does. It's gutting her. But she doesn't blame you for what happened."

"You don't know what you're talking about." There had been so much pain in her eyes.

"I know you're trying to make some big, dramatic sacrifice."

"I'm just ending a partnership." *Lie, lie. Harper, come back!*

"You want her more than you've ever wanted anything in your life. You need her. You're obsessed with her. You *love* her."

Roman shook his head, but he couldn't force the lie past his lips. If he said no...

*No, I don't love her...*That would be a lie.

Because he loved her so much, he was sending her away. Giving her the life she should have. A life not tied to the man who would always remind her of what she'd lost.

"All you have to say in order to get her to stay..." Antony put a hand on Roman's shoulder. Squeezed. "It's that you love her. All you have to do is tell her *that* truth. I was wrong before. When I said that she'd leave when she found out what happened? I underestimated her. She *loves* you."

He heard a door slam. "Harper is leaving. I don't want her to be alone."

"If you want her, fight for her."

"I want her..." Guttural. Broken. "That's why I can't have her."

"That shit makes zero sense." Antony's breath huffed out. "I'll try to calm her down. You drag your ass out of the pity party you're having and realize that you have a chance here. A real shot with someone who doesn't hold your whacked-out past against you."

It wasn't just the past he had to worry about. The threats coming were in the present. He was a danger to Harper.

Antony stormed out. A few moments later, Roman heard the sound of a car pulling away. He remained frozen in the study. The fire crackled. In his mind, he could see Harper's beautiful, hopeful face as she said...

"I want you to know...that I love you."

That hope had turned to pain. Burned to ash right in front of him.

***

"Is everything okay?" Charity bit her lower lip as she held a gleaming emerald in her gloved hand. "You seem upset."

"Everything is fine." *Lie, lie, lie.* "That's another fake. The man really did a number on the museum, didn't he?"

Charity sighed. "We're going to be ruined. Maybe insurance will pay some of the claims but, yes, he destroyed this place. Tomas. His partner. You think you can trust someone..." Charity put down the fake emerald. "This is enough for now. I'm not sure I can handle much more." She stood up, swayed a little.

Harper immediately caught her elbow. "Are you okay?"

"I have low blood sugar." Charity put a hand to her forehead. "I can't remember the last time I ate. Hell, I don't even know what time it is."

"Let's get you something to eat. There's a snack machine down the hall."

"No, I-I want to go home." She looked pleadingly at Harper. "Will you give me a ride, please?"

Harper made some quick calculations. "Sure. My friend and I can drop you off before we leave." Antony had donned his disguise on the way over to the museum once more. Harper had been a bit impressed by how quickly he could adopt the persona of someone new. He'd glued on the beard, popped in some contacts, changed his posture to a lazy slouch, and even used a more rough, gravelly tone when he spoke.

"Your friend makes me uncomfortable," Charity revealed in a sad, lost voice. "I think he blames me. He suspects me. I'm pretty sure everyone at Wilde does. I'm here—helping out the cops, doing everything I can, but people are watching me like a hawk! I'm the innocent one."

Harper let Charity go long enough to scoop up a coat. "If my friend seems suspicious, it's because that's his nature. All of the Wilde agents are still on edge." She deliberately didn't say that her "friend" was a Wilde agent. Because Antony wasn't. "We're still searching for the person who arranged my kidnapping."

"You don't think it was me."

"I—"

Something jabbed hard into Harper's side. "Do you?" Charity demanded as she grabbed Harper.

Harper couldn't reply. Her tongue felt too thick in her mouth. It was swelling. Breathing was suddenly far too hard. A wheezing sound was coming from her and black dots danced before Harper's eyes.

"Because if you do," Charity whispered, "you're right."

***

Antony bounded into Charity's office. When he realized no one was there, he staggered to a dead stop. "Harper?" He'd left her in there just moments before. Where had she gone?

He fished out his phone. Dialed the number he'd programmed in for her. Heard a ringing, one coming from just a few feet away from him. His shoulders stiffened as he turned around.

A phone was ringing, all right—a phone that had been dropped on the floor. He crept closer to it.

Harper's new phone.

Not fucking good.

***

Roman answered his phone on the second ring. "What is it, Antony?" That was his greeting. He'd recognized the number calling him—Antony had programmed his contact info into Roman's phone earlier.

"Look, I'm going to need you to be cool. Can you do that for me?"

"What the fuck kind of question is that?"

"It's the kind of question that's very important. Can you do it for me?"

His hold tightened on the phone as alarm blasted through him. "Hell, no, I can't be cool. Tell me what's happening."

"I'm investigating. I'm pulling up security feeds at the museum. But, right now, it looks as if Harper vanished."

"*What?*" Yet even as he asked the question...

I should have been with her. I knew she was in danger. I should have been there. I—

"I can't figure it out," Antony mumbled. "I saw Charity leave alone on the security footage. Harper wasn't with her. But she isn't here. I found her phone in Charity's office, but there's no sign of Harper."

Breathe. Breathe. His heart thundered in his chest. "Get Charity back there. She knows what happened." Or...Roman's suspicion...

She did something to Harper.

"Working on it," Antony fired back. "Got Wilde agents who went after her immediately but, um, I think she must've had a different car waiting. She...we, they—they found her vehicle abandoned and—"

Roman's phone beeped. Someone was calling on the other line. He almost ignored the call but—

Unknown Caller. He'd pulled the phone back just enough to see the screen. What were the odds that he'd be getting a random call right then?

"Roman, are you listening to me? Harper is gone. I need you to get down here and help with the search. I'm fucking sorry. I know I was supposed to stay with her, but she was just down the hallway, and we both know she can damn well kick ass and take names. I don't know what happened. I don't know how this—"

"Someone is calling my line." The line that only a few had access to. The same line someone had called just days before to say that Harper had been taken. "Hold on," Roman barked.

He switched to the other caller. "Who the hell is this?"

"I will give you an address. If you care about her at all, you'll come to the address in an hour. You'll be alone."

He nearly shattered the phone. It was the same distorted voice from days before. "I want to talk to Harper."

"She's not capable of talking at the moment."

Harper!

"But I assure you, she's alive. Whether she stays that way or not, it depends on you. I will text you the address. You'll tell no one. If you do, if I see anyone else coming—I will kill her. I will put a bullet in her brain instantly."

"Don't."

"Hard, isn't it? When you actually care? When you have a weakness that someone else can exploit?"

"Don't hurt her."

"You'll come to the location. When you arrive, you can trade yourself for her. Harper can walk away and be safe."

You won't let either one of us go. "How do I know you aren't lying?"

"You don't."

The call ended. The phone clicked, and Roman stood there, his whole body tight with fear and fury. The phone automatically switched back to Antony—

"Roman?" Antony snapped. "What in the hell is happening? Roman, talk to me!"

The phone dinged. He'd gotten the text.

"What's going on?" Antony's voice rose. "I need to know what's happening. I can't help if I don't know—"

Roman hung up on him.

***

"Sonofabitch." Antony glared at his phone. His hands were shaking as he hurriedly contacted Dex. His boss/friend/pain-in-the-ass answered after the first ring.

"I hope this is good news," Dex rumbled.

"Bad news. Very bad. Harper is missing, and I'm about ninety-nine percent sure Roman just got a ransom call on her. He shut me down. Hung up on me. That means he's probably about to go for an exchange. I'd lay odds the caller said for him to come alone or Harper would die, and since the guy is in love with her, he'll take any risk and get his fool self killed—"

"Take a breath, Antony."

He sucked in a breath.

"You low-jacked him?"

"You know I did." Not something Antony was particularly proud of. "I put a tracer on her phone and his, but I'm holding hers right now, so it's not going to do me much good."

"We just need his. Let's get a lock on him. We'll stay back until he needs us, but there is no way we're leaving Roman on his own." Dex's voice roughened. "He already thinks I left him alone before. Time to prove to the man that I've got his back."

"You ordered me to low-jack him. I don't know if that is quite the definition of having someone's back. It's more like spying on him—"

"I'm coming to get you, Antony."

"What?" Antony whirled around. "How do you even know where I am?"

"Because I low-jacked you, too."

"Hold on, that shit is not—"

"You and I are going after Roman. And we're making sure that Roman *and* Harper are safe."

"Yeah, well, you need to haul ass. Not like we have time to waste. The last I heard, you'd backed off and gone into hiding. That's why I was sent in, remember?" Though now he got that he'd been set-up. So not cool. Dex had probably stayed close the whole time.

"I'm here," Dex said, confirming his suspicions. "I'll be at the museum in five minutes. Lacey will be with me."

"Wait—Lacey? As in, your wife? Roman's sister? She's—"

Dex hung up on him.

"All right, then." Antony squared his shoulders and checked his weapon. Then he ran for the front of the museum.

CHAPTER EIGHTEEN

"Sorry I had to tranq you."

Harper's eyes slowly opened. Her mouth was cotton dry, and a dull ache pounded behind her eyes.

"For a while there, I was worried I'd used too much. Not like I dose someone with horse tranq every day."

Had the woman just said *horse tranq?*

"Got a friend who works for a vet. I slipped her some cash, she slipped me a small dose." Charity leaned in close toward Harper. "You don't look so good." Her eyes narrowed.

"I don't...feel so good." She didn't have to fake the slurring of her voice. That was real. Harper was trying to take stock of her surroundings. She was in some kind of old house. Paint peeled on the nearby wall. She'd been tied to a chair. Her arms were locked tightly with the rope. So were her legs. Her head had free movement, though, and it was bobbing forward.

"I'm sorry," Charity whispered. She actually *sounded* sorry. "I didn't intend for you to get hurt. When I hired the team to take you the first time, I gave them *strict* instructions not to hurt you. You were a means to an end."

"That's lovely to know." More slurring. More deliberate this time as her head cleared. "Th-thank you?"

"I couldn't believe it when I saw him. He was the last person I ever expected to see. I mean, he was dead. Everyone said he was dead. And some things were different. The hair. Eyes. But she'd told me so much about him. Sent me so many pictures when he was in different disguises that I still knew. He was walking across that crowded museum, coming straight for you, and I recognized him."

Harper was doing her damn best to follow along. The part that was obvious? Charity was the one who'd hired those assholes to take Harper.

"He stared at you like he wanted to eat you alive." Charity curled her hand under Harper's chin. Tipped her head back. Checked her pulse. "How could he do that?" Anger roughened her voice. "How could he look at you that way when he never would love her?"

"Yeah…" Harper licked her lips. "I have no idea what's happening here."

"Heather Madding."

The name rang an ominous bell.

"Has he ever mentioned her to you?" Charity pushed.

"She's dead."

"And?"

"And she's…dead. She was his bodyguard." Harper gave a long pause, as if she was struggling to think. She was actually trying to figure out a good plan of attack. "She turned on him. Got killed."

"She turned on him because he would never love her! He can't love anyone! He's a psychotic bastard who only knows how to destroy!"

Says the woman who gave me horse tranq. "I don't feel good," Harper said fretfully. "My...my chest hurts." It didn't. "Untie me, Ch-Charity. I think s-something is wrong..."

Charity frowned at her. "I'm going to let you go. I am, I promise. The ropes are just for a little while longer. Roman is coming, you see."

Aw, hell.

"He's going to offer himself in your place. That's all I wanted. Justice for Heather. She was my best friend, did you know that?"

How the hell would I know that?

"We met in college. Freshman year. Stayed in contact. Helped each other make a whole lot of money over the years. She'd have clients, people who were looking to acquire special pieces, and I'd facilitate those deals for her."

Harper squinted at her. "Thought...you weren't a thief." Harper was just trying to keep the woman talking while she figured out a plan. If her hands were free, that would be something. But the ropes were tight and strong, and not giving at all. She was twisting and sliding her wrists against the hemp, but she was just making her wrists raw.

"I'm not! Tomas stole from the museum—not me! I found out months ago what that asshole was doing." Her breath huffed out. "Stealing from *my* house!"

Her house?

"He thought he was so clever. He wasn't. He and that idiot he was screwing. They were just going to ruin everything for me! I had shipments coming in that were for me alone. *My* deals. He tried to take one of them. I knew I had to get rid of Tomas then. That's why I suggested to the board that Wilde be brought in with the ruby exhibit. I figured you'd catch Tomas, and you did!" A sigh. "But I never expected Roman. When I saw him, it wasn't like I could just walk away and forget, could I? I owed Heather."

The ropes weren't going to give. Harper let her head sag forward. Her voice turned soft as she sighed, "This is all about a dead woman."

"No." Charity's voice was flat. "This is about a monster. That's what Roman is. He's heartless. He's cold. He is cruel. You don't know who his father was, but Heather told me so many stories...Roman is evil. He will turn on everyone close to him."

"So this guy who is so evil..." Still, her voice was soft. Weak. "You think—what? He'll sacrifice himself for me? That the big plan? Because...it doesn't make sense."

"He—he will. I had my team watching! Those men told me exactly what happened. He rushed into the cabin to save you. He tore the world apart looking for you. I don't know how you did it, but you've tied him to you. He wouldn't love her, but now he's coming after you. And he's going to pay for that. He is going to—"

Harper's laughter stopped her words.

"What's so funny?" Charity snapped. "Oh, wait. Is it the tranq? Do you even understand what I'm telling you?" She curled her hand over Harper's shoulder. "Or, maybe, did you hit your head? I had to dump you in a crate in order to get you out of the museum. That way, no cameras would see you leaving. I might have slammed your head into the bottom of the crate. Sorry about that."

Seriously? Harper whipped her head up, clipping the woman under the chin and sending Charity stumbling back. Charity let out a guttural scream as she wiped blood from her lip.

Aw, poor baby. Did you bite your lip when I head-butted you? Sorry about that.

But at Charity's scream, the door flew open. Three men—all wearing black—rushed inside. The men weren't wearing anything over their faces, though, and it was easy for Harper to see the long, jagged scratches on the tallest of the three men.

"Oh, hi." She smiled at him. "I remember you."

His expression hardened. Then he looked over at Charity. "You okay?"

"The bitch hit me with her head!"

"Name calling isn't necessary," Harper chided.

Charity glared. "I told you it wasn't personal! I told you that I was going to let you go once we had Roman. I told you—"

"That Roman is some heartless monster. Newsflash, why would a heartless monster come here when he knows the whole thing is a trap? Why would he rush to save me? He won't. Sure, I think he'll probably call my friends at Wilde and send them over…"

The men in black looked uneasily at one another.

"But Roman won't come. Look, he didn't love your friend, Heather. And he doesn't love me."

"No, no." Charity was adamant. "I have seen the way he looks at you. I *know*—"

"I've seen the way he looked when I told him that I loved him, and, in return, he told me that his father killed mine."

The man with the jagged scratch gave a low whistle.

"Roman didn't rush to say that he loved me. He let me know that his plan—all along—had been to leave me. I don't exactly see how someone who feels that way will want to sacrifice himself for me." She shrugged—or shrugged as much as she could with the ropes tying her down. "I think this might be the part where you realize you made a terrible mistake."

Charity appeared far less certain. "But I have a client I found…I broker deals…the client will pay millions for proof of Roman's death."

"Yes, sorry." *Not sorry.* "But it's not going to happen." *Keep them talking. Buy time.* "What will happen…Wilde agents will storm in the door of this place any moment. You and your henchmen team will be taken into custody and tossed in jail cells." Harper held her breath after delivering that line. She could see the uncertainty in Charity's eyes, and Jagged Scratch looked as if he might turn for the door at any—

A loud bang echoed from another room. It came again. Again. Pounding. Knocking.

Harper swallowed. "Sounds like someone's at the door. Is it Wilde? Because my money says it is. You're all going to jail, and I'm going home."

Charity pulled a phone from her pocket. She stared down at the screen, and a faint smile tilted the corners of her lips. "No, Harper, *you* have everything wrong. This is the part..." She glanced back up. "Where Roman Valentino dies."

Harper's breath froze in her lungs. *No. I don't like this part.* "No!"

***

The little house was at the end of a dead-end street. No other homes dotted the road. One way in. One way out. Fairly remote. Isolated.

He saw the security camera perched near the front door, and he waved with one finger to whoever was watching him. A moment later, the front door wrenched open. A man in black—with a rough-looking scratch sliding over his cheek—stood in the doorway.

Roman frowned at him. "I have to ask, just how did you get that mark on your cheek?"

"*Did you come alone?*"

"Do you see anyone else with me?"

The guy had a gun in his hand. One he shoved right at Roman.

Sighing, Roman lifted his hands up. "Feel free to search me. I don't have any weapons." He was hauled inside. Searched. Three men total were there. Big, hulking figures in black.

The assholes who's taken Harper from her home?

"I knew you'd come." Charity Hall sauntered toward him. She appeared all smug and satisfied.

But there was no sign of Harper. Where the hell was Harper?

"She told me you wouldn't come," Charity continued with a smirk on her face. "But I knew she was wrong. She said you didn't love her. That Wilde would be coming instead, but I could tell by the way you watched her..."

"I want to see Harper." *She said you didn't love her.*

"Oh, you can see her." She motioned toward the bedroom. "She's in there. See her. Tell her good-bye." She turned on her heel and led the way to the bedroom. "I told Harper I was going to let her go, and I meant what I—"

Bam. Bam.

The gunfire came from behind Roman. He spun and saw the prick with the scratch—he had his weapon up and aimed. He'd just fucking *shot* Charity.

"*Roman!*" A scream that came from the bedroom. Harper's scream.

Roman immediately lunged for her.

"Nope." It was the jackass who'd fired his weapon. The man who'd shot Charity in the back. "In case you missed it, I'm in charge now."

What in the fuck is happening here?

***

"Those were gunshots," Antony whispered. He was about fifty yards away from the house.

Dex nodded grimly.

"What if it was a shot at Harper? Or Roman?" Dammit, he hated not being able to see what was happening in the house. "We need to go in, *now*."

"Damn straight, we do," Lacey—Dex's wife—said. "Because that's my brother in there." She rushed toward the house.

And Dex chased after her.

***

"Roman!" Harper yelled. She could see Charity's slumped body in the doorway. Who had shot her? What was happening? What was—"*Roman!*" She jerked hard, and the chair rocked forward with her—

Just as Roman appeared in the doorway.

When she saw him, relief swept through her so hard that her whole body shook. He was all right. Good. But... "You shouldn't have come here."

"Crazy, isn't it?" A male voice. *Not* Roman's. A voice coming from behind Roman. The voice of the jerk she'd scratched days before. "Crazy that Roman Valentino thought he'd play hero for anyone."

Then Roman was walking into the little bedroom. Harper saw the gun shoved at his back. Roman's hands were up, his palms out, and his eyes were on her.

"Are you hurt, Harper?" Roman asked her.

She wet her lips. "I should probably see a doctor." Her voice sounded weak. That was deliberate. "The woman bleeding out on the floor? She gave me horse tranq. That can't be good."

Then her gaze darted to the man with the gun. "I'm guessing your original plans have changed now, yes?"

He nodded.

"Hurting me? That option is officially on the table?" Harper pushed.

Another nod.

"That is disappointing to hear, but I figured as much. You know, when you weren't trying to hide your identity any longer." Her gaze darted to Charity's slumped form. "And here she probably thought that she could trust you."

"Her mistake," the man with the gun said flatly. He shoved Roman forward. "Were you followed? Did you give Wilde the location?"

"I didn't tell a soul anything," Roman snarled. "Harper's life is on the line. I would never do anything to jeopardize her and I would—"

A shrill alarm cut through his words.

Uh, oh. "What's that about?" Harper asked.

"Company. Guess he doesn't give a shit about you, after all. He didn't follow Charity's orders. Your life wasn't worth enough to him."

Roman whirled toward him. "You don't know a—"

Bam.

The bullet blasted at Roman. "No!" Harper screamed.

Roman stumbled back. Fell.

"Doesn't matter," the man with the gun said. "Neither of you were ever getting out. And whoever is coming? They'll die, too." He hauled Charity's body out of the doorway, yanked the door shut and, a moment later, Harper could hear the sound of his retreating footsteps.

CHAPTER NINETEEN

"Don't you dare die on me." Her foot poked him again. "Get up, Roman. Get the ropes off me, and let's get out of here."

He opened his eyes. Blood soaked his shirt. "The fucker shot me."

"I suspect he's about to do a whole lot more. I heard him *lock* the door. And he said that anyone coming after us was also going to die. So, you know, the whole place just feels like one giant trap. How about we get the hell out of here, *now?*"

Excellent plan. He ignored the burn in his chest. Pushed the pain aside. Grabbed for the ropes around her. He had been lying before—he *did* have a weapon on him. He pulled out the knife he'd hidden, and he sliced through the ropes. Then he tugged Harper to her feet.

She threw her arms around him.

He…held her. Roman couldn't help himself. His arms curled around her, and he held her tight. *God, baby, I love you so much.*

"You shouldn't have come after me," Harper muttered. "I'm glad you told Wilde. At least, they can try to get us out of here and—"

"I didn't tell Wilde." She felt so good in his arms. "I would never do anything to risk you."

Her head whipped back. "What?" Then she blanched. "That's a lot of blood, Roman."

"Barely a scratch."

"You're lying."

"I love you."

Her eyes widened. "What did you say?"

"I'm sorry for what my father did. I wish—I wish everything could be different. I wish I was somebody different. I tried to be, but it didn't work out for me."

"I like you just as you are. Arrogant, too silent, and *mine*."

"Harper—"

"We're getting out of here. Now." She pulled free. "No windows in this place." She grabbed for the doorknob. Twisted. Yanked. "I can probably take off the hinges." She eyed the hinges on the door. "Then we can get out and—"

He curled his fingers around her shoulder. Pulled her back.

Her brows rose. "What are you doing?"

He kicked at the door. Once, twice, three times. The wood shattered in heavy chunks.

"That was nice, but I think you alerted—"

He shoved her to the side just as gunfire erupted. The bullet missed her, but he jerked, hard, when it thudded into him.

***

Dex stilled. "Fuck." Another gunshot. Roman's enemies just weren't going to stop. They would attack and attack until he was dead.

Dex's gaze cut around the secluded scene.

Time to give them what they want.

***

"Roman?" Harper whispered.

"Eric was right about you." His head dipped toward her. "I loved you from the moment I saw you."

She touched his chest—blood. Warm, wet—

He pulled away from her and ran out of the bedroom. He kicked away the parts of the door in his way.

"Roman! Wait for me! You don't leave your partner!" She rushed out after him. Saw that he'd pinned one man in black against the wall and was beating the hell out of him. Well, okay, that took care of one perp.

Where is the bastard I scratched?

She caught sight of him. It looked as if he'd just come out of an old kitchen, and he was raising his gun— "No!" Harper shouted.

His head swung toward her.

Too late. She was already running toward him. Running as fast as her still-somewhat-drugged body could go. She didn't so much tackle him as she flung her body onto his. They crashed together and hit the floor. She rammed her elbow into his nose. Gave him a deep, bloody matching scratch on his other cheek, and she reached for the gun that had—

"Got it, sweetheart." Roman. He had the gun, and it was aimed at their assailant. "You can get off him now."

Before she got off him, she kneed the bastard in the groin. Just because. Then she stood at Roman's side.

"There's one more of them," Roman rumbled. "I think he might have gone outside already. I need you to go track him down. I don't want any of them getting away."

She nodded.

"Here." He slid the gun into her hand. "Take this."

She took the gun.

"I have my knife, and it will be my pleasure to use it if this jackass twitches…" Roman growled. "Now, go, baby. We can't let him get away."

She was going, but she was planning to find a phone and get him an ambulance. Harper raced away. She yanked open the front door.

***

"Who are you?" Roman asked. He looked at the blade of his knife, and then he looked at the man sprawled on the floor before him.

"Christos Hybrek."

The name meant nothing to him. "Let me guess. I did something to you or your family. Or my father did or—"

"No. I just decided to collect the bounty on your head. When you're offered a lottery, you don't fucking walk away." He smiled. "The woman, Charity, she thought I didn't know how much money people would pay for you. She was wrong."

She was also dead. Roman had checked her body when he'd rushed out of the bedroom.

"We should get out of here," Christos said. "Now."

"Because you wired the place to blow?" Like he hadn't considered that possibility. It was the reason he'd sent Harper out.

A shrug. "It was what Charity wanted. She wanted to watch you burn. Said it was the ending you deserved. Nothing personal."

"No? Funny. I take burning to death very personally." He stared down at the man. A stranger who wanted him dead. "There's always going to be someone else. Always someone else in line who wants that lottery." He glanced toward the doorway. Harper was gone.

I told her that I loved her. The words had just tumbled out. But he'd meant them. He loved her. He wanted a shot at a life with her. He sure as fuck didn't intend to die in that cabin.

Harper is outside.

"Come on, asshole," Roman ordered. "Time to go."

The bastard smirked at him. Then lunged up—with a knife of his own.

***

She nearly ran straight into Antony.

He grabbed her. Held tight. "Harper!"

"Roman needs an ambulance!" The words tumbled out. "He was shot, and there's a lot of blood, and I have to get the jerk who ran out because there were three of them—"

"We've got him," a female voice announced. "Don't worry about him. He's unconscious and cuffed."

Harper's head swiveled. "Lacey?" She hadn't seen her friend in weeks. She'd missed the wedding because Harper had been out of the country, and she hadn't even got to meet the mysterious groom who'd swept Lacey off her feet—

Lacey pulled her in for a tight hug. "Where's my brother?" Lacey asked.

"What?"

"Roman," Lacey said as she eased back a little from Harper. "Didn't he tell you?"

Another secret. How many secrets did he possess?

But Harper looked back toward the small house. The front door hung open. "He's inside. He's hurt." Now that she knew things were taken care of out there, she could rush back to Roman. "Come on. He needs us."

She took a fast step toward the house.

And the explosion knocked Harper off her feet.

***

"Completely unnecessary," Roman growled as he watched the flames shoot into the sky.

Harper flew onto the ground.

He immediately surged toward her.

"Dumbass!" Dex grabbed his arm and hauled him back into the shadows. "Are you seriously trying to undo all of my work? Do you know how hard it is to set a scene like this with the zero amount of notice I had going on? I needed hype. I needed witnesses. I need your ass dead. You can't be dead if you're rushing after your girlfriend because she just slipped onto her ass. The woman is okay. Take a breath."

Harper was back on her feet. Trying to run toward the burning house.

"See?" Dex sighed.

Lacey grabbed her. So did Antony. They held her back.

"The two men in the house were dead. You shoved your knife into that one jerk's heart, and I had to take out the second when he tried to jump me. Idiot." Dex's breath heaved out. "When the smoke clears, I'll make it seem that one of those guys was you. The evidence will be overwhelming. You won't need to look over your shoulder any longer."

"Harper is crying."

"Yes, well, that's because she loves you."

"She thinks I just died." She was still trying to get back to the house. Breaking his freaking heart. "I need to tell her the truth. She can't—she can't think I'm dead. I can't...let her hurt."

"Why not? You were going to leave her. According to my sources, that was your plan all along."

He didn't look away from Harper. "Your...sources?"

"You're bleeding a lot. We should probably get you some care before you pass out."

Lacey was dragging Harper back. "Does...my sister know?"

"Well, of course, I told her the plan. Can't very well have my wife getting upset and thinking I let her brother die, now, can I?"

But it was okay for Harper to think that? Roman rounded on him. *"Harper is in pain! We have to tell her—"*

"This is a long time coming, my friend." Dex drove his fist into Roman's jaw.

***

"I want to see the body."

Antony blanched as he stood at the foot of Harper's hospital bed. She'd been brought to the hospital—over her very, very loud protests. The docs had poked and prodded her, and inside, she'd been silently screaming every single moment.

Roman. Roman isn't dead. Roman loves me.

"It was a really hot fire, Harper. They haven't even put it out yet."

She sat up.

"Not all the way," he added roughly. His gaze cut away from her.

Her eyes narrowed. "Where is Roman?"

"Dead, Harper. Roman Valentino is dead."

He wasn't meeting her stare.

"Antony—"

The door flew open behind him. "Antony Kyle!" A woman with sleek, strawberry blonde hair rushed inside. "What in the hell is going on?"

Harper wasn't in the mood for more drama. "I want my partner. I want him now."

"He's dead, Harper," Antony said. He frowned at the other woman. "Ella, how did you know I was here?"

"Because I've been following your phone. You were at a bomb scene earlier. A bomb scene! I heard on the news that some poor man got blown to pieces in that—"

He grabbed her arms. "Not now. Don't say more."

But Harper had heard too much. "It's fake."

Antony and the blonde looked at her. "Excuse me?" the blonde said.

"It's fake." She needed Antony to confirm this for her. "Something you did."

"I...have no idea what you're talking about. I'm a game designer."

Harper looked at the woman he still held. "You're his head of security."

"I—yes. I'm Ella."

"He's lying to you. And he's lying to me." She climbed out of bed. Stupid paper gown. "I know a staged scene when I see one. I want my partner."

Ella pushed away from Antony. "What's he lying about?"

Antony's lips parted.

"Get me Dex," Harper commanded before Antony could reply. "Tell him that I want a private meeting, right the hell now. If I don't get what I want, I will be on the news in thirty minutes, and I will be telling the world a story that no one will soon forget."

CHAPTER TWENTY

"I expected more from you, Harper." Dex had appeared—as if by magic—in Harper's hospital room. Antony had vanished, and he'd taken his furious head of security with him. "Demanding to see me. Threatening to tell some wild story to the media. I know grief can do many things to a person but—"

She stalked toward him. Stopped right in front of Dex. "I know what you did."

His brows climbed. "Saved you. Dispatched the bad guys?"

"He always planned to leave. That's what he said. But using me—making me watch while the house exploded, and I thought he was inside..." Her breath shuddered out. "That was cruel. When he said he loved me, was that just to set the scene? Just so I would hurt more and it would be more believable? Was it—"

"No." Clipped. Quiet.

She wrapped her arms around her stomach.

"He's under the knife right now. His wounds were worse than I thought, or else I wouldn't have slugged the guy when he tried to get to you."

What?

"Roman didn't know what I had planned. The only person who knew was Lacey. I told her at the last minute. The opportunity presented itself—a chance for Roman to die in a dramatic way, a chance for him to be safe—so I took the chance. When Roman realized what was happening, he lost his damn mind. He couldn't stand to see you in pain. He was rushing out of the shadows to get to you, so I had to knock him out."

She bit her lip and felt tears slide down her cheeks.

"He'll pull through. He's too tough and too much of an asshole for anything else." Dex nodded. "Then you'll have a choice to make. You can either stay here and keep your life. From what I've seen, it's a pretty good life. Good job. Good friends. Good home. You can have it. Or you can start over with him. In order to do that, though, you'd have to leave this world behind. Have to become someone new, because that's what he is doing. You'll have to give it all up, and you'll have to be very, very sure...is he worth it?"

Roman isn't dead. Roman isn't dead. "I want to see him. Now."

"Can't happen. He's in a secure location. He's in surgery. He was hit by two bullets, and that Christos asshole drove a knife into his ribs."

Christos?

"You're high profile at the moment. You were abducted—twice—and you were just at the scene of a major explosion. If you disappear right now, that will make things look suspicious. You'll ruin all my hard work. Work that I did so that Roman could be safe. So that *you* could be safe." He held her stare. "He wasn't wrong, you know. Because he cared about you, that put a target on your back. That's something for you to consider. I'm doing everything I can to bury him, but…if you choose the path that takes you back to Roman, there will always be some danger."

Roman is alive.

Dex turned away. "I'll return to you again when things have cooled down. You can tell me your answer then."

"He said he loved me."

Dex paused near the door. "I think that man has spent his whole life wanting someone to love him and thinking that he would never be worthy of love at the same time. So when you make your decision, Harper, be sure. He can handle attacks. He can handle betrayals. But…" He looked back at her. "I don't think he can handle it if he believes he's getting a life with you, then you decide two months in that it's just too much. You decide that it—*he*—isn't something you can deal with. The glow wears off, and suddenly, you're not so sure it was love, after all."

Her chin notched up. She strode toward him. Lifted her hand. Jabbed her index finger into his chest. "There is no fucking glow."

His brows climbed.

"Roman has driven me crazy from the beginning. He's secretive and bossy. He doesn't talk nearly enough, and…" Her voice turned ragged. "*And when I thought he might be in that house, my heart ripped open.* There is no stupid, pretty glow. There is need and pain and a link that cuts straight to my soul. He's mine, and I'm his." She nodded. "You tell him that. You tell him to get well. You tell him that I remember what he said to me, and you tell him to remember this…"

Dex waited.

"I would go to hell and back for him, and if it meant that we could be together, I would enjoy the ride no matter how much it burned."

He blinked. "That's...um, I suppose it could be sweet, in a twisted, screwed-up kind of way."

"Tell him."

A nod.

"And I *will* be seeing you again, Dex."

"Count on it."

***

But five weeks had passed. Five of the longest weeks of Harper's life, and she hadn't seen Dex again. Hadn't seen Dex or Lacey or even Antony. There had been no word from Roman, and Harper was about to go crazy.

So she marched straight into her boss's office. Slammed the door shut behind her. Eric Wilde glanced up. A flash of worry dotted across his expression, and his shoulders straightened as she closed in on him.

"Hi, Harper," he began slowly. "Is there something wrong—"

She slapped her hands down on his desk and leaned toward him. "I want my partner."

"You want a new partner, right. Working on that. I am actually in the process of recruiting a woman who I think will be a great addition to Wilde. She has worked as the head of security for—"

"I don't want a *new* partner," Harper gritted out. "I want my old partner. I want Roman."

He swallowed. "Harper. You know that's not possible."

"I know that it's you and it's me in this office. I also know you're tight with that jackass, Dex. You know where my partner is. I want to know why I *don't* know that." Her heart twisted. "He survived the surgery. Tell me he—"

Eric's right hand closed around hers. Squeezed.

She took that as a yes. For a moment, her head dipped forward. "Then he just doesn't want to see me?" She'd made it obvious that she wanted him.

"Harper."

Her head lifted.

"I...have a new case for you."

"What?" She gaped at him. "Are you listening to anything that I am saying to you?"

"I just got the call on the case a few moments ago. Would you like to hear the details?"

Did she look like she wanted to hear the details?

"It's a long-term position," Eric added as he slowly released her hand. "The client is a reclusive billionaire. He wants round-the-clock protection. He's asked for a live-in bodyguard."

"Find someone else," Harper said without hesitation. "I prefer to guard things, not—" She stopped.

There was something about the way Eric was looking at her...

"You might want to guard this person," he murmured.

Her heart slammed into her chest. "How long term is this position?"

"It's as long term as you want it to be. The client said you could try it on a test run. A six-week probationary period, if you will."

Six weeks. That was how long Eric had originally told Harper and Roman that they would have to be partners.

"I have the case arrangements. You go in for six weeks with the client." Eric's voice held no emotion. "If the job isn't something you wish to continue after that time, you can switch out. New security can be put in place."

She had to blink because her vision had become all foggy. She knew what was happening. Roman didn't think that she'd want to stay forever with him. He was giving her an out. Setting things up so that she didn't have to leave her life behind if she didn't want to keep being with him.

He thinks I'll change my mind. "That's just damn insulting."

Eric's brows climbed. "Sorry, I didn't mean to—"

She straightened from the desk. "I'll take the case. When do I leave?"

"When can you be packed?"

"When do I leave?" she repeated.

A smile tugged at his lips. "I can have you wings up within the hour."

***

Another mansion. Typical. Did the man ever stay in anything else? Harper was in Colorado, the wind was howling around her, and she was staring at what *could* have been a massive hotel, but it wasn't. It was her client's new home. It sort of had a spooky, gothic look. And deep down, Harper had to admit that she loved the place.

Or maybe she just loved the man inside.

Her bags had been dropped off at the door. The driver had left—rushed away. She'd gotten a clipped, former-soldier vibe from the driver, and she'd wondered if he might work for Dex.

Might? Hah.

A shiver shook her as she lifted her hand to press the buzzer near the door. "Come on, come on," she mumbled as she stared into the little camera that she could see. "Do you want me to turn into a popsicle out here?"

The door was yanked open.

A tall, blond, handsome stranger stood before her.

Harper blinked.

No, not a stranger. The hair was a whole lot lighter and longer. The stubble was completely gone from his jaw. He looked thinner. Leaner. The lines near his eyes were deeper. And his eyes were a different color. Bright. He was wearing jeans and a dark sweater. And—

"Harper."

His voice was the same. Just the sound of her name on his lips made her whole body ache. She wanted to throw her arms around him and hold on tight. *Never let go.* But they had to get a few things straight. Rules for the partnership.

"I missed you," he rasped.

"Yeah, can you get the bags?"

He blinked.

"You know what? We'll get them later." She just left them out there. Screw them. She crossed the threshold. Slammed the door. Locked it.

He backed up.

Harper saw that his hands were clenching and releasing. Clenching and releasing. Was that a good sign?

"You came," he breathed.

She lifted one brow. "Five weeks. I trust that you've recovered fully?" Her stare darted over him. "I was worried." Lower. A little angry. Maybe a lot angry. Did he know how many nights she'd stayed up thinking about him? Praying that he was safe and getting stronger? *Every night. Every single night.*

"I've recovered fully." His right hand lifted toward her, then dropped. "I didn't know what Dex had planned. I would never have put you through that, I swear it. I would never want you to think that I had died like that."

She brushed by him. It was either brush by him and get into a room where they had more space or—or just tackle the guy. And once she did touch him—or tackle him—there would be no holding back.

"I tried to get to you," Roman said as he trailed behind her.

There was a fire crackling in the giant, stone fireplace. She winced when she saw it.

"But I was weak from blood loss and Dex knocked my ass out."

Harper spun toward him.

"I would not have let you think I was dead. I would not have let you watch that if I had a choice." His shoulders squared. "Your name was the first word I spoke when I woke up in the hospital. Dex told me you were safe. He promised me that you knew the truth."

"Portions of the truth. I guess with Dex, that's all we get, isn't it?"

His gaze drifted over her face. "You are so beautiful."

Kiss him. Hold him. Never let him go. "I hear you're the new client. A mysterious, reclusive billionaire."

"I thought about you every day." His focus drifted down her body.

"And yet, you only offered me a six-week contract."

His stare snapped back to her face.

"Six weeks." She crossed her arms over her chest. The better not to grab him. "What do you think, that I'll get tired after the first couple of weeks? That I will decide this isn't the case I want?"

He swallowed. "I want you to have a choice. I-I needed to see you, but I didn't want to put you at risk. I didn't want you to have to give up your life. This way, you can have closure if you—"

"Just shut that dirty mouth."

He blinked.

Her breath huffed out. "Don't you talk to me about closure."

"You...don't want closure?"

"Is that why you think I'm here?"

"I don't know why you're here." A flash of hunger, of desperation, slid over his face. "I should have let you go. I should have—"

Screw it. She pounced on him. Closed the distance between them in a flash and grabbed tightly to his arms. "You said you loved me."

A jerky nod. "I do. I will. I will always love—"

"Then why are you talking to me about closure? You love me, I love you. From where I stand, that's not closing anything. It's *starting* everything."

"You love the life you had in Atlanta. You love the job. The people. You—"

"I love you. I want to be with you. I'm not giving up anything. I'm going in a new direction. I'm sure Dex can put both of our talents to work if we feel the urge to do some off-the-books jobs. I'm sure we can meet new people. I'm sure that we can—"

"I have a painting studio set up for you upstairs. The whole second floor. It's stocked and you can work up there to—"

She shot onto her toes. Hauled him toward her. Kissed him as deep and hard and passionately as she could.

Roman.

He kissed her back the same way. His hands curled around her hips. He lifted her up higher. Worshipped her with his mouth. "I missed you," he grated against her lips.

"Don't ever do that again."

His head lifted. He kept holding her.

"Don't doubt me," she ordered him.

His lashes flickered.

"I told Dex to give you a message. Did he?"

"You said you'd go to hell and back for me."

"Damn straight I would."

"I would do the same for you," Roman swore. "In a heartbeat."

She stared into his eyes—different shade, same Roman. Her Roman. Dex had delivered her message, and she remembered the warning that Dex had given to her...

"So when you make your decision, Harper, be sure. He can handle attacks. He can handle betrayals. But...I don't think he can handle it if he thinks he's getting a life with you, then you decide two months in that it's just too much. If you decide that it—he—isn't something you can deal with. The glow wears off, and suddenly, you're not so sure it was love, after all."

When she spoke again, her voice was low and very certain. "I have never felt this way about anyone else. I know our life won't be perfect, but I am not looking for perfection."

"You are fucking perfect to me," he said.

Sweet, but... "I will love you when things are good and when they're nightmares. I'm not going to turn from you. I don't want you to turn from me. The past—you are not responsible for your father's crimes."

The pain that came on his face...*Oh, my Roman...*

She brushed her mouth over his again. "I told you before that we can't change the past. Let's focus on the present. On the future. Our future together."

"I don't want to be like him." Low. Gruff.

"You are not." Certainty. "You never could be."

"Baby…"

"I want you. I've done a really good job of holding onto my control, but it's been a helluva long five weeks. I've thought about you every single day, and I don't want to ever go through that again. This partnership isn't for six weeks. It's for keeps."

Hope. Bright. Burning. It lit his face and had a slow smile sliding over Roman's lips.

"You have the best smile," Harper told him. "It is absolutely gorgeous."

He laughed. The sound was rusty, but warm. "No one has ever told me that before."

"That's because no one else knows you like I do."

The laughter faded. "No. No one else does."

"No more secrets?"

"Not ever from you."

"And no six-week time limit?"

"I thought you might like that. You know, since you tried to get out of the partnership before."

She shook her head.

"No time limit," he whispered.

"And you'll make love to me? Right now?"

"I'll go crazy if I don't."

"Can't have that," Harper said. She twined her arms around his neck. "Definitely can't." They kissed again.

"I have the kitchen stocked with chocolates for you," he revealed. "Every kind you can possibly imagine. Anything that you want—I've got it."

Her lashes lifted. She stared into his eyes. "You're what I want."

"I love you so damn much."

There was no more talking after that. He carried her to the bedroom. She worried about Roman hurting himself because the man *had* been shot, but he just kissed her more. They ripped each other's clothes off. His kisses became even hungrier. Even more desperate.

So did hers.

His hands slid over her body. Teased her breasts. Stroked her nipples. She arched into his touch even as a moan built in her throat. This first time wasn't going to be slow. Their need for each other was far too acute. They could be slow the second time. Or the third. Or the million times after that.

Her fingers caressed his chest. When she found the new scars that marked him, Harper pressed tender kisses to them.

"I'm trying to hold on to my control," he warned.

"Don't."

And he didn't.

He tumbled her back onto the bed. He shoved her thighs apart, and the heavy head of his cock pushed at the entrance to her body.

"Fuck. Need a condom. Sweetheart, hold on—"

"I'm on birth control, but we can stop it when we're ready for a baby."

He froze. "You'd...want a baby with me?"

"Roman, I want everything with you."

"But...who I am...my father...the danger—"

"I want everything with you," she told him once more. "I figure between the two of us, we can handle any threat that comes our way. We can keep our baby safe."

"Harper..."

He drove into her. They both moaned. He withdrew, thrust deep, and her legs locked eagerly around him. The passion was wild. Their need ferocious. There was no stopping or holding back. She needed him too much. Harper knew he craved her with the same desperation.

When the climax hit her, she shouted his name.

And when he came, he kissed her.

She held him tight. Felt her heartbeat thudding far too fast in her chest. And Harper knew, she was finally home.

***

She was asleep in his arms. Roman was afraid to close his own eyes. Afraid that if he did, he might wake up to discover that Harper wasn't really there. She hadn't chosen him. It had all been a dream.

What the fuck would he do then?

Her hand was over his heart. She was warm and soft. And—

"Stop worrying." Her eyes remained closed. Her voice was low. Chiding. "I'm not going anywhere."

So she wasn't asleep. He pressed a kiss to her temple.

"I'm where I belong," Harper continued in her sleepy voice. A sexy voice. "And so are you."

He belonged to Harper. He knew it. When he'd been a kid, he'd dreamed of having a real family. Of having someone who loved him without any limits...

He just hadn't realized how much *he* would love, in return. He loved Harper so much that, sometimes, the feeling scared him. He trusted her completely. Loved her totally. Would die for her in an instant.

Though killing for her would probably be way more effective, especially since he wanted to spend the next seventy or so years with her.

The future. His heart drummed faster. He and Harper were going to have a future together. They would have a home. A child. Holidays. Lazy breakfasts. Candlelit dinners. Slow Saturdays. All of the normal things—they would have them. Everything that others took for granted, he would treasure.

Just as he would treasure Harper. "I love you."

She snuggled closer. "It's not a dream."

"How did you know that's what I was worried about?"

Her lashes finally lifted. "Because I worried the same thing."

His beautiful Harper.

"I'm not going anywhere," she said again.

"Neither am I. I'm exactly where I've always wanted to be."

She smiled. Her dimples winked, and in his mind, he had a flash of a cute, dimpled toddler. A little girl with her mother's eyes and smile.

Oh, hell. He was going to be in so much trouble. Wrapped around their little fingers. In love with their smiles.

I don't deserve any of this, but I will fight like hell for my family. Always.

He pulled Harper even closer, and he made a mental note to send Eric Wilde an anonymous gift of thanks.

You gave me the perfect partner. I can never repay that.

Never.

EPILOGUE

"So..." Eric Wilde studied the woman before him. "You want to take the job?"

Ella Webb gave him a hard, angry smile. "Absolutely."

"You don't sound excited."

"I am. It will be wonderful to work for someone who *doesn't* spend his days and nights lying to me." Ella Webb rose to her feet. Her sleek, straight hair slid over her shoulders. "Before I get started here at Wilde, I want to personally tell my former boss where he can screw off."

Eric lifted his brows. "Um, you'll be telling Antony Kyle to screw off?" God, that would be fun to see.

She nodded. "Long overdue, trust me." Her shoulders squared. "I will be a good employee, I assure you. I have extensive training that will make me an ideal fit at your security and protection firm."

"Oh, you come with glowing references." He was still imagining the scene with Antony. "If anything, though, I feel you should be in a management position, not working as a field agent."

"I want my hands dirty." She nodded. "I need it. I need action. I need something to make me forget—" Ella broke off. "It's time for me to get a fresh start."

He stood and offered his hand to her. "You'll find that start at Wilde."

She shook his hand. "Thank you for the opportunity."

A few moments later, she was gone. Eric glanced at his phone. He thought about giving Antony a call of warning but...

Nah. Things would be more fun this way.

Antony liked to know everyone else's secrets. He liked to control every single thing in his life—it was past time for the man to have a surprise tossed his way.

If only I could be there to see the show...

Because Eric was betting the fireworks would be spectacular.

THE END

A NOTE FROM THE AUTHOR

Thank you for reading ROMAN WILL FALL. Even bad guys can deserve a happy ending, and I had a great time writing a story for Roman. I hope you enjoyed his tale! Next up in my "Wilde Ways" series...Antony will have his story told. THE ONE WHO GOT AWAY is another fun, fast-paced tale, with a guaranteed HEA.

If you'd like to stay updated on my releases and sales, please join my newsletter list.

https://cynthiaeden.com/newsletter/

Again, thank you for reading ROMAN WILL FALL.

Best,
Cynthia Eden
cynthiaeden.com

ABOUT THE AUTHOR

Cynthia Eden is a *New York Times*, *USA Today*, *Digital Book World*, and *IndieReader* best-seller.

Cynthia writes sexy tales of contemporary romance, romantic suspense, and paranormal romance. Since she began writing full-time in 2005, Cynthia has written over one hundred novels and novellas.

Cynthia lives along the Alabama Gulf Coast. She loves romance novels, horror movies, and chocolate.

For More Information
- *cynthiaeden.com*
- *facebook.com/cynthiaedenfanpage*

HER OTHER WORKS

Death and Moonlight Mystery
- Step Into My Web (Book 1)
- Save Me From The Dark (Book 2)

Wilde Ways
- Protecting Piper (Book 1)
- Guarding Gwen (Book 2)
- Before Ben (Book 3)
- The Heart You Break (Book 4)
- Fighting For Her (Book 5)
- Ghost Of A Chance (Book 6)
- Crossing The Line (Book 7)
- Counting On Cole (Book 8)
- Chase After Me (Book 9)
- Say I Do (Book 10)

Dark Sins
- Don't Trust A Killer (Book 1)
- Don't Love A Liar (Book 2)

Lazarus Rising
- Never Let Go (Book One)
- Keep Me Close (Book Two)
- Stay With Me (Book Three)
- Run To Me (Book Four)
- Lie Close To Me (Book Five)
- Hold On Tight (Book Six)

- Lazarus Rising Volume One (Books 1 to 3)
- Lazarus Rising Volume Two (Books 4 to 6)

Dark Obsession Series
- Watch Me (Book 1)
- Want Me (Book 2)
- Need Me (Book 3)
- Beware Of Me (Book 4)
- Only For Me (Books 1 to 4)

Mine Series
- Mine To Take (Book 1)
- Mine To Keep (Book 2)
- Mine To Hold (Book 3)
- Mine To Crave (Book 4)
- Mine To Have (Book 5)
- Mine To Protect (Book 6)
- Mine Box Set Volume 1 (Books 1-3)
- Mine Box Set Volume 2 (Books 4-6)

Bad Things
- The Devil In Disguise (Book 1)
- On The Prowl (Book 2)
- Undead Or Alive (Book 3)
- Broken Angel (Book 4)
- Heart Of Stone (Book 5)
- Tempted By Fate (Book 6)
- Wicked And Wild (Book 7)
- Saint Or Sinner (Book 8)
- Bad Things Volume One (Books 1 to 3)
- Bad Things Volume Two (Books 4 to 6)

- Bad Things Deluxe Box Set (Books 1 to 6)

Bite Series
- Forbidden Bite (Bite Book 1)
- Mating Bite (Bite Book 2)

Blood and Moonlight Series
- Bite The Dust (Book 1)
- Better Off Undead (Book 2)
- Bitter Blood (Book 3)
- Blood and Moonlight (The Complete Series)

Purgatory Series
- The Wolf Within (Book 1)
- Marked By The Vampire (Book 2)
- Charming The Beast (Book 3)
- Deal with the Devil (Book 4)
- The Beasts Inside (Books 1 to 4)

Bound Series
- Bound By Blood (Book 1)
- Bound In Darkness (Book 2)
- Bound In Sin (Book 3)
- Bound By The Night (Book 4)
- Bound in Death (Book 5)
- Forever Bound (Books 1 to 4)

Stand-Alone Romantic Suspense
- Never Gonna Happen
- One Hot Holiday
- Secret Admirer
- First Taste of Darkness

- Sinful Secrets
- Until Death
- Christmas With A Spy

Printed in Great Britain
by Amazon